Edited by Andie Edwards of Beyond the Proof

Cover art by Leni Kauffman

www.oliviahayle.com

how to honeymoon alone

OLIVIA HAYLE

BARBADOS

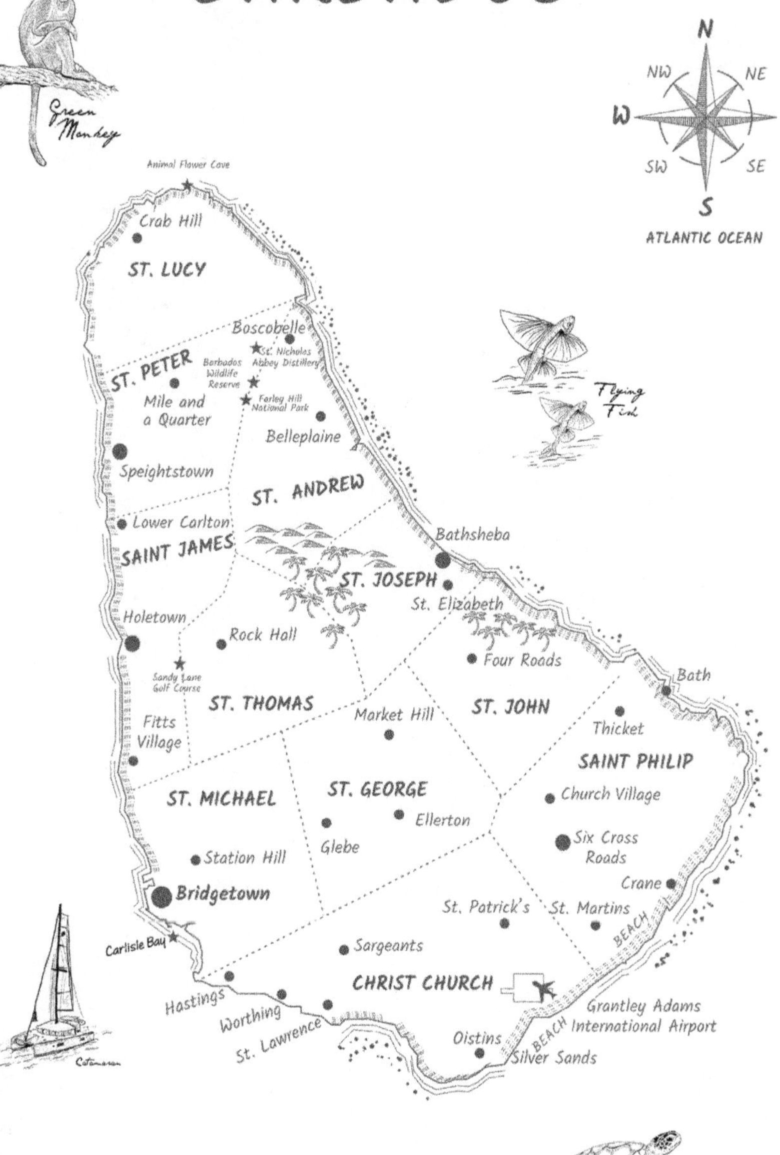

Green Monkey
N
NW
NE
W
E
SW
SE
S
ATLANTIC OCEAN
Animal Flower Cave
Crab Hill
ST. LUCY
Boscobelle
St. Nicholas Abbey Distillery
Barbados Wildlife Reserve
Farley Hill National Park
ST. PETER
Mile and a Quarter
Belleplaine
Flying Fish
Speightstown
ST. ANDREW
Lower Carlton
SAINT JAMES
Bathsheba
ST. JOSEPH
St. Elizabeth
Holetown
Rock Hall
Four Roads
Sandy Lane Golf Course
Bath
ST. THOMAS
Market Hill
ST. JOHN
Fitts Village
Thicket
SAINT PHILIP
ST. MICHAEL
ST. GEORGE
Church Village
Ellerton
Glebe
Six Cross Roads
Station Hill
Crane
Bridgetown
St. Patrick's
St. Martins
Carlisle Bay
BEACH
Sargeants
CHRIST CHURCH
Hastings
Worthing
Grantley Adams International Airport
St. Lawrence
Oistins
BEACH
Silver Sands
Catamaran

Sea Turtle

To everyone whose favorite vacation is a really good book.

Chapter One

Some things are hard to do alone. Putting together large flatpack furniture, for one, or surviving the mean streets of high school. Ordering dinner alone in a restaurant is another one. But my best friend glares at me through my phone screen, unable to comprehend that simple fact.

"Just sit down," she says. "Order and eat. Who cares what anyone else might think?"

I lie down on my hotel bed. "I do."

"No, you don't. They don't matter."

"Yeah. And it's not like I came to Barbados to hide in my hotel room."

"Definitely not. You went to have the best two weeks of your life," Becky says. She's sitting on her familiar paisley couch, with a pregnancy pillow beside her. My future goddaughter is the only reason she couldn't be here with me. "You're going to get back at—no, scratch that. I won't say his name, and you're not even allowed to *think* it."

I salute her. "Yes, ma'am."

"No, you're going to eat dinner at that luscious-looking hotel restaurant, you're going to enjoy the warm weather, and afterward, you can reward yourself by watching old reruns in your room."

"Pregnancy has made you bossy," I say.

Her husband's voice comes through the phone, unseen but close by. "You said it, not me!" he yells.

Becky hushes him. "I'm talking to Eden."

"Hi, Patrick," I say.

"Hey, Eden," he calls back. "Enjoy some sunshine for me!"

"Will do!" I meet Becky's gaze. "But you're right, you know, bossy or not. So what if I'm the only person there eating alone?"

"Doesn't matter at all," she agrees. "It's not like you'll see a single person there again after you come home."

"Exactly." I sit up and look over at my suitcase, half-opened on the carpeted floor. It's spilling colorful sundresses like a store on Black Friday. "I'll wear my red dress."

"That's right," she says. "And Eden? I want a picture of you with a colorful, tropical drink as proof."

I roll my eyes. "Fine."

"Good," she says and smiles at me through the screen. "I wish I was there with you."

"Me, too," I say. "Thanks."

"Anytime. Now go have fun and come back with a tan for me to be jealous of."

We hang up and I'm alone in my empty, quiet hotel room. My windows don't give me a view of the ocean. That had been too expensive. Instead, they offer a view of the beautifully manicured garden of the Winter Resort. The newly opened luxury hotel is everything Caleb and I had hoped for when we booked it for our honeymoon.

And I'm going to make sure I enjoy it all. Even if I have to provide picture proof for Becky as I do it.

The first few weeks after I'd learned about Caleb's extracurricular activities, even getting out of bed had been a struggle. Dragging myself to the coffee shop down the street had felt like running a marathon.

So, as I was speaking to Becky on the phone one day and mentioned what I wanted to cook for dinner, she'd said, *send me a pic or it didn't happen.*

She'd known, even if I hadn't told her, that more days than not it didn't happen.

And so I'd sent her pictures of all of it, and in the three months since my engagement ended, the small, normal acts have stopped feeling like a sporting event. The hurt isn't unbearable anymore. It's not a weight on my shoulders crushing me down to earth. It's a backpack instead, still heavy, but it doesn't slow me down.

Maybe I'll get to take it off entirely one day.

I pull on a red dress and chuck my phone, wallet, and guidebook into a crossbody purse. This is my trip. Mine. I had planned it, insisted on it and dreamed of it for years.

As a teenager, I'd kept a vision board over my desk. It had changed a lot over the years, but a few images had remained —steadfast pillars among an ever-changing sea of dreams.

One of them had been the turquoise-blue of the Caribbean Sea, softly lapping against a white-sand beach and framed by palm trees.

This trip is my first time out of the country, if one doesn't count the road trips from my home in Washington State to Vancouver, Canada, and I don't. Not really. No, this is it. I'm here. I'm doing it.

And the absolute last person I should be thinking about is Caleb.

I run a brush through my brown hair in too-aggressive strokes as if I can comb him out of my thoughts.

I feel calmer when I finally ride the elevator down to the lobby. My walk takes me through the resort's garden, as the softly chirping insects serenade me as I stroll through the open colonnade.

The restaurant opens to the garden on one side and the sea on the other. No windows are needed in the perpetually warm climate.

The air is hot and humid, wrapping around me like another layer of clothing. But the breeze from the sea cools me down in gentle gusts. The *Caribbean* Sea, that is.

A wave of giddiness sweeps through me.

I'm abroad, I think, *and no one can take that away from me.* The magic is right here. It's in the new experiences, the calm ocean, and the sandy beaches. I just need to reach out and grab it.

I stop by the maître d's stand. The linen-clad tables beyond are filled with dining guests and the place looks packed. I rock back in my sandals and peer around. There's no empty table in sight.

Maybe I can get away with room service and binging an old TV show after all.

"Good evening," a smiling host says. "Do you have a reservation for tonight?"

"I don't, no. I can see that you're pretty busy. Is there a space for one?"

"Just one?"

"Yes." I can feel myself shrink.

"Let me check…" He looks down at the screen and taps it a few times. "We do seem to have a table available. You'll get our last one of the night!"

"Oh, that's wonderful. Thank you."

Next to me, a man clears his throat. "There you are," he says to me. "Sorry, I'm late. Table for two, actually."

I stare up at the stranger.

His head of dark-brown hair towers over me by a few inches, and he's wearing a white button-down. He's also watching me meaningfully.

"That's not a problem," the host says and grabs another menu. "Right this way."

He turns and sets off through the packed restaurant. I remain locked in a staring contest with the intrusive stranger.

He raises an eyebrow. "Share the last table?" he asks and motions for us to start moving.

I'm too stunned to do anything but follow the host obediently through the restaurant. He leads us to a two-top right next to the boardwalk and the soft waves. There's a single lit candle on the table, it's flame flickering in the light breeze.

"Here you are," the host says cheerfully and sets the menus down. "Your waiter will be over soon to take your drink orders."

And just like that, I'm left staring at the tall stranger in front of me. He pulls out a chair and takes a seat as if he hasn't just stolen it. There's a hint of stubble along his sharp jaw. He looks closed-off and a bit predatory, like he spends a lot of time getting his way. Just as he is right now.

"Excuse me," I say. "What was that?"

"Maybe I just wanted to get to know you," he says.

Judging by his lack of accent, he's American, too. I cast a meaningful look around the crowded restaurant. "No, you wanted a table in a full restaurant."

"Nothing escapes you." He nods to the chair in front of him. "Have a seat."

"You know, I studied karate for seven years, and I always carry pepper spray. Not to mention we're in public."

"Consider me warned," he says and opens his menu. "They do good fish here, I've heard."

I finally sit down, my movements slow. "Yes. It's in the name."

He gives a low hum. I look down at my menu, but the words bleed together on the page. At least his sudden arrival means I don't need to think twice about what the other guests may be thinking, seeing me here alone.

Across the table, he flips a page of his menu. "Dinner is on me as a thank you," he says. "Choose whatever you want. And no need to worry about awkward small talk, either, if you're not in the mood. I have some emails I need to take care of."

I look at him. "You're going to work?"

He keeps his eyes trained on the menu. "Would you rather we talk about nothing important just to fill the silence?"

"Wow. I… just wow."

He looks up with a faint frown. "What?"

"I don't think anyone's ever spoken to me the way you just have."

"Right. I can be direct."

"No, really?" I ask. Sarcasm drips from my words.

He puts the menu down, and it looks like it pains him. "I'm sorry about crashing your evening. Is it okay with you? Say no and I'll leave, no questions asked."

"It's okay," I hear myself saying because, if nothing else, this is a story to tell Becky about. "I'm just… surprised."

He nods like that's that, and returns to his menu.

The silence stretches between us. I read my menu without really taking in the words and sneak looks at him. I haven't spoken to a man who wasn't my family member, a coworker, or a friend's husband since Caleb and I ended our engagement.

He leans forward, a lock of dark hair falling over his forehead. A heavy watch on his wrist reflects the flickering candle on the table.

"What are you having?" I finally ask him.

He closes the menu with a snap. "The steak."

"The steak," I repeat. "At a restaurant famous for its fish? On an island in the middle of the sea? You do know that swordfish is famous in Barbados?"

"Yes."

"I think I'm having the locally sourced marlin."

He makes that low humming sound again and reaches into the pocket of his slacks. He pulls out a phone and puts it on the tabletop. "I don't want to be rude," he says, "but I really do need to answer a few emails."

"You're working on your vacation?"

His eyes are already on the screen. "Yes."

"Why didn't you just order room service?" I ask.

He doesn't look up at me, but he seems to tense up at my question. "My room wasn't properly cleaned when I arrived. They're fixing it now."

"Oh." That seems… odd at a five-star resort, but okay, then. I entertain myself by reading through the dessert menu, and then the wine list. My eyes graze over the impossible prices of the glass to the bottle. Between mine and Caleb's salaries, this was a once-in-a-lifetime trip.

Staying at the Winter Resort was always going to be a stretch. When I sat down to cancel the honeymoon and learned about the cancellation fees we'd have to pay for the flights, and the deposit we'd lose on the standard double at the resort… well. Caleb already took the wedding from me, and I'll be damned if he takes my lifelong dream vacation, too.

Past Eden wouldn't have considered traveling to a foreign country on her own. But Eden of several months ago thought her maid of honor was one of her best friends, and her fiancé was the man she was going to spend a life with, so she wasn't exactly all-knowing, either.

And apparently, present Eden is an adventurer, willing to dine with a complete stranger in paradise. I feel locked in place at the table. I'm not eating alone, at least, but I'm still nervous. Just for a different reason now.

I glance over at him. He hasn't even told me his name. Judging by the faint lines at the corners of his eyes, I suspect he might be a few years older than me, but not much more. He's frowning while he answers emails.

Work's probably not going great, I think. I'm grateful my kindergarten students barely know how to write. No emails for me to stress over.

The waiter returns to our table. "Ready for drinks?"

"Red wine," the man across from me says. "The Merlot."

"Coming right up. And for you, ma'am?"

"I'd like a rum punch, please."

The waiter's smile stretches wide. "The house cocktail. Great choice. Is this your first time dining with us?"

"First night on the island, actually."

"Really? Welcome!" he says, looking from me to the man

opposite me. "You two will have a wonderful time here. It's the most romantic of the islands, you know?"

The stranger puts down his phone. "It is?"

"Oh, yes," the waiter says with a wink. "So you two enjoy yourself, all right? I'll be back shortly to take your food order."

He disappears amid the tables and leaves the mystery man and me to our own devices. Or rather, him to his device. His eyes are trained on the screen.

I put an arm on the railing. The ocean is shrouded in darkness, and I can just barely make out the softly lapping waves.

"You know, you never told me your name when you invited yourself to my table."

He works on his phone for a solid minute before turning it facedown on the table. Dark-blue eyes meet mine. "Phillip Meyer," he says, extending a large hand across the table. "It's a pleasure."

I take it. "Eden Richards."

He shakes my hand twice, a firm grip, like we're in a business meeting. "Thank you again, Eden, for not relegating me to a convenience store. I appreciate it."

My hand is warm when I take it back. "Sure. I mean, I'm big on charity."

His eyebrows rise, and there's a spark of delight in his eyes. "Charity?"

I'm spared from answering by our waiter's return. He has a rum punch in a tumbler and a glass of red wine, with one beverage looking decidedly more fun than the other. It has a sprig of mint in it and a frozen slice of lemon.

"For the beautiful lady," the waiter says with a smile before turning to Phillip. "You're a lucky man."

I open my mouth to say—what, exactly?—but Phillip beats me to the punch. "Yes, and she sure likes to remind me."

The waiter laughs, and I glare across the table. Phillip,

however, looks back at me with unreadable eyes. "You did me a favor tonight. I'm the luckiest."

I want to roll my eyes, but resist until the waiter's taken our drink orders and left. "So now we're a couple?"

"I was playing along," Phillip says. "Don't worry, I haven't forgotten your seven years of karate. Or your can of pepper spray. How did you get that through customs?"

"Not important," I say. It's easy to smuggle all kinds of things when they're fictional. As long as this doesn't give him any ideas.

But he's already looking back down at his phone.

I take a sip of my rum punch, and it's all spiced goodness. Closing my eyes, I listen to the waves in the distance.

I'm on vacation. I'm in the Caribbean. I'm the master of my fate now.

And I'm going to have the best time.

"Can I ask you for a favor?" I ask. "Since I did you a solid here tonight."

He looks up. "Yes."

I hand him my phone. "Can you take a photo of me?"

"A photo?"

"Yes."

Judgment rolls off him in waves. I ignore it and pose happily, holding up my drink for the camera like I'm saying cheers.

He lowers my phone after a few seconds. "There. I took a few."

"Awesome, thanks."

His jaw works a few times. "You're going to flood your social media with holiday pics, aren't you?"

I shake my head, thinking of all the friends Caleb and I have in common. I'm not planning on humiliating myself further by sharing pics from the vacation they all know was meant for two. "No. And even if I was, is that so bad?"

He takes a sip of his wine instead of answering. The silence speaks for itself.

"I bet that would taste even better if it was a drink with a locally produced rum," I point out.

"It definitely would not."

I find myself smiling. He's like one of the grumpy five-year-olds in my class when they haven't had their nap. Except he's probably a thirtysomething and a workaholic, which means odds are he hasn't had a nap in a decade.

"What?" he asks.

"Nothing much. Just that you're not in a very good mood, are you?"

He's quiet for another long beat, and judging by the faint surprise on his face, I've caught him off guard.

But it takes one to know one. After a flight where I managed to cry not once but twice, and the last few months of moving all my belongings into a new house, this is refreshing. I can't remember a time when the person I was speaking with didn't know everything about my situation.

Phillip sighs, almost reluctantly. "No, I'm not my best self tonight."

"That's okay. We can't be on top all the time." Then, I replay the words in my mind and immediately shake my head. "Sorry, forget I said that."

He leans back in his chair. "Why are you here alone tonight?"

"Why are you?" I ask. My left hand closes around the drink. It's bare without the engagement ring.

The one I'd thrown at Caleb after I found out.

It had been dramatic and satisfying as hell to watch him bend over the cracks on the sidewalk to search for the glittering thing. He always hated getting dirt under his fingernails. I hope he got plenty that afternoon.

Lord knows I felt dirty enough when I found out he'd been having an affair with my maid of honor, the *former* third part of mine and Becky's best friend trifecta.

"I'm traveling alone," Phillip says. "Just here to see the island."

"Well, would you look at that?" I say and give him my widest smile. "That's exactly why I'm here."

He runs a hand along his jaw and looks away from our table, toward the interior of the restaurant. I follow his gaze. The place is packed with people. Most of them are couples, sitting across from one another at candlelit, white cloth-covered tables.

One couple is openly kissing.

I groan. "God, this place is filled with honeymooners."

"They're the worst," he says.

"Something we can agree on?"

"Apparently, yeah."

"You know why they're so bad?" I say, feeling the nerves melt away a little at this sudden common ground. "It's the constant *announcing* of it to everyone around them. Like them being newlyweds matters to the world at large."

Phillip nods, his jaw tense. "At check-in counters," he says. "To flight attendants."

"To the waiters at breakfast, lunch, and dinner. Do you know, when I checked in earlier, I overheard someone tell the bellboy… while he was carrying their heavy bags for them."

"Basically, asking him to congratulate them while he's helping them out," Phillip says. "That's low."

"The lowest," I agree. I take another sip of my nearly empty drink. I feel good. Better than I expected to feel on the first night of my solo trip. "Well, I'm not here on my honeymoon."

"I figured, from your scathing critique of newlyweds," he says. There's dry amusement in his tone. Almost like he wants this conversation to end, but can't quite bring himself to stop engaging.

"Subtle, right?" I say. "But I was supposed to be."

"Oh."

The waiter returns with our food. A steak for the gentleman, fish for the lady; both dishes smell amazing. I find that

I'm hungrier than I felt. The flight, the stress—it all melts away when presented with hot food.

There's another long, polite pause between us, and I take a bite of my fish. It's delicious, well-seasoned, and warm.

"Should I say sorry?" Phillip finally asks.

"Oh, no. It was for the best. Good riddance and all that. But I couldn't *not* go on a pre-planned, pre-paid holiday, you know? Especially not when it's my dream destination."

"I know," he says with a sigh. "It would be a waste."

"A colossal waste. So that's why I'm here."

"Hating on all the newlyweds."

That makes me laugh again. "Yeah. Cynical of me, perhaps."

He shrugs. It's a single lift of his shoulder, dark-blue eyes on mine. "Cynics come out on top, to use your expression."

"Then, I guess I'm a newly converted cynic."

He huffs a half laugh and returns to cutting his steak. It doesn't take long before he's checking his emails again, and the frown is back, but I'm pleased. I got some emotion out of him. And I survived my first solo dinner, even if I know Becky won't give me the win because I wasn't technically alone.

He asks for the check as soon as we're done, and when it arrives, he doesn't give it a second glance.

"Put it on bungalow twelve," he says.

"Phillip," I say.

"Of course, sir," the waiter responds.

"*Phillip,* I want to pay for my share."

He shakes his head, pushing back from the table. "No."

"No? Why not?"

"Because you were kind enough to let me crash your relaxing night out," he says. "Thank you for tonight, Ms…."

"Richards," I say. *He's already forgotten?* "It's Eden Richards."

"Eden. That's right. Enjoy the rest of your trip."

"Yeah, you, too. Don't work too much."

He gives another half snort of amusement and walks out of the restaurant—tall and stoic among the hordes of happy newlyweds.

So he's staying in a bungalow. It's the resort's most expensive option, and one I had looked at briefly when researching. But a single glance at the price made it clear that it wasn't for people like Caleb and me.

I take a sip of my drink, now watered-down and citrusy. *Seems you can stay in a bungalow and still be miserable.*

I might be in the cheapest room at the hotel. I might be nervous every single night I need to eat alone in a restaurant. But I'm here, in this beautiful place, and I owe it to myself to make the best of this experience.

Master of my own fate, I think again. These will be the best two weeks of my life. I deserve that.

Chapter Two

I wake up to a brilliant sunrise. Clouds pass quickly over the sky, creating an ever-changing tapestry. From my hotel room window, I can see the neon-green colors of the resort's garden. Everything seems just a tad brighter here. Even the flowers appear larger, their hues sharper.

Thanks to the incredible laws of jet lag, I'm down at the breakfast buffet early. Sampling all the wonders of the never-ending feast may be the hardest thing to accomplish during my two weeks on the island. Every fruit imaginable, omelets, pancakes, waffles, eggs, toast, croissants, and a granola spread are so impressive, I have to take a picture of it for posterity's sake.

I grab a table by the boardwalk and spend my morning doing exactly four things: eating, watching the turquoise waves, reading my book, and keeping an eye out for Phillip Meyer.

Multitasking has always been my thing.

Even if I'm not sure if bungalow people actually go to the normal breakfast bar. They probably get the whole banquet delivered to their my-monthly-salary-a-night beachside villas.

But I keep my eyes peeled just in case.

I'm on my second glass of mango juice when I finally spot

him. He walks through the breakfast bar with a single-minded purpose, stopping at the coffee station.

He's wearing beige slacks and a blue polo shirt, looking like he's about to close deals on a golf course. I leave my book at the table, get up, and stroll toward him.

Dark-brown hair has fallen over a face that already looks tanner today than it did yesterday, which is unfair on so many levels.

"Good morning," I say.

He turns his head to the side, hands stilling on his coffee cup. "Hello," he says. "Eden, right?"

"Yes, that's it." I find the wadded-up twenties in the pocket of my dress and hold them out. "Thanks for picking up the check yesterday, but I'd like to pay you back."

He looks at my hand like it offends him. "What? Of course, not."

"Yes. It wasn't a date, and we don't know one another. I can't let you pay for me."

"Eden," he says and puts his coffee cup down. He speaks my name with emphasis on every single letter. "I imposed on you. There's no way I'm taking your money."

I give him my best smile. "You know, I'll have to chase you across the resort if you won't take this. Don't forget that I know which bungalow you're staying in."

The grown man in front of me rolls his eyes. "Right. And you know karate, too, don't you?"

"Black belt," I lie brightly. "So, here. I was raised to pay my own way."

Phillip looks like it pains him, but he takes the money from my outstretched hand. "Fine. If you truly want to…"

"I do."

"All right," he says. "But I want it noted that it's against my will."

I grin. "Noted. Well, I hope you have a good holiday, then. Don't forget to schedule some non-work, too. It's a beautiful island, you know."

He nods. "I have things planned."

"Good. Have fun!"

"You, too," he says and smoothly slides the money into his back pocket.

I return to my table, and when I look back, searching for where he's had a seat, he's gone. So is the coffee cup by the station.

An entire smorgasbord, and all he wanted was a cup of java.

I open my book again. *Bungalow people,* I think.

Lounging on the beach alone is a lot easier than eating one's dinner solo at a restaurant, I discover. It's almost seamless. Except for being unable to reach some parts of my back with sunscreen, there's virtually no downside to Caleb's absence. There are, however, a multitude of pluses.

For one, I can read my book in peace. It's about two people who shouldn't be together but brave all the odds to—well, I'm pretty sure they will—overcome the obstacles in their way.

I've been wanting to read it for weeks.

I get through a page. And then another. And discover that I can't focus on the story at all. There's an interaction between characters I typically enjoy, but I can't follow it. I'm too intrigued by the conversations around me.

The kind of guests who stay at the Winter Resort could probably fill the pages of a murder mystery novel all by themselves. I keep my book open and my sunglasses on and, behind the cover, I let my eyes wander.

The couple beside me appears effortlessly elegant. He's got windswept hair that looks too dark to be a natural color. She's lazily flipping through the pages of an interior design magazine and chewing gum.

They'd be excellent suspects. I'd name them something delicious. Fitzgerald as the last name, perhaps, or Huntington. They'd come here to repair a faltering marriage.

I tap my finger against the spine of my book and wish I'd brought a notepad.

There'd be a romance, too. Two visitors to the resort would be drawn to one another. Maybe one of them could be a suspect in the murder…

And who'd be the victim?

I look out over the beach and the array of tourists around me, each more interesting than the next. For the first time in months, I feel the itch to write. To turn my surroundings into stories.

I've lacked a seed for so long.

Although maybe not, I admit to myself. Seeds might have been everywhere, but I hadn't seen them. The desire to nurture ideas until they blossomed into fully-grown stories had been missing.

If I'm honest with myself, it had been muted even before I discovered Caleb and Cindy's dirty little secret. I'd been stressed about planning a wedding while my fiancé did nothing to help.

An affair.

Maybe two of these people are having an affair. Maybe that's the case with the people next to me. I glance at them from the corner of my eye. *She's married, and she's here with her lover, the dyed-haired man.* Maybe she bumps into someone she knows at the resort… someone who discovers her secret.

That's the motive right there.

I dig through my bag in search of a pen but I don't find one. I make do with my phone instead. The ideas pour out of me into a note, strings of thoughts, little snippets that could bloom into more if given the time.

Murder in paradise is a good premise.

I slip my left foot off the lounge chair and dig it into the warm sand beneath. The soft sound of waves against the shore is the soundtrack to my outburst of creativity.

It's been almost a year since I finished writing my last book. It had been a murder mystery with a strong romance at the center. A romantic thriller, or romantic suspense, as some may call it. A combination of three of my favorite things: true crime, a bit of mystery, and a love story to rival the historical greats.

And just like the books I'd written before, it's now consigned to a folder on my laptop.

I haven't shown a single person my writing for almost seven years. Not since… well. The-event-I-don't-like-to-think-about happened. It's my own personal Voldemort.

The-thing-that-must-not-be-named.

I dig my toes deeper into the sand and catch sight of two women standing by the shoreline. They look like they're arguing. One woman's hands move in a swan dance as she makes her point, while her companion's expression is set in hard lines.

Sisters, I think. Here, after the death of a parent, on an all-inclusive trip paid with a vast inheritance. They could throw a few wrenches into the plot…

A wrench or two is something I know about. Cindy and Caleb had thrown one into my life.

I'd had it all mapped out before they did.

The rest of my life, essentially, or at the very least the upcoming two decades. Caleb and I were saving for a bigger house together. In two or three years we'd start trying for a baby. House, kids, jobs, two cars, and maybe a dog. Predictable, stable, and safe.

And now I'm left with an expanse of time, the collapse of a comfortable relationship, and the question of who I am on my own.

Even worse is the prospect of dating again. Of going on apps and meeting men online. The mere thought of online dating makes me shudder.

I tap my fingers against the side of my phone and watch the couple next to me again. That could be it. The murder victim could be here to meet someone they only know from a dating app. That would seriously slow down the investigation, too, because my characters could only find that out by accessing the murder victim's phone. Which, of course, will be locked.

My fingers fly over the screen with strings of ideas and nuggets of a story.

I'm broken out of my reverie by a familiar voice.

"—no, that won't do. You know it won't. Those papers need to be airtight if they'll want a—"

It's Phillip, the disturber of the peace and stealer of tables. He's walking across the white-sand beach with a phone in hand and headphones in his ears.

I watch him stroll to the end of The Winter Resort's stretch of beach. He turns on his heel at the perimeter and begins heading back, bare feet leaving footprints along the shoreline.

There's an air of annoyance about him. Even in the distance and with sunglasses on, his face looks tense. Seems he's graduated from answering emails at dinner to making work calls on a Caribbean beach.

I curl my legs up and return to the notes app on my phone. There's something about him marching back and forth, hands gesturing, that triggers my imagination.

Maybe he can be the manager of the resort in my story. There's a secret, something he's keeping from the guests and staff…

Or maybe he's a high-profile visitor who fled from New York or London where his business has just collapsed? He has to be a suspect, for sure.

I catch a snippet of his conversation as he passes me. "Briggs, that's not my problem. It's yours. You're the one the client requested, though I can't understand…"

This happens three more times. It gets more amusing with every pass. He's going to make a great base to build a character on. Grumpy and rich, and with a large secret that comes out at the very end. Maybe it will be one that'll affect the two main characters and their romance…

He stops right In front of my chair. His back is to me, and he's staring out at the horizon.

"…okay. Send over the paperwork and I'll read through it… yeah. Bye."

He turns around in my direction and halts at seeing me.

I give him a small smile and raise my hand in hello. Grump or not, he's now a part of my cast of characters.

He's statue-still for a second before he nods in greeting. It's a curt clip of his head as if we're business acquaintances passing by one another in a hallway. Then, he flips his phone around in his hands and strides back across the beach, toward the bungalows. I watch his retreating back disappear between the luxury villas and the jet-setting denizens who stay there.

That's one part of the resort I still have to explore.

I reach for my lemonade and take a long sip. Two weeks here might not be so difficult after all.

Chapter Three

It's the next morning, and I'm back to finish my survey of the breakfast buffet. My conclusions… The fruit is a must, especially mangoes grown here on the island. And, as good as they are, the waffles aren't worth the space on the plate, not when the cooked-to-order pancakes are fluffy as a cloud. By the end of my trip here I'll have my breakfasts down to an exact science.

I eat on the resort's patio. It overlooks the crystal-clear, blue waters, with gently swaying palm trees casting a cooling shade over the space. I've been sitting here a while now, eating and reading the first of the three books I brought with me on this trip. Out of the corner of my eye, I'm also watching the other guests.

The sisters from yesterday are back, and while they aren't arguing over breakfast, there's a certain sharpness in their movements. Of course, I don't know if they're sisters. I don't know anything about them at all, and that gives my imagination plenty of space to spin fanciful stories.

The secretive businessman-who-might-be-the-villain-in-my-new-story doesn't show up.

The morning is pleasantly warm, but humidity is still present, and I'm forced to corral my long hair into a braid. Little tendrils escape around my face, curling in a way they never care to do back home. With my dark eyes and light-brown hair, one might think I tan well, but there's always a pinky stage before I reach any kind of summer tan.

As the morning moseys into midday, I change into a bikini and a cover-up, and grab my beach bag and guidebook. As I head through the lobby, I take a deep breath of the citrusy scent that always lingers in the hotel's common areas. Five-star service right there. My first booked excursion is tomorrow, and I want to make sure I know exactly what to expect.

There's a line at the front desk, so I take my place behind a couple with huge bags that are likely checking in. I don't mind the wait. I only want to confirm the pickup spot tomorrow, to make sure I don't miss my snorkeling cruise.

An annoyed sigh sounds behind me. Apparently, not everyone's okay with the wait. I glance over my shoulder.

It's Phillip Meyer.

He hasn't noticed me yet. His gaze is laser-focused above my head at the single attendant working at the front desk.

I can't help myself.

"In a hurry?" I ask.

His focus shifts to me, jaw clenched tight. But then his eyes clear in recognition. "Hello, Eden. I didn't see you."

"Hiya."

"You'd think a place like this would have two receptionists."

"Maybe they do," I say calmly. "Maybe one got sick or had to step out for an important call..."

He's quiet for a moment like he hadn't expected a real answer. "Yes. I suppose so."

"Are you checking out? I think there are boxes over there where you can leave your key card. You know, if you're in a hurry."

"I'm not checking out."

"Oh, okay." I shift my guidebook over, gripping it with both hands, and search for something to say.

He beats me to it. "You aren't either, are you?"

"No."

"Thought so. No bags," he says and looks down between us. His gaze stops on my hands. "Is that a guidebook?"

I glance down at it and the colorful Post-it notes that stick up among the pages. "Oh, yes. I've been reading up on the island."

"I'll say." His lips curve in one corner. "How long are you planning on staying? Two months?"

"Two weeks," I say. "But it never hurts to be prepared. Those who fail to plan—"

"Plan to fail," he cuts in. "I couldn't agree more."

"Oh? Where's your guidebook, then?"

He holds up his phone. "The accumulated wealth of human knowledge, right at my fingertips, and probably more up to date than a book."

"You do seem very attached to your phone," I say in a brilliant retort. It's my wittiest moment to date.

But he just snorts. "The disease of the modern age. What are you in line for, then? Is your Wi-Fi also shit?"

"No, it works. Is that why you're here?"

He nods. "Seems like the network doesn't reach all the way to the bungalows, at least not reliably. I was on a video call for work this morning, and it kept cutting in and out."

"Did you try turning off the video? Sometimes that helps."

He looks at me with a patience that feels entirely put on. "Yes. I did try that."

The grumpy five-year-old is back. "Take your calls in the lobby," I suggest.

"I'll have to do that going forward." A frown appears between his dark eyebrows. "So, why are you in line?"

"I've booked a snorkeling cruise for tomorrow. It will probably be the highlight of my entire trip. I can't wait to see the sea turtles and just want to double-check the pickup spot so I don't miss it."

"Is it a sunset cruise?"

"Yes, should be. I think it departs from the Bridgetown

Marina."

"Have fun," he says.

"Thanks. I'm planning on it. Oh, we're moving."

The couple with the large suitcases in front of us shuffles up to the sole receptionist, who welcomes them warmly. The woman speaks first. Her voice is loud and reverberates through the lobby. "Thank you. We're so excited to finally be here. It's our honeymoon!"

I can't stifle the low groan that escapes me. Phillip snorts, and it sounds just as cynical as mine.

"Honeymooners," he mutters under his breath.

I shake my head. "They're everywhere."

"It's already knocked a star off my review," he says darkly.

The deadpan delivery makes me laugh. It's only a chuckle, really, but Phillip's eyebrows rise at the sound.

"Oh no," I say. "I bet this multi-million dollar resort will hate that."

He looks away, but that curve of his lips is back. "They better. I can write *very* strongly worded reviews."

The honeymoon couple wraps up their check-in, and is sent on their way with a cheery *Welcome to The Winter, where it's always summer.* It's cheesy enough that I'm willing to bet it's a line the employees are taught during training.

"How can I help you?" the receptionist asks me with a wide smile. And just then, another employee appears out of the staff door, walking quickly to the front counter.

He locks eyes with someone behind me. Phillip, presumably. "I can help you right over here, sir. Sorry for the wait."

I resist the urge to glance over at Phillip. I'm sure the look in my eyes would be shouting *I told you so* if I do.

I have a feeling that he hears the words all the same.

By the time I'm done with my questions, he's gone, and the lobby is once again empty. I exit the lobby through the side door, leading to the garden and the wooden path beyond that snakes down to the ocean.

Only about half of the evenly spaced lounge chairs spread across the white-sand beach appear to be occupied. Without my sunglasses, however, I wouldn't be able to see a thing thanks to the bright sunlight bathing everything in sight. The water is clear and turquoise, and just this side of choppy. It's the first day I've seen the sea as anything but a mirror of perfection.

My lounge chair is still free. Not that it's mine, but after a day, it's already starting to feel like it is. Creatures of habit, aren't we?

The thought sparks an idea.

Maybe two of the characters in my story would be arguing over something on the beach. Others will take note, and after the murder, suspicions will rise among them. But it's just another red herring… because the argument was just over the lounge chair. *This is mine. Yours? There was no towel here! No, but I* always *use this one. And how was I supposed to know that?*

My poor book lies unopened beside me as I make notes in the notepad I'd remembered to bring today.

It's been months since I felt this geared up, since my surroundings were a source of inspiration instead of frustration. Maybe all I needed was a change of scenery.

Becky calls while I'm still consumed by my manic scribbles. I'm fleshing out the side characters and trying to figure out the murder victim, but the couple meant to fall in love while solving the crime is noticeably absent. I can't see the shape of them or their love story.

"Hey," I say.

"Oh, that's your focused voice."

I chuckle. "I said one word."

"Yes, and it was a very focused one. Is this a bad time?"

"No, of course, not. I'm on vacation. I have *oceans* of time."

"Well, I've seen that guidebook of yours, and I don't know if *oceans of time* is exactly the right description. You're packing a lot into these two weeks."

"I'll have you know, I've taken it very easy these first

days."

"Oh?"

"Yes. And I've even spoken to another guest here, at the hotel."

Becky draws in a mock gasp. "Spoken? Oh my. Was it in an elevator? And was it about the weather?"

"No, and no, you smart-ass. I ended up sharing a table with him the other night."

As expected, the conversation devolves shortly after in a flurry of details. I look over my shoulder to make sure there's no tall, dark-haired, scowling man to overhear me, but he's nowhere in sight. The people around me have all cleared out, too.

I realize why ten minutes later.

The sea had been disturbed before, but it's positively choppy now. There's not a single swimmer in sight. Above me, the clouds are heavy and moving fast, blocking out the sun and blue sky.

I gather my things and tuck my phone between my ear and shoulder. "How are you feeling? Feet still sore?"

"That's the least of my problems now. Sore feet, the fiercest of heartburns, aching back, and I have SPD, which basically means my pelvis is ripping itself apart. And I've not even gotten to the giving birth part, yet."

"That sounds wonderful."

"Oh, it is. I highly recommend it. Patrick is so jealous that he can't do it, too."

I chuckle. "You're almost at the end of it. I wish I could make it better, but—"

"But I did this to myself," she says miserably, with the dry tinge of humor I love so much. "Well, Patrick helped, but I knew what I was getting myself into."

"Doesn't mean you're not allowed to complain."

"Thank you. You've had to listen to a lot of it."

I sigh. "Well, you heard a lot about Caleb and Cindy."

"Hey, I was angry about that, too. Still am. Darn, I have to go. Well, if I can get off this couch."

I smile. She always cheers me up. "Talk to you later."

"Already looking forward to it," she says. "Enjoy turning real people into fake people."

That makes me laugh. "You make me sound like a psycho."

"Aren't all writers?" she asks, and the line goes dead. I'm still smiling when I trudge up the white sand to the pool area.

Maybe we are. Maybe I can test it out here, in this new place, with enough space to be anyone I'd like for the rest of these two weeks. An entirely new version of myself that could never have existed back in Pinecrest, Washington.

The mention of Cindy had sent a pang of pain through me. It'll pass like it always does, but I stop at the pool bar to get a mojito to help it along.

I quickly discover that the people who left the beach because of the turning weather just migrated to the pool area. They're sprawled in cabanas and lying beneath umbrellas. The place is packed.

I grab my mojito and beach bag and walk around the long side of the pool. There's a single free lounge chair at the very end, protected from the potential rain by the oversized umbrella.

If no one else takes it.

I soldier on in my flip-flops, my eyes on the prize. This place is a veritable gold mine of inspiration, and I can't wait to get my notepad open again.

I'm so focused that I miss the small kid who races in front of me. I hear his excited scream before I make contact with the inflatable he's carrying.

It all happens very fast. I take a step to the right to avoid hitting the kid and sacrifice my balance in the process. I tilt toward the only thing close by.

A lounge chair. A currently occupied lounge chair.

My knees brace against the cushioned seat, and I come to a graceful stop. No harm, no bruise, no damage except for the painfully overpriced mojito in my right hand. The plastic glass tumbles out of my hand and spills its icy contents all over the lap of a man and the laptop he's currently working on.

"Oh no," I say, reaching out to grip the pole of the umbrella for support. "Shoot. Hello. Gosh, I'm sorry."

Phillip is staring at me like I've just grown two heads. "Eden?"

"Yes. Shit, did it get on your laptop?"

He looks down. "Yeah. Wait, it's not too bad…"

He starts to wrap his towel around it, but I beat him to it, throwing my own across it with frantic movements. "I'm sorry. I promise I'll get you a new one if this one is ruined."

"No need."

"I mean it. It's just, I didn't see that kid, and then—"

"Not your fault," Phillip says. "This resort is marketed as kid-free."

"It is?"

His voice darkens. "Yes. It was one of my very few requirements. I don't know why they've made an exception for this one family, but…"

"Is your computer okay?"

"It'll live," he says, but he doesn't sound enthused by the prospect. He sets his laptop on the side table next to him and it does look fine. Usable.

"The spill mostly missed it, thank God," I say. "But then… oh. It got on you."

We both look down at his legs, and his trunks, and the beige polo he's wearing. There's a lonely mint leaf garnishing his right thigh, and I can see ice cubes trapped between his knees.

"Sorry," I say. "Really."

He gets out of the chair and shakes himself off. I watch the tiny mint leaf sail to the ground. "Stop apologizing."

"Let me get you another drink."

He stares at me. "Eden, you spilled your *own* drink."

"Oh, that's right. Sorry." I chuckle in apology and pick up my bag from where it had fallen on the ground. "Let me get you a drink in apology, then."

"That's not necessary. It wasn't your fault."

I give him a wide smile. "Come on, let me. What do you want? Oh, were you working?"

"Yeah. The Wi-Fi is better out here." He runs a hand through his dark hair. It looks more disheveled now than it ever has before, as if he just toweled it off after a swim.

"Right. Did you get it sorted in your room?"

"There's someone there now, checking on the router."

"That's good," I say, nodding once, nodding twice. "Very good. So uh, do you like mojitos?"

He sighs like I'm being stubborn. "Yes."

"Good. Wait here, I'll be right back."

"Watch out for kids," he says.

I do. I'm super careful on the way there *and* on the way back, carrying two overpriced mojitos. I'm so busy focusing on where I'm stepping in my death-trap-flip-flops that I don't notice until I get back that he hasn't opened his laptop again.

He's watching me instead.

I set the mojito down on the table for him. "There we go! Sorry about that. Is your laptop not working?"

His eyes are locked on his drink. "What's that?"

"A forgive-me-mojito. A… forjito."

"No, the pink umbrella in it."

"Oh, that? The bartender added it. I guess it's a sign of being on holiday, and that you're enjoying yourself." I slowly smile, thinking of the dinner the other night. "Want me to take a picture of you drinking it?"

He gives me a dry look. "Absolutely not."

"You could send it to your colleagues."

"They'd hate me," he says and takes a long sip of the minty cocktail. His fingers struggle to hold the umbrella off to one side, and I have to hide my smile behind my own tumbler. "More than they already do, at any rate."

That's… an interesting comment. At least he gets a high score for self-awareness.

"Well," I say. "Enjoy your business meeting, then."

He nods. There's still a wet stain on the bottom of his polo shirt, and I can't look at it too long without feeling guilty. Everyone around the pool must have seen what happened. Maybe they even awarded points. *Seven-point-eight for that pathetic performance.* Thank goodness no staff saw that disaster, or they'd have been here with extra towels and kind smiles, and I would have felt even worse.

"I will," he says. "Enjoy your… guidebook."

It's almost a mean comment, the way he says it. But there's something in his tone that makes me suspect he means it to be a dry joke. Maybe he's just unused to making them.

"I will." I raise my glass in a mock salute and head away from him and toward a tantalizingly empty lounge chair on the other side of the pool.

I make it under the umbrella just before the first heavy raindrops fall from the sky. The tropical downpour is torrential. The droplets bounce off the stone deck, leaping back up like they're trying to rejoin the cloud they came from.

I curl up on the lounge chair and listen to the thunderous pitter-patter against the umbrella canopy above me.

Even with the rain, it's still warm. An earthy, floral scent rises off the surrounding vegetation, while slight mist forms over the hot stones of the pool deck.

It's magical.

A smile breaks across my face. *I have to put this in my book.* Maybe the couple will hide somewhere, forced together into a makeshift shelter where they can confess their feelings.

The rain is so heavy, I can't clearly see the other guests through it. On the opposite side of the pool, is a familiar shape, a smudge of a beige shirt and dark hair. I can't make out his expression, but it's probably a frown. And that only makes me smile harder.

The only thing I can see is that he's turned toward me.

Chapter Four

It's easy to get used to a five-star breakfast buffet and endless time to enjoy it. I spend the next morning at my usual table—overlooking the ocean—with a plate of fresh fruit, eggs, and bacon.

It's not a hardship.

The real suffering will be returning to the five-minute granola bar routine in my car before arriving at the school for my first lesson. I look around the restaurant at the other guests enjoying their meals and feel grateful to be able to experience this kind of luxury, even if it's just for a short time.

I open my notepad and write *Game Plan* at the top. If I'm serious about this story, the one I'm inspired to write more than any other in previous years, I need to do my research. The Winter Resort website will give me inspirational images, of course, but there's no accounting for personal experience.

And authors are supposed to *experience* things.

Some of the great authors have gone to war, traveled, or drunk their way from one country to another. My sojourn into the lives of the rich isn't *quite* so harrowing, perhaps, but it's immersion nonetheless.

I tuck the notepad, complete with the rough character sketches I've drawn up in the last two days, into my bag and walk around the resort. The lobby. The gardens. The outdoor pool. A lot of it is familiar, but there are areas I haven't seen. The hotel gym, the spa, the concierge desk.

I save the best for last. The bungalow section.

Even from the outside, they look luxurious and private, offering guests a taste of secluded exclusivity. The path between the buildings is paved in wide, sand-colored stone, and is just large enough for a golf cart to get around. I'd seen a few of these vehicles parked by the lobby earlier. They must be for transporting bags and guests to their private accommodations. The path is fringed by low hedges, and a gate blocks off the entrance to every unit.

The bungalows have names, too, etched on the wooden plaques by each entrance. One bungalow is called *The Sandpiper.* From reading my guidebook, I know it's a bird. A very tiny one with a long beak, often found flittering around the shoreline. I walk by *The Green Monkey, The Leatherback, The Bullfinch,* and *The Whistling Frog.*

The bungalow labeled *The Hawksbill* catches my attention. That's the name of one of the turtle species mentioned when I booked my snorkeling tour set for later this afternoon. This bungalow looks no different from any of the others. Dark wood stairs up to a large door and the perfectly landscaped plants in pots on either side.

It's beautiful. I walk around it to where a stone path cuts between *The Hawskbill* and its neighbor before leading down to the sea. The water is a glittering turquoise band, edged by the white sand, to which the bungalow guests have near-private access. It's so beautiful, it tears at my heart a little.

I could live here forever.

There's not a single cell in my body that longs for the cold winter in Washington.

I stand between two bungalows that blend beautifully into the landscape. I snap a few shots of the area for my inspiration before heading to the beach.

That's when I hear a voice coming beyond the hedge to

the right. "Shit," a person's saying. "Okay. How did you get in there?"

There's no reply. Curiosity gets the better of me and I rise on my toes, peering over the shrubbery.

The bungalows have private patios. I catch the back of a man's head and then a pair of shoulders before he bends over.

It looks like Phillip.

He straightens again. And yup, that's a button-down shirt and dark hair.

He's holding an empty five-gallon water jug. Each bungalow must get its own, not like in the main hotel building where the watercoolers are evenly spaced in the hallways. I catch a glimpse of something tiny, green, and moving frantically about inside the container.

A lizard? Or a frog?

"I'll set you free in this hedge here..." The words are barely audible, speaking to himself as he is, but I catch them all the same.

I duck out of sight and continue down to the beach, my smile stretching even wider.

Seems like this place brings out the best in everyone.

I have another hour until my snorkeling trip. I spend it on the beach, sitting with my feet in the sand, and send a few quick pictures to my parents and to Becky.

By 3 p.m., I'm waiting outside the hotel lobby. My long hair is securely braided down my back, my cap is on tight, and I have the underwater camera Becky gave me in my bag. Emailing the trip organizer to change my booking for the snorkeling cruise from two people to one hadn't hurt *quite* so much when I'd searched for images of it afterward.

Turquoise waters. Underwater shots of sea turtles. The sunset is seen off the bow of a boat. Being heartbroken on a boat on the Caribbean Sea is infinitely more preferable to crying in between my kindergarten lessons in Pinecrest.

The minivan picks me up from the hotel lobby, and I cram

in next to a pair of Dutch tourists. It takes us twenty minutes to drive to the marina in Bridgetown. I pull my cap lower on my head to shield my eyes from the intense sun and look at the boats waiting for us.

And all the tourists.

Turns out, we're two entire minivans worth of people scheduled for the open bar, and the intimate dinner and snorkeling cruise.

My stomach sinks as I let my gaze wander over the assembled excursionists. Half of them are my age or younger. Two women in bikinis are posing in front of the boat, while a third takes pictures of them. Beside me, a British couple is standing with their arms around one another, talking in hushed tones.

I'm the only one here alone, and I can feel it.

One of the deckhands must see the expression on my face. "Yeah, it'll be a cozy one today," he says with a grin. "I think we might get a proposal, too."

"A *proposal*?"

"Yes," the deckhand says. He flips over a page on his notepad. "It's fairly common. Pretty setting, lots of drinks to celebrate. Now let me just see... yes, we're waiting for the final minivan."

I look down at the line of people who are eager to board. "Is this peak tourist season?"

"Nearly," he says and looks at me. His smile widens. "Don't worry, miss, we'll take good care of you. Once we're out there, you'll have the wind in your hair and not a care in the world."

I smile back at him as happily as I can manage. The people are one thing, but a proposal?

Something twists in my stomach.

I should head down the dock, to join the line waiting to get aboard the gently bobbing catamaran, but my feet don't feel like moving. Somewhere on board, speakers turn on, blasting upbeat dance music.

I just want to see the turtles.

"Eden!" someone calls.

I look over at the deckhand checking off names. But he didn't call my name. No, the loud voice comes from the dock next to ours.

Phillip Meyer is striding across the small pier toward me.

"Hey," he says, slightly out of breath. "You're scheduled for a snorkeling cruise, right?"

I blink at him. His cheeks are flushed with color, darkening his skin. "Yes."

"Good. I have one scheduled, too. Similar route and itinerary: snorkeling and dinner. Skip the other tourists and join mine instead."

I stare at him. "Where's yours?"

He nods to the catamaran anchored next to the one I'm supposed to be boarding. It's just as large—a white giant throning on the turquoise waves—but nearly empty. Two crew members are untying the ropes keeping it tethered to the dock, but I don't see a single tourist.

"That's *your* boat?"

"For the next four hours, yes." His voice sounds strained around the edges. "It was booked for two, so there's an already-paid-for spot available."

My brain takes a long minute to work through what he's saying. "But we barely know one another."

"We've had dinner together," he says. "There's a private tour guide on board and several crew members. We're stopping to snorkel with the turtles."

"You're sure?"

"Yes," he says. "Don't you want to sit on the bow by yourself? Rather than beside all those people?" He glances at the group of rowdy twenty-something-year-olds beside me who, if I were a betting woman, probably started drinking around noon.

For me, the cruise appealed because of the open-water snorkeling and the beautiful views. For others, it seems the open bar was the selling point.

"Eden," Phillip says. "I have an entire catamaran for myself, with three crew members. They're going to cook me dinner. *Just for me*."

"Wow," I breathe.

His face holds a stressed edge. "You won't be in the way. You would actually be doing me a favor."

"I would?"

"There are rose petals all over the deck."

Everything clicks into place, from the flushed cheeks to the tight mouth.

He's embarrassed.

Just like I will be on a boat chock-full of happy couples, with me being the lone person without someone there to share the experience with. Except he will be surrounded only by the crew, but they will all will know that it was originally meant for two. Because rose petals can only mean one thing.

Phillip gestures to his catamaran. "On or off?"

"On," I say, "if you get rid of the rose petals."

"I've already chucked them overboard."

Chapter Five

The boat is huge.

Where it might have felt crowded with three minivans full of people, with only two guests, this catamaran feels positively enormous. I could avoid Phillip the entire trip, and without lifting so much as a finger.

I join him on board and receive wide smiles from the crew. If they were curious about Phillip racing across the docks to pick up a seemingly random woman not originally meant to be here, they don't show it.

Professionals.

"Welcome on board, Ms...."

"Eden," I say. "Please call me Eden."

Giant nets stretch between the hulls at the bow of the boat. I unfold my towel on one of them and lie back. The boat starts moving, and beneath me, the waves dance. We're full speed ahead cruising down the coastline toward Carlisle Bay.

"Here you go," Jamie says with a smile and hands me a virgin piña colada. He'd introduced himself as the lead deckhand and let both Phillip and I know that he'd be happy to make us any drinks or snacks we might want. His crisp white polo shirt stands out in sharp contrast to his dark skin.

"Thank you, that looks incredible."

"Anytime," Jamie says and looks over his shoulder at

Phillip. He's sitting on a low bench across the deck, wearing dark-tinted sunglasses and looking down at his phone.

He must be doing what one apparently does best on a boat in the Caribbean. Answering emails. How does he even have internet out here?

At least Jamie's expression makes it clear I'm not alone in wondering.

I keep my eyes on the horizon, savoring the warm air and the spray of ocean off the waves against my face. I feel alive, more alive than I have in weeks. All the anxiety leading up to this trip was worth it, just for this.

The catamaran takes us into the calm, light-blue waters of Carlisle Bay. The captain halts the boat at the first stop and throws a light tether over the buoy anchored to the sea floor.

"Ready to get in the water?" Jamie asks me. "We've got all the snorkeling gear you'll need."

"I wouldn't miss it for anything," I say.

Seems like Phillip won't, either. He comes walking toward us, steady on the softly undulating deck.

"You'd like to as well, sir?"

Phillip nods and reaches for buttons of his shirt. I look away as he tugs it off. I don't have the gift of tanning easily—the elusive skill that evolution bestows most unequally—and I'm very aware of how pale I am next to Phillip.

There are abs. I see them out of the corner of my eye. Distinct lines chiseled into a flat stomach and faintly smattered with dark hair that disappears into his trunks.

Annoyance flares in my chest. Of course, he has a sculpted body, the perfection marred only by his frequent scowls. I love my lilac bikini, but it suddenly feels too small and covers far too little. I don't exactly spend my evenings slaving away at the gym.

So, I focus on adjusting my goggles and try my best to ignore the tall and muscled man beside me.

"We've stopped away from the other tourist boats," Jamie says, "but there should still be plenty of turtles here.

Green turtles, mostly, but we might see a hawksbill if we're lucky. I'll join you guys in the water with some food for them."

"No leatherbacks?" I ask.

He smiles in surprise. "They're rare here on the west coast, so probably not, no. You know which species we have?"

"I read up beforehand," I say. "Isn't it also the hatching season right now?"

"Sure is," he says. "So make sure you look twice before lying down on the beaches. Nests are clearly marked and currently protected by volunteers. Ready to get in the water?"

I make my way to the platform at the back of the catamaran. Turquoise water laps softly at the edge of the platform, and beneath the surface, I see only the sandy bottom—far, far down. It looks gorgeous.

A feel a shiver of fear at the sight of so much deep water, surrounding us in every direction. But it's clear, and it'll be warm, and I let myself linger in a frisson of anticipation. Adventure. That's what I'm on.

An adventure.

Phillip comes to stand beside me on the diving platform. He's been quiet since we came on board, but now he speaks up, his voice dry and teasing. "You were a teacher's pet in school, weren't you?"

I look sideways at him. "You'd rather answer emails than enjoy the expensive catamaran cruise you've paid for?"

"Answering emails is my way of enjoying the cruise," he says, deadly serious. But then he breaks and a half smile curves his lips. "I'm kidding," he says and pulls the goggles over his face. "Now come on. Let's get in the water."

"Right," I say and look back at the wild expanse of ocean. "The turtles wait for no one."

The water is colder than I expected and really salty, making floating on my stomach an easy feat. Beneath me, I can see the sandy ocean floor. It's so very far away. *Barbados has never had a shark attack.* I'd researched this very thoroughly.

The waves are soft and gentle, and I bob with my head in the water, breathing through the tub of my snorkel.

Jamie dives into the water with us. He shouts and I look up, seeing him waving a few feet away. "There!" he calls and points to a spot in front of us.

I swim in his direction, my eyes glued to the waters beneath us. And there it comes.

A large sea turtle glides quickly beneath the waves. It pumps its flippers once and ascends, taking a dried piece of fish from Jamie's hand before diving away again. As graceless as they are on land, here they're aquatic gymnasts, and this is their realm.

One turtle turns into three, all drifting beneath us in the turquoise water. They're larger than I thought they'd be and much more curious. A turtle comes up close, inspecting my feet, and I tread the water as carefully as I can. Happiness explodes in my chest.

I'll remember this forever, I think. *Forever, forever, forever.*

Thirty minutes later, my little underwater camera is full. I climb up onto the platform, sea droplets sluicing off me.

"That was incredible!"

Jamie chuckles and reaches for my snorkel set. "They're Bajan turtles," he says. "Of course, they are."

I twist my braid around and squeeze, letting the water drip back into the turquoise depths. "Green turtles, right?"

"The very ones," Jamie says.

Phillip pulls himself up the ladder after us, arms flexing, and comes to stand beside me on the platform. Water runs down his body in rivulets, following unseen paths over his arms and muscled chest. He pushes the wet strands of hair back off his forehead, and his stomach flexes with the movement.

"That was awesome," I say. He might be the surliest and richest workaholic I've ever met, but even *he* can't say anything snarky about swimming with ocean giants.

"You brought a camera?" he asks. The sun glitters off his wet hair, now near-black.

"Yes. I don't think the quality will be great, though." I hold up the plastic square. I'll have to get the film processed when I get home… if there are still places that process analog film.

He looks at the camera for a long second. "Preserving the turtles for posterity?"

"Yeah. I promised my students pictures of my trip."

Phillip steps up on the catamaran deck, and I follow him, puddles forming beneath us on the shiny deck. "Your students?"

"Yes, I'm a teacher."

"Ah," he says. There's a whole world in that word, as if it explains everything about me. "Let me guess. It's not high school."

"No, I teach kindergarten."

His lip curves again and he grabs his navy towel, rubbing it over his head. I look away from the vigorous movement of his hands. The action feels intimate somehow. Like he's just stepped out of a shower.

"Kindergarten?" he says. "I have to say, you're my definition of a hero."

My eyebrows shoot high. "A hero?"

"Dealing with two dozen small kids every day? Half of whom can't sit still, and the other half who want to eat glue? Yes." He tosses the towel onto the catamaran's deck and drops down, stretched out on top of it.

I grip my towel more closely. There's so *much* of him, strong, long legs and tanned stomach, and eyes that meet mine. It's easier to handle him when he's focused on his emails. But like this? I feel intimately aware that he's a man, a stranger, and objectively a very attractive one at that.

I carefully lay my towel beside him and sit down cross-legged. In a bikini. *Don't think about it,* I tell myself. What he might think or not think about me doesn't matter.

Below deck, the boat hums to life. We're heading up the west coast now, turquoise waters splashing beneath the boat's hulls.

"It's fun, though. I love kids."—I look over at him, unable to resist adding—"Besides, being a teacher means I don't get to work on vacations."

"You took pictures of turtles for your students," Phillip says without opening his eyes. His hands are beneath his head. He looks relaxed while soaking up the sun, with a faint smile stretching over his lips. "So you're working, too, Ms. Goody Two-shoes, and don't try to pretend otherwise."

"So, what do you do for a living, then?"

"I'm an attorney."

My mind conjures up an immediate image of high-rises and conference tables, and endless nights in front of the lit-up computer screen. "Wow," I say, drawing out the vowel.

"Whatever you're thinking—"

"Is probably correct, right?"

There's silence beside me. And then, the admission. "Probably."

I chuckle. "Good thing you treat yourself to nice holidays then. Did you enjoy your drink with the little umbrella?"

"The drink, yes," he says.

"Want another one?" I get up off my sprawl and start making my way back toward the galley. We haven't taken full advantage of the open bar.

"Eden!" Phillip calls. "No umbrella!"

"I can't hear you!" I call back.

He gets an umbrella.

Three of them, in fact, in three separate rum punches. I'm on my second when the dinner is served at the back— the stern—of the boat. Anchored in a turquoise bay on the exclusive west coast, not far away from the Winter Resort, with the setting sun as our backdrop.

I sit down on a chair with a small sigh of wonder. I can't

believe I'm here. I can't believe I'm doing this, seeing this. *I can't believe I'm here without Caleb.*

Phillip clears his throat. It breaks me out of my thoughts, and I look across the table to see him extending a hand.

"Pardon?" I ask.

"Give me your phone," he says. "You'd like a picture of yourself here with the sunset, wouldn't you?"

"Oh, good thinking! Thanks!"

He mutters something about having a lot of practice, but there's a half smile on his lips, too. The drinks have served their purpose.

Jamie and a fellow deckhand, Aaron, serve us grilled mahi-mahi, salad, roasted potatoes, and another round of drinks. It's one of the best meals I've ever had—fresh from the ocean, on a boat floating softly on the waves.

That's when I strike.

"So," I say, cutting through my fish. "There were rose petals on deck?"

Phillip groans. His hair has dried, curling slightly at the ends, and he brushes it back off his brow. "Yes."

"You know, I've made some assumptions about that."

"Of course, you have," he says and reaches for his drink. "Think you could stop?"

"Not likely. So, Phillip Meyer. Are you here on your honeymoon, too?"

He looks out over the waves and doesn't answer me. It had been a guess. It could have been any kind of couple's trip, really, but his silence…

"Oh, you are," I say. "Damn."

He waves a hand as if to dismiss the entire subject. "Yeah, this trip was planned for two."

"I'm sorry."

"Don't be. What happened happened," he says. But his gaze is on the water like he's expecting it to throw him a life buoy.

"I never thought I'd meet anyone else here in the same position as me."

"Someone who didn't want the vacation days they'd so painstakingly carved out of their schedule to go to waste?" he says. "Because that's me."

That makes me chuckle. "But you're still working, though."

His eyes flash to mine, but then he sighs. "Yes, but not as much, and with a much nicer view. Chicago this time of year is… well."

"I totally get that. I'm from Washington State, and it's not exactly sunny," I say with a shrug. "I don't know about you, but we couldn't get refunds on anything. Not the flight and not most of the hotel stay."

He makes a humming sound and then falls quiet. There's something about his impossibility and unpredictability—*Who sits down at another person's table? Who invites them along on a private catamaran cruise?*—that makes him easy to talk to. It's like he exists apart from my usual life, apart from the rules of the universe I know and accept.

"Does that mean your ex-fiancé is here, too?" he asks, fingers drumming on the table. "Hiding in a different hotel room and on different catamaran cruises?"

"Oh God, no. I told him I'm keeping the honeymoon. Going to the Caribbean had been my dream. I've planned this trip and done the research. I was the one who read the guidebook cover to cover." I shrug, a bit embarrassed about the force in my words. "Teacher's pet, you know?"

On that vision board as a teenager, I had a Caribbean beach, yes. But beside it, there was also the Eiffel Tower, the logo of my dream college, my favorite Virginia Wolfe quote, a woman enjoying her run, and various other things I thought I wanted out of life. I never became a runner, and I haven't been to Paris.

But damn it, I'm finally in the Caribbean, and it's a tick on my bucket list.

Phillip is still tapping his fingers along the edge of the table. "I get it. You really wanted to come here."

I nod. "I really, really did."

"Well, my entire itinerary is planned for two."

"No refunds for you, either?"

"None," he says with a half smile. "Eden, you should take advantage of it."

"Of your itinerary?"

"Yeah. All of it is pre-paid. You haven't been too annoyed by me today, have you? On this giant boat?"

"Only when you spend time on your phone instead of the views."

His smile widens. "You can put me in a time-out then. But think about it. I have more things planned during these weeks."

I nod, my teeth digging into my lower lip. It's not a bad idea. But it's definitely outside of my comfort zone. Everything about him is… and everything about this trip is... Challenge after challenge. Socializing with strangers, snorkeling in the deep-blue ocean, and exploring a place so different from the one where I grew up.

But maybe that's the point. I've been complacent and sad for too long. Perhaps the thing I need is excitement and just a tinge of fear to spike the adrenaline.

I lift my rum punch in the air. It takes him, this stranger in front of me, a moment to follow suit. All I know of him is his name, his job, and that he saves lizards if they're trapped. But it's a good start.

"To honeymooning alone," I say.

He shakes his head like he can't believe I just said that, but touches his glass to mine. "To honeymooning alone."

Chapter Six

The beach is glorious. There's no other word for it. I'm lying on one of the Winter Resort's lounge chairs, part of my body beneath the shade of an umbrella, watching the turquoise waves lap against the sand. Even I hate myself a little for how good of a time I'm having.

Thanks to the tech gods, the Wi-Fi from the hotel stretches all the way over here, and I'm halfway through the newest episode of my favorite true crime podcast. Beside me is an ice-cold glass of lemonade, courtesy of the gentleman who just walked across the beach selling drinks.

Perfection.

My phone buzzes with a text. It's Becky.

Omg. I'm at the grocery store and just saw Cindy.

My stomach tightens reading the words, but the familiar feeling of nausea doesn't come. It's been three months, after all, and the time has helped dull the initial pain.

What did you do? Did you duck behind the produce?

No. I'm too pregnant to hide behind anything but an elephant, probably. I gave her the evil eye.

I smile at the screen. Becky had taken my side right off the bat, even though I hadn't asked her to. The three of us had been a team since high school. Through different colleges and cities, we'd stuck together—regular phone calls and girls' trips. *You have your own relationship,* I'd said carefully to Becky. *I don't want you to feel like you* have *to—*

Becky had cut me off right then and there. *Someone who'll sleep with their best friend's fiancé is not a friend I want.*

And that had been that.

Maybe Becky will change her mind someday, but she's the most "law and order" person I know, and for now, she seems to be more outraged than me. Hard to believe, that.

What did Cindy do?

Her and I haven't had a proper conversation since that explosive day back in November.

She was the one to duck behind the produce! I just realized I shouldn't have texted you about this. SORRY! Enjoy beautiful Barbados and forget about everyone here in Pinecrest. Send me a picture of the beach and I'll cry over my swollen ankles.

I snap a picture of my legs in the lounge chair, along with the beautiful waves in the background. Two sailing boats bob peacefully out in the distance. My phone quickly pings with her response.

You deserve it.

I lean back in my lounge chair and try not to think of Cindy. Not of Caleb, either. And definitely not of the two of them together. No, I don't want that image here.

Happy place. This is my goddamn happy place and my dream vacation.

I succeed somewhat. It helps to have the soothing voice of my favorite podcaster narrating a gruesome double homicide in my ears. It never made any sense to Caleb, my fascination with true crime. But he's gone, and the podcast is still going, so who really serves me best?

Let it go, I tell myself. *You're on vacation.*

I people-watch instead. Look at the other tourists on the beach. A couple of retirees a few chairs down are both sleeping in their loungers. Further away, a young man is industriously rubbing sun lotion on the back of a young woman.

Probably newlyweds.

A sharp voice cuts through my peaceful podcast. Someone's on the phone. Because I'm nosy, I lower my volume to better eavesdrop and crane my neck.

It's Phillip's voice. He's walking along the shoreline again, wearing a pair of swim trunks, no shirt, and Bluetooth headphones in his ears. The sharp features of his face are drawn. He's arguing with someone.

He walks the length of the beach once. Then twice. And then, one final time, turning so his back is to the ocean. His arms are crossed over his chest.

I lift my hand and give a little wave.

His eyes land on me. For a moment, I don't know if he'll even acknowledge me. But then, he nods—a sharp jerk of his chin, so different from the looseness I'd observed in him on the catamaran deck.

I raise the volume on my podcast and lie back. My bikini is navy with little white dots today. Perfectly decent. And I have a bit more of a tan than the other day, courtesy of the cruise.

A shadow falls over me, and I look up.

"Hey," Phillip says, his headphones gone.

I straighten on the lounge chair. "Hello," I say. "Um, want to have a seat?"

He looks down at the free lounger next to mine like it offends him. But then, he sighs and sits down. "Yeah."

"Is everything all right?"

"Yes," he says and puts his phone face down on the chair with more force than necessary.

I decide to tempt fate and use a tried-and-tested method. It's calmed down many people. They were mainly kindergarteners and not grown men with more money than sense, but I'll try it anyway.

"I get the sense that you're not feeling like your best self," I say. "If you want to talk about it, I'm a good listener. But it's perfectly all right if you don't want to."

Phillip stares at me for so long that I get uncomfortable. There's only sternness on his face, like I'm an opponent across the negotiating table. Do attorneys even negotiate? I admit, I get most of my ideas about their work from television shows.

Then, his lip curls. "You're using your teacher's voice on me, aren't you?"

"Yes. Did it work?"

"No. But it was impressive."

"Darn," I say. "If only you were five years old."

He snorts and runs a hand over the back of his neck. "You could have given me a pair of scissors and I'd be happy again."

"I do usually carry a pair on me," I say, and it's the absolute truth. "Sometimes, I also have a glue gun or glitter. I'm pretty sure you won't believe me, but there are very few problems a bit of glitter can't solve."

There's a light in his dark-blue eyes. "I'll have to think about that if I go to court any time soon."

My smile widens. "The judge would be so impressed."

He runs a hand along his jaw. "Add some stickers to the evidence reports."

"I've found that gold stars can be very motivating."

"I'll bear that in mind," he says. The tightness around his eyes is gone, but the smile from yesterday isn't quite back. He nods to the book lying beside my lounge chair. "Is that your infamous guidebook?"

"Yeah," I say. He reaches to take it while a protest is born and dies on my tongue. I take my headphones out instead and watch in silence as he flips through the pages.

"Wow," he finally says.

"I know how it looks."

"There's no glitter, at least." He flips a heavily annotated page. "No gold stars, either. But look, you've used a highlighter. I didn't know it worked on these sorts of pages."

"You have to get a special kind," I murmur.

He flips through another chapter. There are tiny Post-it flags that mark important parts. To the casual observer, I must look like a complete lunatic to have done so much research before a trip.

"So, are you actually scoping out the island for a future movie shoot or something?" he asks. "Was the honeymoon thing a ruse? Tell me the truth. You're really undercover."

I shake my head. "I wish that was it. I just got a bit obsessed."

"I'll say." Phillip stops at a particularly annotated page. "There are asterisks here. *See more in…* no. You have *more* info?"

"Just some links in an online document."

"You would make a great paralegal or assistant," he says.

"Um, thanks?"

He looks up at me. "Oh, I don't mean… just that you're very thorough. It was a compliment. This kind of note-making is impressive."

"Thanks." I play with the edge of the beach towel I'm lying on. "This trip became my lifeline after the whole non-wedding, you know? It felt like it, at least. I wanted to be as prepared as I could be. Honestly, I probably went a bit overboard."

He closes the guidebook. "Well, you've done ten times the research I have. No, a hundred times."

I smile. "You didn't plan your itinerary for two, then?"

"God, no."

"So your ex did," I say, gambling again.

He shakes his head. "No, we used a professional for that."

My mouth forms a tiny *o*. I can't imagine the life you live if you use someone else to plan your vacations. Our paths would never have crossed back in the States. Even if we'd lived in the same city, we would still be two countries apart.

"Wow," I say. "Did they provide you with your own guidebook?"

He snorts. "No. Just eight pages of itinerary with the relevant booking details of each excursion."

"Were the headings highlighted, at least?"

"No," he says. "There was shockingly little glitter, too."

I give him a look of mock outrage. "Sorry to say it, but I think you got taken for a ride. I wouldn't hire them again."

He chuckles, the first sound of joy I've gotten out of him. "Right," he says and looks back down at his phone. Turns it over and then over again, like he can't bear to see the screen. "Do you like to fish, Eden?"

"To fish?"

"Yes. Pole, line, bait."

"I know *how* it's done," I say, and something sparks in his eyes. "But I've only tried it once or twice when I was a kid. My uncle had a cabin in the woods, next to a lake, and we'd go sometimes."

"Did you like it?"

"I was eight," I say. "I liked everything except broccoli. Why?"

"I've got another thing for two planned this afternoon. If you're interested." He inclines his head to my lounge chair, eyes briefly flitting from my bare legs to the bikini top. "Unless you've got an important date with the sun planned."

"Where are you going fishing?"

"The ocean," he says, voice deadpan.

I roll my eyes. "*Phillip*," I say. His name feels intimate on my tongue.

"I'm being picked up from the Winter Resort pier."

"Oh. Wow."

"It's a three-hour trip up the coast. The guide specializes in fishing mahi-mahi and swordfish." He shrugs. "Someone told me that swordfish is a specialty in Barbados, but maybe she hadn't done her research properly..."

I swing my legs over the side of the lounge chair. "I'll go with you," I say. "What time?"

"Three." He grabs his phone and stands, forcing me to crane my neck. He looks stupidly tall from this angle. "Don't burn yourself to a crisp before then."

"Very funny," I say. "We can't all be olive-toned!"

He snorts and heads away, and I can hear him mutter the word *olive-toned* under his breath like it's the most ridiculous thing anyone has ever said.

Chapter Seven

The motorboat speeds along the endless blue waters, and I have to tug my cap down against the wind. Phillip is sitting across from me. He's in shorts and another button-down, a thick watch on his tanned wrist. Sunglasses on. No smiles and all seriousness, just like he usually is, and there's no open bar or a guidebook to help ease our conversation this time. I'd texted Becky earlier, telling her about my outings with him.

> Have you lost your mind? He could be a serial killer! But didn't you say he was attractive? Because if so, remember some risks are worth taking.

It was a typical Becky text. My response was a peak vacation me, which is apparently someone who embraces spontaneity.

> If he kills me, tell everyone back home that I loved them very much. Also, I'm in a blue sundress if you need to identify my body over the phone.

Got it. I'll make sure your case becomes the best podcast episode ever. Also. HOW HOT IS HE?

I didn't answer her all-caps question.

It's a tricky one. Objectively, yes, hot would be the right description of the man sitting beside me, his face turned toward the waves and a strong arm draped along the backrest. But it's the cold, impersonal kind of handsome I've always struggled with. He's a bit taller than the norm, hair a bit wavier, perhaps. His face is sterner than a man his age should have.

Yeah. He's hot. And absolutely nothing like my ex, or any of the guys I've had crushes on before Caleb.

Our fishing guide's name is David. He's a fifty-year-old Bajan with an easy manner and a teasing glint in his eyes. He slows down the boat and lets it come to a rolling stop amid the turquoise waves.

"You ready?" he asks us. "Because I have to warn you, you're both going to catch something."

I eye the fishing rods David is holding. "I'm ready, I think."

"Don't worry," Phillip says at my side. "It doesn't take a lot of skill."

"Thanks?"

His mouth tips into another one of those small, almost-smiles. "That's a good thing."

I get up off the bench. "You've done this a lot?"

"Once or twice." He accepts a rod from David that is nearly as long as he's tall. "To be honest, I did this a lot as a kid."

"Really? Did you like it?"

"Yes."

David hands me a rod of my own. He's well acquainted with the fact that I'm a beginner and finds a lot of amusement in instructing me how to grip the rod, and how to flick and cast it.

David and Phillip take turns instructing me how to rhythmically tug on the line as I slowly reel it in, to mimic the swimming of a real fish, and draw in the bigger ones.

"Do fish really swim like this?" I ask them, my arms growing tired. "In weird bursts of energy?"

But neither of them thinks my question merits a lot of consideration.

Phillip catches the fish first. He gets the second one, too, and then David catches a marlin. It's too small to keep, unlike Phillip's two barracudas, so it gets gently put back into the water to swim another day.

My arms are thunderously tired when something finally tugs on my line.

"Oh my God. I think there's a fish."

"Just a nibble?" David asks. "Or is it hooked?"

"Uh, what's the difference?"

"Is it tugging?"

"Yes," I say, my arms going taut. "I think it's hooked?"

"Reel in the line," Phillip says. His voice is coming from close by, his own rod forgotten. "Slow and steady. That's it. Reel it in just like that."

"It's heavy," I say. Adrenaline pumps through my veins. Maybe this is what they like? The thrill of the chase? "Can you see it?"

He leans over the side of the boat. "No… yeah. David, are you seeing this?"

But David's ready with the net. Up comes a large, yellow-green fish. It has a blunt face like a pug.

"Oh my God! What's that?"

"You caught a dolphin," David says.

"A *dolphin?*"

"Yeah. Dolphinfish. You guys will often call it mahi-mahi," he says. The fish gives a mighty wiggle. "Look at that! Your first catch!"

"Should we throw it back?"

"No, no, this will feed an entire family. Yes, please!"

Next to me, Phillip's words are quieter. "Great job, Eden."

"All I did was hold a stick," I say.

"No, you rhythmically tugged on it, too," he corrects. "And that made all the difference."

That makes me laugh.

Fifteen minutes later, and our fishing trip is concluded. David suggests we both take pictures with our catches. Phillip is pretty unwilling, but as I pose with my giant dolphinfish that's decidedly more fish than a dolphin, I'm grinning. *Another check on my "explore Barbados" list.*

Behind the camera of my phone, David frowns. "I can't get you and the fish in the shot. Can you back up?"

I take a small step. "Like this?"

"More."

I back up. Then, I back up a bit more, until the back of my legs hit the railing of the boat. I'm thrown off balance. My arms flail, but there's a giant fish in them, and I can't straighten up. The mahi-mahi slips through my grasp and lands on the deck… just as I start to tilt backward.

"Eden!"

I claw towards the railing as I flip over it. But it's no use. I go overboard.

I hit the dark-blue surface of the sea. Lukewarm water surrounds me, and I quickly kick back up to the surface. We're far enough off the coast that I can't see the sandy floor in the depths.

Phillip laughs. I've never heard it before. He laughs so loudly that it echoes across the waves, but sounds entirely genuine. Even when he bends over the side of the boat to extend a hand, he's laughing—deep chuckling sounds that soothe the worst of my shock.

I tread water and reach my hand up to wrap it around his. "You okay?" Phillip asks, still smiling widely. It lights up his face.

I nod, and he pulls me back onto the boat.

"Yes. Oh my God, I *never* want to do that again, though!"

"The dolphin's revenge," David says with a glance down at the fish, prone on the deck. "It made you take a sea bath."

"Gosh, it really did." I stand, dripping wet. My sundress is soaked through and through, and thank God the sandals on my feet had straps or they'd have been lost to the deep.

Beside me, Phillip chuckles again. He's taken off his sunglasses, and in the late afternoon light, I can see the creases at the corner of his eyes because of how wide he's smiling. "Thanks, Eden."

"I know what you're going to say."

His smile grows. "Do you?"

"Yes. I just gave you a whole lot of entertainment, didn't I? Free of charge, too." I grab my hair and twist it around, water dripping on the deck. I don't want to look down. My dress must be molded to my body, showing off every curve.

He's already seen me in a bikini. Besides, any sex appeal I might have had was probably lost the moment I mentioned I was a kindergarten teacher. Or when he saw me geek out about turtles and my underwater camera. Not to mention when he saw my annotated guidebook.

Lots of options to choose from.

"Yes," Phillip says, "you did. David, do you have a spare towel onboard?"

Our fishing guide digs out a frayed towel. The fabric is rough but dry, and I wrap it around myself.

"You'll get cold," Phillip says behind me.

"We're in the Caribbean."

"The moment we turn on that engine…" he says.

I get what he meant five minutes later. Heading back to the Winter Resort is awful. I get more chilled with every second as the wind assails my soaked-through dress.

Phillip digs through his bag. "I thought I packed another T-shirt," he mutters.

I look down at his form, bent over his backpack. "Oh,

thank you, but that's okay. We're almost back at the hotel." I look down. "Besides, I'm… actually, will you hold this?"

He accepts the towel. "Yeah. Why?" His eyes drop to my hands, clasped around the hem of my dress. "Oh. Right."

I peel it off my body. Phillip looks away, over to where our fish lie packed together in a bucket of ice. His smile is gone.

With the wet, cold fabric gone, I already feel five times warmer, even if goosebumps still spread across my bare skin. "Much better. Can I—"

He shoves the towel in my direction. "Of course."

"Thanks." I wrap it around myself and pull my wet hair out so it drapes down my towel-clad back. "So, where did you fish?"

"What?"

"Where did you fish? When you were a kid?"

His eyes refocus on mine, and then he clears his throat. "Lake Superior."

"Outside of Chicago?"

"Yes." He clears his throat and leans back, silhouetted by the setting sun. "We used to have a cabin by the lake, and we'd go up there in the summers and on the weekends."

"That sounds lovely. Did you fish with your siblings?"

He shakes his head. "No, my sister never liked it. My father did, though."

"Did you two catch a lot of dolphins?"

That draws out another half chuckle. "Not a single one, no. Either kind."

"Do you still fish up there?"

"No, I haven't for years. I'm almost as much of a novice now as you."

"Well, you missed the part about falling in," I say. "That's key."

"Oh, is it?"

"Yeah. To celebrate a successful catch, you know. It's a ritual to give thanks to the ocean. But don't worry," I say and reach out to pat his arm. His skin is warm beneath my fingers. "You'll get there eventually."

He raises an eyebrow. "Thank you for the encouragement."

"Anytime."

"So, what else is in your little guidebook?"

"What else?"

"Yes. What other sights are a must for you?"

I smile at him. "You're asking for a monologue. You know that, right?"

A dimple appears on his cheek. It's there and gone again, almost like it never existed at all. "Monologue away."

"Okay. So, you know they produce a lot of rum in the Caribbean?"

"I may have heard about that, yes."

I roll my eyes but continue undaunted. "Right. Well, the oldest brand of rum is produced here on the island."

"It is?"

"Barbados is home to the oldest distillery, but there are several others. So, one of the things I really want to do while I'm here is to go to a rum tasting, try a ton of different cocktails, and maybe learn how rum is made."

He runs a hand along his jaw. "You know, I might've seen something about rum in my itinerary."

"Really?"

"Yeah. It was a private tour of a distillery and a rum tasting."

My mouth opens. "A *private* tour?"

"Yes. Still want to rag on my trip planner?"

I pretend to lock my mouth shut. "I swear I'll never talk badly of them again!"

Phillip nods again, the dimple flashing. "Well. I think it's scheduled for this weekend. Want to come along?"

My answer is immediate. "Yes. But I have to pay you back somehow. I mean, with this fishing trip, the catamaran cruise. I can't just—"

"Absolutely not," he says. "Everything was already booked."

"But I can't just impose like that."

His arm stretches out along the back of the railing, his hand close to my shoulder. "Eden."

"Yes," I say. "Phillip."

"I didn't decide to actually go through with this trip until the day before my flight."

"Oh."

"And I fully planned on blowing off half of the itinerary," he says. His gaze drifts from me to the waves, and something works in his jaw. "Tell me something. When you checked in, did they congratulate you on your wedding?"

"Yes," I whisper.

"Right. Well, they did the same to me. That's why I was at the restaurant on my first night, crashing your table rather than ordering room service. I asked the staff to clear my bungalow of rose petals and celebratory champagne." He shakes his head as if he's dislodging a memory. "You're not imposing. Not even a little bit. Do I strike you as a man who'd invite you along just to be nice?"

"Want an honest answer?"

"Always," he says.

"No, you don't."

He nods. "Exactly. I'm not short on cash, either. So you're not paying me back for anything."

I find myself nodding. "Okay. But I have the guidebook."

"Yes, you sure do."

"And I'm not afraid to use it. I'll pay you back in knowledge."

His lips twitch. "You're going to make me regret this, aren't you?"

"Probably," I say. "But I'll make sure you learn a lot of useless trivia along the way."

He runs a hand through his windblown hair. Around his

eyes, laugh lines appear with his almost-smile. "Sounds like an ideal vacation," he says.

Chapter Eight

The hotel is quiet as I make my way back to my room.

The vending machines down the hall are stocked with chocolate, and for days, I've stayed strong. But not tonight. It's 11:30 p.m. and I should be asleep, but the movie on my computer is interesting, and the chocolate craving hit me hard after a full day of sun and an afternoon of sea fishing.

Armed with a packet of M&Ms in hand, my foraging is complete. I've hunted and gathered, and now return to my hotel door.

And I can't open it.

The key card is not in the pockets of my fluffy bathrobe and it's not tucked into the bralette I'm wearing under my T-shirt. It's also conspicuously absent from the pockets of my cotton shorts.

I lean my head against the door. "Shit."

It takes me another minute to swallow my pride. Once it's gone down, tough as it is, I head to the elevators. Hopefully, most of the guests are either at the restaurant or in beds, and not lingering in the lobby, ready to judge me for my attire.

I tiptoe into the lobby in my flip-flops, which isn't the easiest of feats.

It's empty. There's not a single person, employee or guest,

in the spacious lobby of the Winter Resort. I tap my foot on the stone floor a few times before looking over the giant granite front desk. "Hello?"

It's quiet as the grave.

I raise my voice. "Excuse me? Hello?"

Someone is probably taking the time for a little bathroom break, I think, walking around the lobby. Why did I have to wear my bathrobe out?

I push open the doors leading to the hotel garden. Might as well walk around a bit before coming back to see if anyone is manning the check-in desk. Or maybe they're out here, enjoying a cigarette.

They're not, but the air is pleasurably warm compared to the intense sun of the day. Well-placed lighting illuminates the meticulously sculpted garden with its low box hedges, palm trees, and tropical flowers. This place truly is stunning. The most beautiful resort I've ever visited.

I tie the belt of my bathrobe tighter and stroll along the colonnade. The path opens up to the outdoor hotel pool in the distance. The pool closes at 8 p.m., with a large sign informing guests that no swimming is allowed at night.

But I can hear splashes.

Too curious to resist, I walk down to investigate.

A man is swimming laps.

He cuts through the surface in a crawl, dark hair plastered to his head.

Odd that I should recognize the swimming style so easily. We'd only been on one snorkeling cruise together. But it's definitely Phillip.

I sit down on one of the lounge chairs. They're all empty, the area abandoned. Decorative lights illuminate the desk, and the sound of tropical nightlife is heavy in the air. I've learned from my guidebook that it's not cicadas, as one might suspect from the sound, but tiny whistling frogs.

Phillip notices me halfway through another lap. He shifts mid-stroke and turns to tread water.

There's a surprised look in his eyes.

I give a little wave. "Hello."

"You're hiding in the darkness, watching me swim," he says and takes two large strokes toward the edge of the pool. "That's not creepy at all."

"Swimming past 8 p.m.," I say. "That's not forbidden in the least."

"And you're not about to do the same thing?"

"No. Oh, because of my robe?" I shake my head. "This is embarrassing."

He rests both arms on the side of the pool. "Then, you have to tell me."

"I locked myself out of my hotel room."

A half smile illuminates his face. "You don't say?"

"Yes."

"You're a constant source of amusement, Eden."

I groan. "Why does this stuff always happen to me?"

"After watching you fall into the ocean earlier… I'd say it's an absolute mystery."

"Funny. Why are you violating the sacred hotel rules?" I rest my head in my hands, bracing my elbows over my knees. "Just had to get your evening workout in?"

"Something like that," he says.

"You're a good swimmer."

He nods, but it's not gloating. Just self-awareness. "I swam competitively growing up."

"Oh, that explains a lot," I say. "The drive, the self-control."

"You know something about my self-control?"

"You're an attorney, right? That means college, law school, and a lot of paperwork." I shrug. "Maybe your life isn't like the lawyers I've seen on TV. But if it is, it takes discipline, a lot of coffee, and hot paralegals. Probably a bit of casual sexism, too."

He looks at me for a long few seconds. "You know, you're one of the strangest women I've ever met."

My eyebrows shoot high. "Me?"

"Yes."

"I don't know if I should take that as a compliment."

"Me, either," he says, but the half smile is back. "It seems that you say exactly what you think."

"Not always," I counter. There have been many thoughts I haven't shared over the past few months. About myself, about Caleb, about Cindy. Question of why. *Why, why, why?*

"Oh? Should I be scared to hear the ones that don't make the cut?" he asks.

I shake my head. "I'm a perfect angel."

"Of course, you are," he says. "Now come on. Get in."

"Get into the pool?"

"Yes. You're here, aren't you? Why not?"

"Because it's… crazy. And because I'm not wearing a swimsuit."

"So wear your underwear. It's not like anyone can see anything in this light, anyway." He turns onto his back and pushes away from the edge of the pool, floating on the water. In the distance, I can hear the waves beat the shore, mingling with the serenading insects and frogs.

Phillip resumes swimming laps, on his back this time. I watch him complete two full laps while my hands played with the belt of my bathrobe.

Of course, he's the type to do laps. It makes perfect sense, with his semi-serial killer vibe and repressed sense of personality.

This should be in my book. Maybe it's how the two lovers meet. The pool at midnight. Or maybe it's someone's alibi… only there's no one about at that hour to confirm it. That'll be good.

I take a deep breath. So far this trip has been all about craziness. About saying *screw it,* about embracing my vacation self, about taking risks and shaking off the rut I'd been in.

"I can't believe I'm doing this," I say and tug off my robe.

"There are no sea turtles to photograph here," he says. "So, so am I."

"Very funny. Is it cold?"

"Not really. It's cool."

"Which probably means it's freezing." I dip my foot into the water. It's lukewarm. Likely a welcome reprieve during the blistering hot days, but now with the sun gone, it feels a bit chilly.

I don't let myself think as I tug off my pajama shorts and shirt, standing there in my underwear for a heartbeat, before stepping into the pool. Phillip is at the other end anyway, swimming again, cutting through the water in strokes that I could never replicate.

The water is brisk against my skin. I take a deep breath and sink down to my shoulders.

It's nice. Well, it will be nice. In about two minutes.

Phillip surfaces a couple of feet away from me.

"I can't believe I'm doing this," I say.

"Breaking the rules? Or swimming?"

"Both."

"Well, rules were meant to be broken."

"Is that your professional opinion, as a lawyer?" I say. "Because that doesn't seem right."

He shakes his head, water droplets flying from his wet hair. They ripple the surface around us. "No. I'm off hours."

I stretch out in the water. It's luxurious—being here, doing this. The sky above is peppered with stars, and exhilaration courses through my veins. *I want to stay here forever*. The moment feels big, and unusual, and awe-inspiring.

Phillip starts to swim again.

I wait until he does a few laps before I speak again. "How old are you?"

He takes a few leisurely strokes before answering. "I don't understand how your brain works."

"I'm just curious. I can ask something else if that's too

sensitive. Did you send your dad the picture of you with the fish?"

"No, but from your question, I take it you've sent one to yours?"

"Yes. My parents were very impressed with my mahi-mahi slash dolphinfish."

"Did you tell them you fell off the boat three seconds later?"

"I might have left that part out."

He chuckles. It's the second time I've heard him laugh, and both of them have been today.

And both have been about me falling off.

"Smart. Well, I'm thirty-two," he says. Then, he pushes off the wall and swims an entire lap with quick strokes, like that the end of the conversation.

I lie back in the water and stare up at the sky again. There are so many stars visible here, more than I can see back home, and no wonder. There must be very little light pollution on a small island in the middle of the sea.

Thirty-two. I thought he was older at first, but that might've just been my reading of a tense facial expression. But those faded away on the fishing boat, singed by the sun and swept away by the wind.

"I'm twenty-eight," I volunteer when he's back in my part of the pool.

He pushes a few wet strands of hair back off his forehead. "Right. Met your fiancé in college?"

"No, we went to high school together," I say. "But we didn't get together until one summer when we were both home from college."

"I see."

I look at him across the water. He hasn't told me a single thing about the woman he was meant to marry, or why the wedding didn't happen. I'm only *moderately* curious. It's not like it's eating me alive or anything.

"Don't ask," he warns me.

I use my most innocent smile. "Wasn't about to."

"Yes, you were," he says. "I can see it in your eyes. But it's too nice of a night."

I push off the side of the pool. "Yes, it is. Is that why you're out here so late?"

"Needed to clear my head," he says.

I swim to the other end and rest my arms against the edge of the pool. Tipping my head back, I stretch out in the water. "Well, don't let me stop you if you need to do a few more laps."

He grunts a response and kicks off into an impressive crawl. I close my eyes and listen to the sound of rhythmic splashing. It's past midnight in this beautiful place, and I'm enjoying every minute of it.

The sound gets louder on my left but then suddenly stops. I open my eyes to see Phillip beside me, long arms stretched out like me.

"So," he says. "What are you doing next?"

"Tonight? I have a hot date with my hotel bed, as soon as I find someone to help me unlock the door."

"Damn. Don't forget to use protection."

"Wow."

He runs a wet hand over his face. "It was a joke. I didn't mean to upset your delicate sensibilities."

"Do I strike you as someone with delicate sensibilities?" I raise a hand. "Actually, don't answer that."

"I won't," he says, and it sounds like he's smiling. "But I meant what's next on your grand tour of the island."

"Oh. Well, during the day tomorrow I'll be on the beach again. But I'm considering going to the fish market later. It's Friday night."

There's skepticism in his dry voice. "Fish market?"

"Yeah. It's a pretty famous thing on the island, apparently. You can get grilled fish and drinks, there's live music... It's down past Bridgetown."

"How are you getting there?"

"Well, I haven't really figured it out yet. I read in the guidebook about taxi-buses. So, I'm considering that."

"Taxi-buses," he says. "And you'd go alone?"

"I was planning on that, yeah. Unless you have a taste for fish? I don't think they serve steak at the fish market, buddy."

"Buddy?"

"Yeah, it felt wrong the second it came out of my mouth. I take it back. I un-buddy you."

"Thanks," he says and turns back toward the stars. "Want company?"

"Sure, if you want to go. But don't feel like you have to. I know it might not be your scene, you know."

He pushes off the edge and swims to face me. "No, I don't know. What do you mean?"

I give him an apologetic smile. "I mean, bungalow twelve? Exclusive itinerary? You probably had a lot of things planned that were golf course related or involved private tours, and not buses and fish markets."

He shakes his head. "I don't know what I hate more, that you think that... or that you're right," he says. "But count me in for tomorrow."

My smile widens. It had been something I very much wanted to do, but I'd been reluctant to try it on my own. "Really?"

"Yes."

"Okay, perfect. We can meet in the lobby?"

"Yeah."

"I'm not sure how we'd—oh." I look across at the security guard approaching with a flashlight. He shines it toward the pool, and I fall silent. My rebellion was short-lived, and I'm instantly filled with regret. I hate breaking the rules.

The guard sighs, the sound audible across the quiet pool area. "I'm sorry, but I'll have to ask you two to get out of the pool," he calls. "No swimming allowed after 8 p.m."

The flashlight flicks across the water until it illuminates

us. Me—arms crossed over my wet bralette. Phillip—calmly treading water close by.

"Please," he repeats.

"I'm sorry!" I shout, swimming as fast as I can toward the ladder. "We won't do it again, I promise."

"Good," the guard says. He looks pointedly away from me. "Have a good evening now, ma'am. Sir."

"Thank you, you, too." I pull myself out of the pool to the man's rapidly disappearing back.

The night air is warm, but I still reach for my bathrobe, sweeping it around me. The elastic in my underwear is doing a heroic job of supporting clothes that were never meant to be worn wet, and I'm not in the mood to challenge it further.

Phillip gets out of the pool behind me. He reaches for his towel and starts to dry his hair in quick, hard movements.

"We got off pretty easy," I say with an embarrassed chuckle.

He loops the towel around his neck and shoots me an amused look. "How awful did it feel to get scolded?"

I grimace. "Terrible."

He chuckles. "You survived. We didn't harm anyone. It's all good, Eden."

"Yeah, I suppose you're right. Oh, damn!"

"What?"

"I should have asked him about my key card!"

"There should be someone at the front desk. Come on, I'll walk with you."

"Aren't the bungalows in the other direction?"

"Yes," he says and heads past me toward the lobby. "But you have a hot date you need to make it to."

I scoop up my abandoned clothes. "Oh, that's right. My bed."

"What were you doing out, anyway? Why'd you lock yourself out?"

"I went to the vending machines for a late-night snack."

His eyebrows pull together. "There are vending machines?"

"Um, yes. In the main part of the hotel, anyway, with the standard rooms," I say.

"Right." He holds the lobby door open for me. I must look like a drowned rat, with half-wet hair and waterdrops running down my legs. I'm leaving small puddles on the floor as I cross toward the check-in desk.

Beside me, Phillip walks through the lobby like his wet skin is a pressed suit, completely unbothered. I keep my eyes away from the long form of his body and the well-toned physique that now makes perfect sense. Competitive swimmer, indeed.

The receptionist is back, and she immediately hides the phone she'd been scrolling on when she sees us. "Good evening. Did you two go for a midnight swim?"

"Yes," Phillip says. "In the ocean."

I glance at him out of the corner of my eye. The man is smooth.

Five minutes later I have a spare key, and the lady wishes us a good night. Phillip gives me a farewell nod.

"Enjoy your date," he says, fully within earshot of the receptionist. Judging by the glint in his eye, he knows that had embarrassed me, too.

"Uh… thanks. See you tomorrow."

His mouth curves. It's not quite a smile, but it's close. "Until tomorrow, Eden."

Chapter Nine

"One of *those?*" Phillip says. He's standing beside me on the road as a route taxi whizzes past. The minivan looks packed. It's Friday night, and the route we're taking is a super popular one.

"Yes."

"Let's take a taxi," he says. "A real taxi."

I take a deep breath to calm my nerves, because damn it, I'm nervous. This is my idea and my initiative. I'm excited *and* hesitant, of course, but it's a heady mix all the same.

Phillip is standing beside me, all silent judgment at my plan. He's in navy slacks and a blue linen button-down, like we're going to a sit-down restaurant, even if the sleeves are rolled up and his top button undone.

He also looks handsome. Masculine in a way Caleb rarely was, with his sailing shoes firmly planted on the cracked sidewalk.

"We can take a real taxi home," I say. "But this is part of the experience."

The next route taxi stops, and a guy jumps out of the front seat. He opens the sliding door to a minivan packed with Bajans and tourists alike. Loud soca music blasts out of a hidden speaker.

"There's no space," Phillip says.

"Oh, there sure is! Yes please!" the guy says and pulls down a foldable seat from the wall. Three people are already seated next to it. "Gentleman first!"

Phillip sits, hesitancy in his movements. The guy beside us gestures for me to hop on in after him. But there's no space.

"Um, where, exactly?"

"On his lap!" the guy says.

On the street around us, someone honks. We must be holding up traffic.

I get in, crouching to avoid hitting my head on the vehicle's roof and leaning over Phillip. I can't sit on his lap, can I? The guy pulls the sliding door closed and jumps back onto the front seat. A second later the route taxi starts moving again, pulling out on the trafficked road to the heavy beats of music.

"Come on," Phillip mutters behind me and puts a hand on my waist. I'm tugged backward, and then I'm there, sitting on his lap.

I turn. "Sure this is okay?"

There's a yes somewhere close to my right ear. The half-open window sends air through my hair, whipping it back. It's hard to think over the loud music.

"I'm sorry," I say and tug it around to my right shoulder. "You okay?"

There's no response, probably because he can't hear me. I'm perched on the very edge of his knees. This must be so uncomfortable, and I'm abruptly regretting this whole thing. Suggesting it, bringing him along, being so set on this. He must be wondering how the hell he ended up in a packed minivan with a weird girl sitting on his lap.

A hand curves lightly around my waist, and then his voice is by my ear. His breath tickles my skin. "Sit back properly, Eden," he says. "It's safer."

The words send a shiver down my spine. I'm about to ask him again if he's sure about that when the hand at my waist tugs, just slightly. So I do what he says. I shift over his thighs and rest my back against his chest.

I'm mortified.

I twist my head to say that I'm sorry only to find the sharp edge of his jaw. I twist further toward his ear, and the scent of shampoo and cologne hits me.

"I'm sorry about this," I say.

He shakes his head. It's a tiny movement. "It's fine."

"Sure? I'm not too heavy?"

His scoff reverberates through my body. "No."

I settle back against him as one song blends into another; this one has a beat that rattles the sides of the van.

We drive past houses and hotels and take a curve. I shift sharply to the right, only to be stopped by an arm around my waist. Phillip's hand rests lightly on my upper stomach.

"This okay?" he murmurs.

I can't breathe. "Uh-huh."

He's warm behind me and big, and the strong thighs under me carry my weight. I tilt my head back and rest it against his shoulder. As if in response, the arm around my waist tightens a bit more. *That's okay, too,* I imagine him saying.

It's the first time I've touched him, I realize, if you don't count the hand he'd given me back up onto the fishing boat. The tanned arm around my waist feels strong. Fitting.

"You're my seatbelt," I say.

"Huh?"

I have to tilt my head again, my lips close to his ear. "You're my seatbelt," I murmur. It sounds even stupider a second time.

But he gives a small chuckle. "Yeah."

The loud music drowns out most of the sounds from the engine and surrounding traffic. At the next turn, we shift together, like a unit, rocking sideways. His left hand lands on the side of my thigh.

I glance down only to see it still there. His fingers are long enough to reach the hem of my dress and brush against my bare leg. My entire body focuses on that innocent touch.

It's nothing. He's just resting his hand and holding me steady. Doing me a favor on the way to a place he'd never planned to go to in the first place. But my body can't seem to stop focusing on that spot.

Phillip's voice returns to my ear. "Relax," he says again. "You okay?"

I let out the breath I'd been holding. "Um, yes," I say. And then, because my brain loves to sabotage me, I blurt, "You smell good."

The fingers at my waist tighten, as if in surprise. But he doesn't answer. So I twist my head toward the view outside the window and relax into his grip. He probably didn't even hear me above the sound of heavy music.

One can hope, at least.

It isn't until the route taxi stops to let off the family of three next to us that he speaks again. "So do you."

There's space beside us. I don't have to sit on his lap anymore, but as the sliding door closes shut, and the van starts to move, we stay put.

All the way to our stop at the Oistins Fish Market.

"This is us," I say. I have to use both arms to tug at the sliding door. As I do, Phillip's grip around my waist disappears. After paying the driver, we emerge into the chaotic bustle of a Bajan sidewalk.

"Thanks for the ride!" I say. The route taxi throws itself back into traffic, a reggae song blasting out of the half-open windows.

"Wow," I breathe. "That was..."

"Yes," Phillip says, his eyes meeting mine.

No more words are needed, and I have to swallow hard before I can speak. "So... are you hungry?"

We make our way among the stalls. The place is packed in the most wonderful of ways, with tables set up between the booths for people to eat and drink. Tourists and locals alike seem to be gathered here. Behind one of the venues, a band starts to play soca music.

The energy is palpable.

"So many people," Phillip mutters beside me.

I grin at him. "It's amazing, isn't it? Come on, let's find the stall with the red roof… I've heard it's the best one."

"You've read about the *individual* stalls?"

"Yes. Come on!"

He mutters something behind me that sounds a lot like *too much free time,* but he lets me tug him through a group of people standing in line.

I spot the stall with the red roof. Their grilled swordfish and mahi-mahi are supposed to be the best on the island.

It takes us a solid half-hour to get our fish, sides, drinks, *and* a spot to sit. On my paper plate, my grilled mahi-mahi is the size of my face. Beside it is a heaping side of macaroni pie.

It smells absolutely divine. "How am I supposed to eat all of this?" I ask.

Phillip holds up his wooden fork. "With this."

I roll my eyes. "Very funny."

"Thank you. I thought so, too."

"You're dry, you know," I tell him and point my fork in his direction. "Funny, but dry. It's a sneaky kind of humor."

"Thank you," he says seriously. "That's the nicest compliment I've ever received."

I chuckle. "Right. Tell me, does your sarcasm ever get you in trouble?"

"Never," he says.

"See, now I can't tell if you actually mean that or not."

He raises an eyebrow. "Doesn't that answer your question?"

"Yes, it does. It gets you in trouble a lot then. I can see that." I narrow my eyes at him. "Doesn't work well in court though, does it? The judge must get so annoyed at you."

He rolls his eyes and digs into his swordfish. "I don't go to court very often. Great attorneys rarely do."

"How come? Isn't that where you make your bombastic speeches and appeal to the juries, and... and... have little sidebars with the judges?"

"You watch too much TV," he says. "No, it's mostly meetings."

"You settle before going to trial?"

"I mostly work with contracts, in mergers and acquisitions. Not lawsuits."

I take a long sip of my rum punch. It's strong, and we have two each, courtesy of a happy hour. "You must be a good attorney," I say. "Even though you're a nice person."

Phillip spears his grilled fish. "I'm not that nice."

"You are," I say. "You agreed to this, didn't you? Although," I add, tapping a finger on my chin, "I suppose you wouldn't be able to afford a bungalow for two weeks without a bit of blood money."

He reaches for his drink. "Now you're getting it."

"Do you like it? Attorneying?"

"*Like* it," he repeats and gives a half laugh. "That doesn't seem relevant."

I chew my piece of fish and macaroni. "It doesn't seem *relevant?* Are you serious?"

"Yeah. What does it matter? Everyone needs a job, and I'm good at mine."

"Well, considering how much time we all spend at our jobs, I think, liking what we do is pretty important. I love my job, even if it's challenging at times. There are definitely days when I want to take a week off work just to sleep. But overall, I like it. Do you feel that way, too?"

He stretches out a leg next to the table and braces his hand against it. His free hand holds the fork in a tight grip. "I'm good at finding solutions to problems that don't appear to have any. It's what my clients need, and they pay good money for it, too."

I smile at him. "Not what I asked."

"Sure," he says and rolls his eyes. "I *like* that part of it."

"A ringing endorsement from Phillip Meyer!" I say. "It's his absolute dream job!"

He shakes his head. "You're impossible. It's an okay job. It's a lot of work, but I like to work hard. There's not much more to it than that. Besides, it's a job with very clear winners and losers."

"And that's... something you like?"

"Yes," he says. "I'm competitive. Winning suits me just fine."

I chuckle. "Wow. Just the other week, I spent the evening making participation trophies for every kid in my class."

Across the wooden table, Phillip makes a sound of disgust and cuts into his fish. My eyes land on his large hands. One of them had been on my bare thigh.

"—that's wrong with society today."

I blink at him. "Sorry. What?"

"Participation trophies," he says and raises an eyebrow. "You okay?"

I take another big gulp of my rum punch. "Yes. This is strong."

He chuckles. "Yeah, it sure is, Eden."

We get two more drinks, rum sours this time, along with a slice of rum cake. I feel full and happy and sway in tune with the music blasting from the stage. A man plays on the drum kit while another sings. People, locals and tourists alike, dance in front of the stage. The whole place feels filled with life.

When it's time to leave, I slip my arm through Phillip's and sing along to the music. The band is covering an old pop song now.

He keeps walking. "Told you the rum was strong."

"I'm not drunk," I say. "I'm tipsy. There's a massive difference."

"Mm-hmm," he says, and we come to a stop next to the busy road. "Now, I'm going to insist on this—we're taking a regular taxi back to the resort."

"You didn't like your job as a seat belt, did you?"

He gives a non-committal harrumph and raises his hand. A taxi slows to a crawl, and Phillip opens the back door for me. As I'm sliding across the back seat, I hear his muttered reply, half of it is lost to the haze of music and traffic.

"—liked it far too much."

Chapter Ten

I rock back on my heels, standing on the Winter Resort dock. It's a beautiful day. The sun shines down on me from a cloudless sky.

Phillip should be here soon.

He has an excursion booked for today on his planned itinerary. This time, it's a private boat tour out to one of the many shipwrecks along the coast of Barbados. The ruins have long since been reclaimed by nature, and it is now a teeming coral reef. The tour guide will let us snorkel above it.

You're not nervous, I tell myself. I'm my brave vacation self, one who doesn't need a playlist of forest sounds to fall asleep, and the one who loathes routine and plunges headfirst into every adventure.

In another week I can go back to my safe existence, my new house, my job, and writing in my spare time.

You're not nervous. You're excited.

But it doesn't matter how many times I tell myself that, my anxiety refuses to go away.

Something had shifted yesterday, in that route taxi, as we drove over the streets of Barbados toward the fish market. Amid the deafening beats of soca music and the curves hastily taken...

We'd touched.

And, somehow, that has turned Phillip from merely a person I'm having unexpected fun with during my vacation to an *actual* man with a capital M. The kind of man I haven't let myself think about since my engagement had ended.

Not that he likely sees me as a capital W woman. Or if he does, it's a new thing, and it might even run counter to his own instincts. *You're one of the strangest women I've ever met,* he'd said during our midnight swim in the pool. That can't exactly be a recipe for attraction.

But do I even want him to be attracted to me? The question sets off another burst of nerves in my system. That would turn this whole little enjoying-my-not-a-honeymoon project on its head.

"Hey," a voice says.

I startle. "Oh. Hi!"

Phillip pushes his sunglasses up and comes to stand beside me on the dock. "You're daydreaming?"

"Yeah. I do that a lot," I say like a complete idiot. Not once have I thought about my daydreaming habits.

But he nods as if that makes perfect sense. His eyes meet mine, and even though he's not smiling, there's something in his gaze. Something that speaks of a crowded route taxi and his hands on my body.

"Hi," I say again.

His lips curve. "Hello again, Eden."

"Um, I think the boat is here. Is it this white boat with a giant engine? Your honeymoon planner didn't spare any expense, did they?"

He lowers his sunglasses, hiding his eyes from view. "She was told specifically not to."

"Oh," I say.

He leads the way toward the boat and I follow, my beach bag on my shoulder. "Does it pay so well to be an attorney, then? I probably chose the wrong profession."

He shrugs. "It pays well if you're an excellent one."

"Well, excuse me," I say with a smile. "Are you sure

there's space for all of us on this boat? You, me, and your ego?"

He chuckles. The sound is warm, and those nerves are back, flipping my stomach. "It'll be a tight squeeze," he says, "but I think we'll manage."

Our guide ushers us aboard a boat that was clearly built for speed and comfort. I tuck my bag safely inside a small cabin below deck and head back up.

Phillip is already there, sitting on a bench. His phone is nowhere in sight. I can see the faint hint of a five-o-clock shadow in the sunlight. He must have skipped shaving this morning.

I look at him for a few seconds too long.

"Hey," he says and looks up. "How are—oh."

I can't see his eyes behind his dark sunglasses. But I notice the tilt of his chin, and my cheeks flush when I realize he's looking at my bikini.

He runs a hand along his jaw. "Had a good day so far today?"

"Yes," I say. I sit down next to him on the seat and pull my cap down tight on my head. It has stupid writing on it, an inside joke I shared with Becky and Cindy in college. "I spent the morning at the beach."

"I can see that," he says and nods toward my shoulder.

I glance down. "Oh. Yes, I got some color, didn't I?"

"Yes, you did. Does it hurt?"

"No, not yet anyway. I tried my best to get my back with the sunscreen, but it's... hard, you know. I wasn't about to ask the staff for help."

"I'm sure they would have obliged you," he murmurs.

"Maybe," I say, "or maybe I would have been thrown out for sexually harassing resort employees."

"Well, we can't have that. I would have bailed you out of a Bajan prison, though."

"Oh, that reminds me. I wanted to ask you something yesterday, but I thought of it after we got back from Oistins."

His eyebrow lifts. "Did you?"

"Yes. Do you ever work with criminals?"

He's quiet for a moment, and then he laughs, quiet and deep. "No, I'm a corporate attorney, Eden. I don't prosecute and I don't meet criminals."

"Oh, right."

"You know, that's never disappointed a woman before."

"I'm probably a weird one. I listen to a fair number of true crime podcasts," I say.

A fair number sounds saner than *all of them.*

"Ah," he says. "My sister does that, too. What is it with women and true crime?"

"I have a theory," I say.

Below deck, the boat's engine roars to life. We start moving away from the dock. As we head farther from the coast, the massive architecture of the Winter Resort grows smaller. It's so clad in greenery that it almost disappears into the surrounding landscape.

Phillip leans back against the seat, his posture more relaxed, and stretches out his long legs. "Tell me."

"Well, I think women are drawn to true crime because it lets us explore the dark side of human nature from a safe distance. It's like a puzzle we can be a part of solving." I tilt my head. "I've also heard that some can feel empowered, weirdly enough, since women are most often the victims in these stories. Like, listening to true crime is almost instructional, on a subconscious level."

He's frowning. "Fuck, that's dark."

His frank tone makes me chuckle. "Yes. I'm not sure if that's why I like them, personally. I find true crime fascinating and entertaining at the same time, and I love the ones that are solved. It feels like I'm listening to justice being done, you know?"

"Right," he says. "Maybe it's analogous to guys who love watching documentaries about World War Two."

"You know what, that might be it, exactly."

"My sister says true crime podcasts help her sleep. She's probably a psychopath," he says and shakes his head. "I've suspected it for a long time."

"Oh, have you?"

"Mm-hmm. She's a dentist," he says like it's the final nail in the coffin.

It makes me laugh. "Okay, I can sort of get your point."

We fall into a comfortable silence, there on the boat, moving fast across the open ocean. I push my sunglasses higher on my nose and look around for my bag. "I should probably put on some sunscreen."

"Yeah," Phillip says.

"Could you help me with my back this time? If we're going to be in the water, you know..."

He gives a slow nod. "Yeah," he says. "I can do that."

Five minutes later, I'm sitting with my back to him, looking out at the swell of the waves, and waiting for the first touch of cold lotion.

Silly, I think to myself.

Amazing, the other part of me says.

I'm flirting. I'm actually flirting, and I'm doing it on what would have been my honeymoon. There's nowhere I want this to go, and nowhere for it *to* go. And maybe that's just what I need. To dip my toe infinitesimally into the metaphorical pool, with no one knowing but me that it's been dipped.

A first step into the world of singledom.

Warm hands land on my shoulders and brush my long hair out of the way, pushing it over my left side.

Goosebumps erupt on my arms.

"This'll be cold," he mutters, and a second later I feel cold sunscreen on my bare skin. His hands are large and strong on my back. They move in sweeping motions, over my shoulder blades, along my spine, and beneath the band of my bikini top.

I close my eyes. It feels weird, and it feels good, and perhaps it feels weird *because* it feels good. Even when we're not in the cramped confines of a minivan. Phillip runs a hand over the small of my back, his pinky grazing the top edge of my bikini bottoms.

"This good?" he asks.

"Yes, I think so."

"Good." His hands return to my shoulders and run in slow strokes down my arms. I shiver at the touch.

He notices, his hands stopping just below my elbows. "Still okay?"

"Mm-hmm. Yes."

He continues down to my hands, resting above my wrists for a second before removing them. He clears his throat, and I feel the cushion beneath us shift as he moves back.

"Thank you," I say.

"Yeah. No problem." He looks out at the sea and not at me. "Can't have you burning on my watch."

"Nor on your boat," I say.

His mouth curves. "Right. Well, you know, we're almost through with all major activities on my itinerary."

"Oh?"

"Yeah. There are a just a few left, including the rum tasting." He waves a dismissive hand, and I wonder at the attitude of skipping pre-paid things. If my parents and I had planned to go to an all-you-can-eat buffet for dinner, none of us would have eaten lunch that day. That's my point of reference.

"Now who's being dismissive of your travel agent's hard work?" I ask.

"Trust me, she got paid her fair share."

"Who's idea was it to go to Barbados for your honeymoon?" I ask and kick my legs out in front. My feet are close to his, mine bare beside his sailing shoes.

I know nothing about his ex-fiancée. He's not sharing breadcrumbs, he's hoarding entire *loaves.*

And I'm starving with curiosity.

But he just looks out over the waves, his voice calm. "We

decided on the Caribbean early on. We'd both been to the area before, on other islands."

"Oh."

"A travel agent suggested a few hotels across the region, and the newly opened Winter Resort looked good." He shrugs and runs a hand over his nape. "I also represented the company in a settlement a few years back."

"Ooooh. So this is a perk?"

"It's not."

"I'm sitting on a nepotism boat?"

"I'm not related to any of the owners."

I grin. "But you know them."

"I met one of them. Once. That's it." He raises an eyebrow. "I also work out of Chicago now, not New York anymore."

"But you used to?"

"Yes," he says and sighs. "Is this twenty questions?"

"Maybe. Why'd you move back home to Chicago?"

His lips flatten. "She was also from there."

"Ah."

"Besides, my firm had an office there, and I was tired of New York. It was a good opportunity."

"How'd the two of you meet?" I ask.

He shakes his head. "We haven't had a single glass of rum yet today."

"You haven't? I drank four piña coladas for breakfast. You should really try the buffet. It's incredible."

"You didn't, or you'd be overboard by now. Again."

I cock my head. "Why don't you eat at the breakfast bar? I never see you there."

He turns to face me fully. "You've been looking for me?" he asks and sounds inordinately pleased by that fact.

"I watch all the guests. They're fascinating."

"You mean you hate-watch the honeymoon couples?"

"Yes," I say. "Two of them fed each other chopped mango yesterday morning, and I almost committed double homicide with my grapefruit spoon."

"Good thing you have an attorney present on the island," he says.

I dig my teeth into my lower lip to hide my smile. "Would you take my case pro bono?"

"I don't know," he says. "I might ask for some form of payment."

"Oh yeah?"

"Yes. Your guidebook, for one."

My eyes widen. "My guidebook?"

"Yes. Your annotations could save me from a mediocre restaurant experience one of these nights. I'd rather have an excellent one."

"Don't mock the guidebook."

"Oh, I would never," he says. "I'm considering making it the holy text of my new religion."

"All right, that's it, Meyer." I shove at his shoulder, forcing him away from me on the bench.

He lets me push him two inches before he braces himself, becoming an immovable, half-smiling statue. "This right here is violence. You just admitted to having homicidal thoughts, too. I think I should report you. You're a danger to society, and I take my civic duty seriously."

"I told you that in confidence! Attorney-client privilege."

"That only applies after you've committed a crime," he says. "Not before."

"The guidebook told me all about the shipwreck we're headed to," I say. "I was planning on sharing that information with you, but now I won't. I'll just let you swim over it like an ignorant dork."

His eyebrows shoot up. "An ignorant dork?"

"Yes. I know that sounds stupid, but I stand by it."

"Right," he says. "You know, I've never had as weird conversations as I have with you."

"The feeling is mutual," I say.

That's the exact moment the boat comes to a slow standstill. We're in the deeper blue waters off Carlisle Bay again, close to where we'd seen the sea turtles.

I know from my reading that there have been hundreds of shipwrecks over the centuries in the shallow waters surrounding the island, and six of them are in this bay. The oldest is from 1919 and the most recent happened in 2003. which was deliberately sunk to create a habitat for coral, but none of that is information I'll share with the ignorant dork beside me.

The very *handsome* ignorant dork pulling off his T-shirt. He's tanner every day I see him, and has a dark smattering of chest hair across a muscled torso that I do my very best to avoid looking at.

Our guide anchors around a buoy and helps us grab our gear. He'll join us in the water, he says, and starts telling us all about the shipwreck we're going to be snorkeling on.

Phillip gives me a triumphant look, his goggles in his hands. *I'll get all the info anyway,* his dark-blue eyes say.

I try to narrow my eyes back at him, but I doubt he can see a thing through the thick plastic of my snorkel mask.

The water is lukewarm and soft against my skin, and so clear I can easily see the sandy bottom several feet below.

Together with the tour guide, we swim toward a large, dark shadow in the water. It's only a little scary, but once I can look beneath the surface, my fear becomes wonder again. Just like it did the last time, with the turtles.

There's an entire world beneath the surface.

The shipwreck is home to a coral reef now. The boat itself is still clearly visible, resting against the sandy ocean floor as if it's just sleeping. But in its slumber, it's been taken over by the ocean itself, covered in coral and seaweed. I spot a school of bright yellow fish emerging out of a porthole. At the far end of the wreck, a lone sea turtle feasts on some seafood growing off the ship's bow.

I'll remember this for the rest of my life. It's like looking at magic. We're not alone at the shipwreck, but the other group of tourists from a chartered cruise keep to the other side. The ocean is large enough for us all.

Something big passes under me. I flinch on instinct before I recognize the person. Phillip. He's swum beneath the surface and is holding something out in my direction.

Is that a…?

We both surface.

"What's that?" I ask, treading water.

"It's an action camera," he says.

"Did you take a picture of me?"

"Yeah." He hands it to me above the surface. The thing is tiny, with a string that goes around my wrist. "Press the right button… there, yes."

I stare at him across the softly undulating waves. "I can *borrow* it?"

"Yeah. There's a turtle down there. Take some pictures for your class back home."

Delight swells up inside me, and I grin at him. "You don't trust my cheap underwater camera, do you?"

"Not one bit," he says.

A loud shriek echoes across the waves. We both turn towards the frantic splashing. In the distant turquoise waves, a man is flailing. His head dips beneath the surface before emerging again, spluttering and yelling. The closest tourist boat is another hundred feet away. He must have come from there.

"Phillip," I call. "What—? Oh God."

Phillip's eyes are trained on the man. When the distressed man resurfaces another time, panic clear in his ragged breaths, Phillip tears off his mask and tosses it in my direction.

Then, he sets off, cutting through the water in a crawl.

I scramble to catch his snorkel before it slips beneath the surface and watch Phillip's rapid advance. I pegged him as a competent swimmer in the pool that night, but it's nothing to what he's doing now.

He's halfway to the panicking snorkeler before the tour guide from the other boat reacts.

I swim closer, but while I can breaststroke with the best of them, it's no championship crawl. I watch as the man dips below the surface again. Phillip doesn't stop. He barely even looks up. He just parts the water like he's made for it.

Phillip reaches the flailing tourist before anyone else. He twists smoothly in the water and shifts into a rescue, holding the man up by his elbows.

"Wow," I whisper, watching him swim them both back to the other snorkeling cruise.

Ten minutes later, we're both back on our boat. In the distance, we can see the commotion on the other boat's deck. I can just about make out the man Phillip helped on the deck, sitting down with a towel around his shoulders.

Phillip is toweling off beside me. Agitation is clear in his form and his quick movements. "Foolish," he says. "Snorkeling cruises always offer life vests and noodles. *Use them* if you're not a strong swimmer."

"Did he say what happened?"

He shakes his head. "He was too panicked. Not unusual, all in all."

"Good thing you were close by," I say.

Phillip drops the towel and sits down on the bench. His bare feet are tan against the light wooden deck. "Yes," he says. His mouth is set in a grim line. "Not the first time I've seen that with tourist cruises."

"Oh?"

"No."

I put my hands on his shoulders, curving them over the muscles that connect to his neck. His skin is already sun warm. "Not the first time you had to play a knight in shining armor, either?"

He grows still as a statue beneath my hands, but it still takes me another second to realize what I've done.

My hands freeze on his shoulders. "Gosh, I'm sorry."

"Don't be," he says. He looks up at me with serious blue eyes, and my brain short-circuits. He's so close, and I'm only in a bikini, standing right in front of him. And he's only in his swimming trunks.

My thumbs dig softly into his muscles. "It was an instinct."

"Yeah," he says. His voice has deepened. "I get that."

"We should—"

"I got you some bottles of water," our tour guide says. He pauses with a bottle in either hand, his smile grows brighter when he sees us. "Right! You two are newlyweds. Can I get you anything else?"

I drop my hands from Phillip's shoulders like I've been caught shoplifting. Not that I ever have been. Shoplifting, that is, not caught. "Thanks."

"That's all," Phillip says and gets up to accept his water. "Thank you."

"Anytime!"

I focus on unscrewing the tight cap of my water bottle. "Sorry."

"Eden," he says and takes a step closer. A notch appears between his eyebrows, giving him a look like there's something he wants to say. My fingers stay locked on the tight cap, my body stone-still once again.

"Yes?"

His mouth softens. "The rum tasting is tomorrow."

"Oh. Yes, I remember."

"Good," he says. "Don't forget."

It sounds like a promise.

"I won't," I say.

Chapter Eleven

I check my watch. It's ten minutes past our meeting time, and he's not in the lobby. I shift on the sofa and grimace at the chafe. Despite my diligent use of sunscreen and Phillip's help on the boat, I've missed a few spots. The backs of my thighs and my backside are a lovely shade of pink. Tomorrow it'll be deep red.

There are just some areas a girl struggles to reach, and asking Phillip to help there too had been… well.

Better to burn.

I glance at my watch again. Phillip hadn't been at the restaurant last night, after our boat trip. And this morning, the breakfast buffet had been as full as always… with him just as absent. It still feels like a crime not to indulge in that spread.

In the absence of my illusive companion, I'd spoken to a lovely middle-aged couple from Manchester instead. They are here to watch the cricket tournament, which necessitated a deep-dive online into *cricket,* and then refining the search term for *sport* after I got pictures of insects.

I get up off the couch. Maybe I should check outside, in case he decided to wait there.

Just then, the large wooden doors to the lobby open, and

Phillip comes walking in. He's wearing tan chinos, a blue linen shirt, and a scowl.

"There you are," he says.

I smile. "Hey."

"I've been waiting."

"Oh, you have? Where?"

"In front of the lobby."

"Gosh, I'm sorry," I say. "But I thought you said to meet you in the lobby?"

"No, in front of. Let's go," he says and turns to walk back toward the parking lot. The man from yesterday's boat ride feels miles away.

I follow him with a frown. "It was a misunderstanding. We're only ten minutes late."

"Yeah," he mutters and runs a hand through his dark hair. It's wet at the ends, as if he's just had a shower. The dark mood radiates from him like a cloud.

"You told me to wait for you in the lobby," I say quietly. "I'm sorry it made us late, but I'm not going to let that ruin our day. Are you?"

He pulls the door open to the car and doesn't answer. It's like he's back to his asshole ways, and I'm not having it. I've got enough of my own shit to handle.

"Because if you are, I'd rather not go," I say. "Thanks, though."

His hand on my arm stops me. "Wait. I shouldn't have… I won't let it ruin the day."

"Are you sure?"

"Yes. I shouldn't have taken it out on you." His jaw works, just once. "I'm sorry, Eden. It's just been a long day already."

"Okay, then. Let's try to make the rest of it good."

He nods and lets his hand fall back to his side. But the expression on his face doesn't change, and the serious lines remain etched into the handsomeness.

I get into the back of the car. So far, this trip has been very little *lying on the beach doing nothing,* and a hell of a lot of risk-taking. Which is probably what I need. Looking back on the past few years and my relationship with Caleb, we took remarkably few risks. Maybe, if we'd have taken more together, he might not have gone out seeking some of his own.

I can hear Becky in my mind, admonishing me for the thought. She doesn't like to talk about the why's behind Caleb and Cindy's actions. In some ways, she's even angrier than me, because she has no hurt feelings involved to temper the fury. Not like me, who'd needed explanations. In the beginning, it had been all I'd craved.

Just tell me why. *Why, why, why?*

Of course, there had been no why. No explanations that fit, no justifications that I could accept.

Beside me in the car, Phillip is quiet. He's looking out the window. I wonder about his dark mood. He was supposed to have been on this trip with his fiancée, or rather his wife after the wedding, so if they broke up right before… what's he thinking and feeling?

The taxi takes us through the shifting landscape of Barbados. Away from the main road with hotels and restaurants and into the interior of the island. We drive past a golf course and come up on sugarcane fields, stretching as far as the eye could see.

During the wondrous trip, I forget all about the man beside me and his terrible mood.

I'm in a foreign country, with new sights, culture, and history to explore, and my eyes are glued to the passing landscape. The music on the car radio shifts to an upbeat soca song, and I can't stop the wide smile stretching across my face.

The driver pulls into a beautiful driveway, leading to a large stone mansion. The name of the rum company is proudly displayed across oak barrels by the entrance.

We're greeted by a smiling young woman with long black braids falling in an intricate pattern down her back.

"Mr. and Mrs. Meyer," she says. "I'm Angela, and I'll be your tour guide today. I'm happy to welcome you to the property. We'll start with a tour of the grounds before heading to the distillery. How does that sound?"

Phillip and I both nod, neither of us correcting her. Of course, this tour was meant for Phillip and his bride. I glance at him out of the corner of my eye as we follow the hostess. He looks more relaxed now than he did in the car, but there's still something unreadable in his expression.

"So?" our tour guide asks over her shoulder. "What do you know about the history of rum?"

Not much, it turns out. She seems delighted by that and launches into the story while we walk across the beautiful grounds. She takes us to a platform by a vast sugarcane field, lets us sample raw sugarcane, and weaves in the history of the property.

We finally escape the blazing sun by entering the large building that houses the distillery.

"Feeling better now?" I whisper to Phillip, as we pause in front of a giant steel watt of distilled alcohol.

He looks at me sideways, his eyes narrow. Does he need clarification?

"Your bad mood?" I add.

He's quiet for a long beat, long enough that I wonder if he won't reply at all. But then, his shoulder nudges mine. "I'm better. But I'm looking forward to the tasting."

I chuckle, but stop when our tour guide ushers us onward. I take as many pictures as I can. Phillip doesn't ask this time, just extends his hand for my phone, and I pose in front of a giant copper tub.

We see the barrels, learn about the different vintages, and the fermentation and aging processes. Phillip asks a couple of detailed questions about the distilling methods, his arms crossed over his chest.

I can't resist commenting on that. "If I didn't know better,"

I tell him as we walk back toward the main house, "I'd think you were a teacher's pet in school, too."

He's wearing sunglasses and I can't see his eyes, but a smile curves his lips. "I was valedictorian once."

My mouth opens. "You were?"

"Told you I was competitive," he says, and there's a touch of joking arrogance in his voice. It makes me smile.

Our tour guide drops us on the deck of the main house, overlooking a beautiful garden of native plants. She hands us off to the bartender and tasting guide, Ryan, who presents us with four glasses of rum, each a different blend.

And they're not small glasses, either.

I follow Ryan's instructions, carefully sampling one after the other. The alcohol burns going down my throat, and by the end, my head has taken on a light cottony feeling.

"These portions are too big," I tell Ryan. He's got closely cropped hair and brown skin, offsetting a pair of light eyes behind wire-frame glasses. Judging from his explanation of each vintage's flavor profile, this isn't just his job, but his passion.

"They're Bajan-sized," he says with a chuckle. "I use rum in everything. Cakes, cookies, barbecue marinade, potato salad. I even used it in my cereal once."

"Really?"

"Oh yes. Curdles milk, though. It might be one of the few things not improved with rum."

At the end of the official tasting, we get two cocktails each. A planter's punch and a rum sour, both served in beautiful glasses with garnishes. Ryan tells us we can stay as long as we want and brings out a small bowl of chips before leaving us in the shade in our half-drunken state.

I lean back in the chair. "God, that was a lot of rum."

"We've got two drinks left."

"I don't often drink this much. Especially, not rum. Not that there's anything wrong with rum, you know. It's a great liquor."

"Ryan's not listening," Phillip says.

I chuckle. "You're funny sometimes, you know, when you're not being curt." Then, I frown. "Not that you're... sorry."

He takes off his sunglasses. There's a glint in his eyes that makes it clear he's not unaffected by the rum, either. "No, I told you I like honesty. And I was an asshole earlier."

"Okay. Then, yeah, you kinda were."

He runs a hand over the back of his neck. "I get that way sometimes, especially about punctuality. It's not something I'm proud of."

"It's okay. We all have our flaws."

"I'm pretty sure you have none," he says. "Well, except that you probably like glitter far too much. Maybe you're too-trusting, too. And too talkative."

I open my mouth in outrage. The *too-trusting* one had hit a nerve. "You tell me I don't have any flaws and then come up with three off the top of your head?"

Phillip reaches for one of his drinks. "Two of those are arguably virtues. You know, like how people in job interviews say they're workaholics?"

"I bet that's how you got your current job."

"You think I'm a workaholic?"

"Let's just say I'm surprised you haven't checked your emails in the last five minutes."

His mouth tips into a smile. "I'm pleasantly distracted."

Oh. I take a long sip of my planter's punch to avoid answering, only to get spice right up my nose. I burst out coughing. Across the table, Phillip pushes a glass of water my way.

"Lovely," I wheeze. "Now the rum is trying to kill me."

"I think that's alcohol's game in general," he says. "Maybe that's why we all drink it. It's poison, and we all know it, and yet, most of us win the bouts."

I stare at him.

"What?" he says.

"That was rather profound."

He snorts. "It was not. I've had just as much to drink as you, even if I'm handling it slightly better."

I cross my legs. It hurts, my thighs burned to crisps. But it's easy to ignore the ache when there's someone so fascinating in front of me. There are so many things I haven't been able to ask, yet. Things you don't really ask a new acquaintance, at least not one as ornery as him. But being in this beautiful place and drinking all this rum has made the questions feel possible.

"So why were you so annoyed earlier? It can't just have been us being a bit late."

He taps his fingers against his glass. "No," he finally says. "I got a phone call right before, and it didn't exactly go great."

"Ah. Did you find out one of your clients is going to prison?"

The gaze he levels on mine is dry. "I'm a far better attorney than that."

"Also, you don't really work on criminal cases."

"Well, that, too," he says. "But mostly, the I'm-great part."

"So what was the call about, then?" I ask.

He twists the glass in his grip. One-quarter rotation, and then another. "Your curiosity is bottomless."

I give him an apologetic smile. "Yes. There are a ton of things we don't know about one another."

"Most things, yes. It's a natural consequence of just having met."

I look down at my drink. Somewhere in the distance, a bird sings. Despite being in the shade, I can feel the warmth of the sun on my bare arm. "Was it your ex?"

"No," he says. "It was my sister. She couldn't resist saying 'I told you so.'"

"Oh. About the non-wedding?"

His mouth curves into a smile that's only a little amused. "Yes, and about my ex in general."

"God, I can see how that might put a damper on your mood."

He shrugs, his voice dry. "Maybe, but I wasn't angry at her. She was right."

Something dawns on me.

"You were angry at yourself," I say slowly, "for not seeing what she saw?"

He looks down at his drink before looking up at me, his eyes guarded. But then he nods. "You're good at reading people, Eden."

"You're an interesting person to read."

He chuckles. "God help me, then."

That makes me laugh, too. I take a sip of my planter's punch and relax back in my chair. The air between us feels calm and unbothered. Most of all, it's easy. "Are you buying a bottle or two of rum to bring back with you?"

"I hadn't thought about it," Phillip says. "Are you?"

"Yes. I have to give one to my parents and one to my best friend Becky, even though she's pregnant. She'll have to wait like a year until she can taste it," I say. A dark thought strikes me, and I smile. "Maybe I should get one for my ex, too."

Across the table, Phillip's hand pauses in midair. His eyebrows pull down low over his eyes. "You'd do that?"

"Probably not. But it's a fun idea. Like, 'look what you missed out on, you idiot.' Maybe with a printed picture of me in a bikini." I put a hand over my face. "God, I'd never in a million years do that."

His voice sounds amused. "But it would feel good, wouldn't it?"

"Yes. Probably even better if I keyed his car while I was at it."

Phillip's laughter is short, but it's there. Dark and delicious. "I'm imagining the worst now if he's gotten someone like you to consider violence. What did he do?"

I rest my head against the back of the chair and look up at

the nearby house. It's easier to tell the story if I'm looking at interlocking bricks and not at the man in front of me.

"It's embarrassingly cliché, really. He said he worked a lot with a corporate branch in a city a few hours away, and it required a lot of late nights and the occasional weekend trip. Funny, how most of those trips lined up perfectly with my best friend Cindy's out-of-state visits to her parents."

"Damn," he says. His voice is not amused now.

"Yeah. She was supposed to be my maid of honor. Becky declined because she is pregnant… we joked that she was my lieutenant and Cindy was my general." I look over at Phillip. He's silent, watching me. Listening.

The rum makes it easy to talk.

"But one weekend, the lies just didn't add up. I was naive enough that I didn't realize the reason why. Becky's the one that did, actually. So I called Caleb and asked him if Cindy was in the hotel room with him… He was quiet for a few seconds before the excuses poured out of him." I sigh. "It was right under my nose the whole time."

"It usually is," Phillip murmurs, looking down at his drink. He swirls the glass around, and the ice clinks softly. "How long ago?"

"Three months, roughly. Want to know the craziest part?"

He nods.

"Caleb actually thought we could still go ahead with the wedding. He promised he'd stop right away, and that he'd be a better husband than he'd been as a boyfriend. As if I'd ever agree to that?"

Phillip takes a sip of his drink. "He sounds like a fucking idiot."

I let out a surprised chuckle, and soon I'm laughing so hard I have to put down my glass. The matter-of-fact delivery of that statement couldn't be more accurate.

"Yes," I say. "God, yes."

"How long were you together?"

"Seven years."

"Shit." Phillip stretches out his long legs beneath the table, his shoe resting next to my sandal. "I'd say I'm sorry, but you're better off without him."

"That's what I think, too. And that's why I had to go on this trip. I have to enjoy it. I *have* to. Because… because I was the one who dreamed of a trip to the Caribbean. I wanted this expensive honeymoon. And I booked it, and planned it, wrote out our itinerary, and paid my half. It was my *dream* vacation. How could I let him take that away from me, too?"

"Revenge by enjoyment," Phillip says.

"Exactly. And if I don't enjoy this, there's no point, you know?"

"I know," he says, and it sounds like he truly does. "That's the most devastating thing you can give him. Your happiness."

Chapter Twelve

I'm giggly in the car back to the resort. Phillip is more stoic, but there's a smile lurking in the corner of his mouth, too. *All thanks to the rum.* Maybe the sun and the tour, and the lovely day, too.

My head is floating. It's the most pleasurable feeling, like I'm in that pool at midnight, afloat on my back and staring up at the star-ridden sky.

We make it out of the car and end up in front of the resort's giant wooden doors. It's late, but not late enough for bed, the sun just having set. The last thing I want is to return to my little room. Alone.

So, I turn toward the garden and the path that leads down to the beach. "I'm going for a walk."

Phillip chuckles behind me. "Think you're sober enough for that?"

"I'm not drunk. I'm just a bit tipsy," I say and demonstrate this by walking away from him in a wonderfully straight line.

He follows me at a leisurely pace. "You're not going for another midnight swim, are you? Because it's far from midnight."

"Another? You're the one who tempted me into the first, you know."

"That's right. I'm a bad influence."

"The worst," I say. My meandering takes me to the very edge of the beach. I slip out of my sandals and stand barefoot in the sand. "Isn't this place just amazing?"

He makes a low humming sound in agreement, his hands in the pockets of his pants. "Have you seen the entire resort?"

"Most of it, yeah. I mean, your area is pretty gated."

"Only the individual bungalows," he says. "Come on, let me show you."

We amble past the empty lounge chairs toward the path that leads to the bungalows. Soon enough, we reach the gate beyond which are the villas, built in a staggered row. Hedges separate them from one another, and I catch sight of a small pool. I had missed that during my snooping.

"You really have your own pools?"

Phillip nods and pushes open the gate. "Want to see?"

The paved pathway takes us past two small bungalows. They're private and closed-off, and it isn't until we've walked to the far side that he turns onto a smaller path behind a bungalow. A quick swipe of his key card and a gate unlocks, revealing a private backyard.

"Oh my God," I say. "This is stunning."

"It is," he says. He's holding the gate open, his eyes on me. It's an invitation.

I step inside the backyard of his private bungalow. It's small but cozy, with a miniature version of the hotel pool right here. It's surrounded by planters of flowers, and it's only a stone's throw from the beach. A beach that starts right at the edge of the bungalow's property.

Behind me, Phillip unlocks the porch door. Through the glass window, I glimpse a large room and the edge of a bed. I can't imagine staying in a place like this for a honeymoon. If I did, I wouldn't need an itinerary. I'd just stay here—in the garden, on the beach, in bed.

My cheeks heat up. I'm in his hotel room. Well, not inside it. But right on the fringe.

Phillip returns to the porch. The top buttons of his linen

shirt are undone, revealing a hint of his tanned pecs and a sliver of chest hair.

He's holding a bunch of small bottles in one hand.

"I raided the minibar," he says.

I grin. "That'll cost you a fortune."

"It'll be worth it," he responds and hands me one of the small rum bottles. "There's a chaser, too. Let me grab it."

"Your bungalow really comes with all the bells and whistles, huh?"

"Yes. Do you want two hundred rose petals, too?"

I laugh. "No, thanks, I'm good."

"I figured."

I sit down on the edge of his pool and sink my feet into the water. So this is bungalow twelve.

He lowers onto the other edge of the pool, directly across from me. There's something so composed about him that it's just shy of intimidating. Like even when he's relaxed, he's still guarded, watching his words and his actions.

I lean back on my hands and look up at the heavens. It's dark, but not all the stars have come out quite yet. I can't wait for them to illuminate the sky again. It's a wonderful sight.

"Can you believe we've already been here more than a week?" he says.

I raise my small bottle of rum. "To surviving half of our honeymoons."

His eyebrows draw together, but he raises his own bottle. "To our first week," he says.

We make it through two full mini-bottles each, sitting beneath the sky, with our feet dangling in his private pool. "I don't understand your ex," I say. "If I was her, I would have fought tooth and nail for this vacation."

"Mh-mmm. But you're *not* her," he says. "And a vacation like this isn't a big thing to her."

I frown. "Not a big thing?"

"No, she's..." he shakes his head. "Doesn't matter. We

wouldn't have gone on a vacation together after the way things went down."

"How did they go down?" I ask. "I mean, if you want to talk about it. It can be therapeutic."

Phillip runs a hand along his jaw. He's quiet for a long moment, and I wonder if I've overstepped. If he's going to tell me off.

But then, he looks over at me. "We changed our minds last moment."

"Oh," I breathe. "That's… intense."

He chuckles, but the sound isn't humorless. "Yeah."

Silence falls between us again, and I'm burning with questions. I want to know more. It's hard to picture him in a relationship. Him with someone… else.

I clear my throat. "I didn't see it coming, with my relationship. Did you?"

His eyes feel unusually heavy on mine. "I should've," he finally says. "We lived very different lives."

"Was it enough for you?"

He turns the bottle over in his hands, and it looks tiny in comparison. "I thought so at the time. We weren't a couple for as long as you and your dipshit."

I stare at him for a second before chuckling. "Dipshit?"

"He'll never be anything else," Phillip says. There's a curve to his lips, but his voice is serious.

"It does make you rethink things. Like, you see the relationship differently. In the beginning, I only thought of things I missed… but now, the list of things I'm glad to be rid of is so much longer," I say.

He puts a hand on his knee, supporting himself. "All right. One shot per good riddance you can think of."

"You have to do it, too," I say. "Okay?"

"All right. But you're starting."

I push my hair back over my shoulder. "Well, used gym socks everywhere. I don't miss that even a little bit."

"Cheers to that," he says, and I take a shot of the rum. It

burns going down. I don't think I've ever had this much rum before—or probably ever will again—in one week.

"Your turn," I say, grimacing. "Ugh, that's strong."

His eyes find the horizon again and the softly swelling waves. The sea is barely visible in the darkness, illuminated only by the moon and stars.

"I can't believe… okay. Well, I won't miss the constant texting to let someone know where I am, *all the time.*"

That makes me chuckle. "You guys had that kind of relationship, did you?"

He runs a hand over his face. "If I was working late and forgot… well. I'm not going to miss that."

"That sounds stressful."

"Yeah." He shrugs like he wants to get rid of the memory. "Come on, what's your next one?"

"Well, he *hated* quiet nights in. Like, something always had to happen. A big movie night, dinner with friends, or going for a run." In the last couple of years, our differences had become stark. I'd want to spend the evening on the couch with a book, and he'd call me boring or lame.

Phillip frowns. "What? That's the best."

"Going for a run?"

"No, having quiet nights in."

"Right?" I smile, shrugging, too. "Anyway, what's your next good riddance?"

He holds the small rum bottle up to his lips. "Dating someone who is constantly checking their social media," he says and drains the bottle. "Good fucking riddance to that."

I laugh. "That would drive me nuts."

"Trust me," he says, his eyebrows lifting high, "me, too."

A comfortable silence descends. My fingers play with the tiny label on my rum bottle, carefully peeling it away. I feel warm, inside and out.

"So," Phillip says. "Tell me your next good riddance. What did the dipshit do that you won't miss?"

I tear the label clean off. "I won't miss—um. Wait," I say,

shaking my head. A blush is creeping up my cheeks. "Never mind."

"What?"

"No, it's nothing."

"Oh," he says, voice amused. "I get it."

"You get what?"

"What you were going to say." He raises an eyebrow, and there, on his cheek, his barely-there dimple winks at me. "So Caleb wasn't the best in that department, was he?"

I can't look at him. "Wow. That's not what I was going to say."

"No? Okay, then." He takes another sip from his bottle, and it's clear in the silence that he doesn't believe me.

"I mean… yeah, I'm not going to miss the five-minute sessions."

"Five minutes," Phillip mutters. "Right. So, with the dipshit, you had participation trophy sex?"

I blink at him. "Sex doesn't have winners and losers."

"Oh, Eden, it definitely does," he says. "I like winning… and I like making sure the woman I'm with wins, too. Several times."

I have to swallow before answering. "Oh."

"And the matches last longer than five minutes." His tone is the same matter-of-fact one I'm used to. His eyes meet mine with a hint of humor, laugh creases appearing at the corners… but on his knee, his fingers are tapping away.

Like he's not quite as unaffected as he's letting on.

"So, you don't miss it at all, then?" he asks.

"Sex with Caleb?" I ask. "Or sex in general?"

"Both. Either."

Heat creeps up my neck, but I consider the question. Consider the man in front of me. It feels like we're veering into a territory that's less beach and more quicksand. "Both, in the beginning. Now just the second one. The, um, last option. Sex in general."

Phillip's lips lift into a curve. "Tough subject?"

"No," I say. "Well, maybe a little."

"We can change it."

I shake my head. "No, no. Do you? Miss it, I mean?"

He gives a slow nod. "Yeah, I suppose."

"Mmm," I say. Breathing feels hard. "That's natural, I guess. In your relationship then… you two didn't have… that problem?"

Phillip doesn't look away from me. "No, but we had plenty of others, don't worry."

"Oh. Right."

He tips his head toward me. "So how long has it been?"

"Since I had…"

"Yes," he says. The unspoken word in my sentence seems to expand in the empty space between us, growing until it's all I can hear.

"Well, over three months at least," I say.

He frowns. "Painful."

"Well, in the beginning, I was too sad to notice any kind of lack, really."

"That makes sense," he says. "And what do you—"

My phone chimes loud enough to make me jump. I reach over to where my bag is lying and dig it out.

The text makes me grin. "Oh my God, the turtles are hatching tonight!"

"What?"

"The turtles, they're hatching tonight."

"Did they text you to tell you that?"

I roll my eyes. "No, Jamie did."

"Jamie?"

"From the catamaran cruise. You remember, right?" I stand up and look back down at my phone. "He's sending me the location, too. There will be a bunch of volunteers there… we can join them!"

There's a groan from Phillip's direction.

"Don't you want to?" I ask, grinning. "It's a once-in-a-lifetime thing, you know."

He puts down his bottle. "God, you're crazy."

"Yes, but you like a bit of vacation crazy, don't you? Oh, come with me. It's going to be amazing."

He looks at me with something like amused resignation in his eyes. "Fine," he says. "But I'm holding you personally accountable for the outcome."

I'm already slinging my bag over my shoulder. "Come on. You can tell me your good riddance on the way."

Chapter Thirteen

The front desk calls a taxi for us. Apparently, it's not normal for the Winter Resort guests to order one at 10 p.m. to drive to the east coast, because she looks at us as if we've lost our minds.

Phillip seems to agree with her.

But he doesn't say a thing as we get into the car, or when he hires the cab driver to stick around when we get there.

We arrive at the coordinates Jamie had sent, but the place looks dark and deserted. I can hear waves, though, so the beach must be close by.

"We're probably about to get robbed," Phillip says calmly by my side, and I can't tell if he's joking or not. I *think* so, but his sarcasm is tough.

"Oh, of course we're not!" I say. The rum of the last couple of hours has settled into a pleasurable buzz in the back of my head, like a song you can't help but tap your foot along to. "Jamie and I spoke about this organization during the sunset cruise."

There's a surprise in his tone. "You did?"

I nudge Phillip's shoulder with mine. "Yep. You were on your phone, I believe. Now let's find this group…"

We walk around the dense shrubbery, and the ground turns from packed dirt to fine sand. The moonlight casts a silvery shadow over the landscape, and through the thickets, I hear waves breaking against the beach.

And then, voices.

"Over here!" someone calls. "It's starting!"

Excitement burns in my stomach. "We're definitely in the right place."

"It's damn dark," Phillip mutters. "Does no one have flashlights?"

"Oh, you can't use flashlights. It would disorient the hatchlings." I reach for his hand. It's warm and dry around mine. "Come on, let's find the others."

We find Jamie by a dune, standing with the other volunteers next to a foldable table laden with hot beverages. Phillip and I are welcomed like we're not just two random tourists, offered coffee, and instructed on the different nests on the beach.

"There are many on this beach," Jamie tells us, pointing to a few flags. The orange color is just barely visible in the moonlight. "They've been percolating since this evening."

"Percolating?" I ask.

He grins. "Yeah, the sand is shifting. Means they're digging from below. They'll be out in a few hours, most likely."

Phillip has a cup of coffee in his hand, his eyes steady on Jamie. "Is a hands-off approach best?"

"Yeah, we can't do the digging for them. They need to imprint on the sand. That's how they know which beach they should come back to in a decade to lay their own eggs."

Oh my God. I can't wait to tell my students about this. "Do you guys know which species of turtles are going to hatch here?"

Jamie nods. "This beach has leatherbacks."

"Really?"

"Really," he says and grins. "So, why don't you two have a seat and keep an eye out?"

"Of course. And what are we looking for?" I ask. "I mean,

is there anything we can do to help?"

Jamie scratches at his tightly braided hair. "Look out for the stray dogs, mongooses, and big birds. They'll try to grab a quick meal later, and we gotta force them away. But remember, no touching the turtles."

I cross my heart. "And no light?"

"None."

We walk toward a part of the beach without volunteers but that has a few flags. I dig through my bag for the beach towel I'd packed. Phillip watches me in silence as I spread it out on the sand for us, right next to a thicket, but with a great view of the beach.

"We can patrol from here." I sit down on the towel. He doesn't, looking down at me.

"What?" I ask.

"We weren't robbed," he says. He looks mildly surprised.

"Yeah. Did you really expect us to be?" I lean back with my hands in the now-cool sand. "I thought you were joking."

"Mostly," he says. "But I still didn't quite believe... Do you make friends wherever you go?"

"Sometimes I do, but not always. I just like meeting new people and learning new things, even if I can be naive at times." The word hurts to say. *Naive.* Like I'd been with Caleb and Cindy for months.

Phillip shakes his head. "Not what I meant. Just that, we were always bound to end up here, weren't we? Once I asked to share your table."

I smile up at him. "Sure was, and if my memory serves, you didn't really ask. Now sit down. You're too tall, and you'll confuse the turtles."

He gives a quiet huff but does what I ask, sitting down beside me. "What does that mean?"

"They need the landscape to be as unchanged as possible. Navigating with the moonlight, the look of the waves, and the sands. You'd throw off the entire coastline."

He shakes his head. "I can't believe you just said that."

"It's the truth. Come on, Phil. Lighten up."

He glances at me from the corner of his eye. "Phil?"

"Don't people call you that?" I say, unable to hide my smile.

"No," he says. "They don't."

"Well, maybe you're more of a Phillip. Phil feels so relaxed. Like a dad at a barbecue."

"Right," he says, as if that makes any sort of sense, and reaches inside his jacket. I hear the telltale sound of glass against glass.

My eyebrows fly up. "You didn't?"

"I sure did," he says. "Want some rum in your coffee?"

"Yes. Though, I don't think I've ever done that before."

"When in Barbados," he says and tips half the bottle into my paper cup. My feet are beyond the edge of the towel and I bury my toes in the sand. Waves beat softly against the beach, darkness stretches out in front of us, and the stars are a blanket above us. And somewhere beneath us, in this sand, under the carefully placed flags, hundreds of sea turtles are starting their lives.

"I think," I say, "that I've never been happier than I am right now. Can you feel it? What a beautiful night we're having?"

He's quiet for so long that I doubt he'll answer. I rest my head on my knees and look out over the sand. Watching out for stray dogs. Patrolling.

"Yeah," he says softly. "I can."

I twist my head to look at him. He's a dark shadow in the moonlight, thick hair falling over his forehead.

He's looking back at me. "What's the plural of mongoose?" he asks.

A slow smile spreads across my face. "You know where my mind goes."

"Yes," he says, "I know. And I figured it was the kind of question you'd like."

"It can't be mongeese, but oh how I wish it was."

He takes a sip of his rum-laced coffee. "The world is a non-sensical place."

"Yes." I glance at the closest orange flag waving in the wind. "Aren't you glad you sat at my dinner table?"

"I would have missed out on the high-quality conversation, that's for sure," he says. "Not to mention the entertainment on a Hollywood-like level. Do you get up to this much trouble back home? Washington, was it?"

"Yeah, and absolutely not."

"No falling off boats," he says, "and no charming strangers left and right?"

"This is my vacation self," I say. "I can promise you that I'm decidedly less social back home. And a lot more stable on my feet."

"Your vacation self," he repeats.

"Yes. Like, I packed a sun hat and a colorful maxi dress for this trip that I'd never wear at home. That's part of my vacation identity." I brush his shoulder with my own. "Come on, Phillip. What's yours?"

"Well, I forgot my sun hat at home," he says evenly. "My maxi dress, too."

I chuckle. "What a shame."

"Very. I can definitely rock a polka dot." Then, he shakes his head and lifts his coffee cup to his lips. "Fuck, that was stupid."

I chuckle. "Yes, but I appreciate it."

"That's my vacation self," he says. "I'm doing a shit ton of things I never had any intention to."

"*Enjoying yourself* is a great vacation goal for you." I touch my cup to his. "Mine is to challenge myself."

He lifts a dark eyebrow. "Challenge yourself, huh?"

"Yes. I have to start living again, you know? After my wedding got called off, and the relationship imploded, well…" I shake my head. "It took a toll. But even though I love sitting at home in my pajamas most evenings and watching old movies, I can't *only* do that."

"Hmm," he says. And then, says nothing more at all.

I lean back with my hands on the cool sand. Maybe it's the days we've spent together, or maybe it's the rum. But I can almost feel how he's thinking.

I tap his foot with mine. "Say it."

"How do you know I was about to say anything at all?"

"I just do."

He runs a hand through his hair. "I was just thinking that you wouldn't like me if we'd met Stateside."

"Do you know what? I find that very hard to believe."

"It's the truth," he says.

"Well, you wouldn't look at me twice if we met back home, so I guess we're even."

His brow furrows. "What does that mean?"

I take a long sip of my drink. It tastes like coffee set on fire.

"It doesn't matter," I say. "But I guess that means it's a good thing we met in Barbados, then. As our vacation selves."

"Mm-hmm. Although I can imagine—you're cold," he says, eyes on my arms. Goosebumps race across my skin.

"Just a bit. It's okay."

He sets down his cup in the sand and shrugs out of his thin jacket. I catch a sliver of muscled back as his T-shirt rides up a bit.

"Here," he says.

My fingers dig into the soft material, warm from his body heat. "Won't you be cold?"

"No. I'm my vacation self," he says and rests an arm behind us. "And my vacation self is excellent at homeostasis."

I stare at him.

"What?" he asks.

"Nothing," I say. "Just that you're very funny. You just don't let on."

He snorts. "Honor my sacrifice and put on the jacket, Eden."

I wrap it around myself. It smells like him, like soap and

warm skin, and man. I wonder why men's scents are often described in overwrought sentences, like a dewy morning or musky pine, when that's never what they smell like. They smell so much better.

"Something wrong with it?"

I stop sniffing. "No. It's warm. And, um, very nice fabric."

"Good," he says. There's amusement in his voice. "So, we could be here all night then, waiting for the turtles to emerge?"

"Technically yes, I think. But that's a small sacrifice."

"Turtles hatched without our involvement for centuries," he says. "I'm sure they'll keep hatching during the next century, too."

"Well, now there are all kinds of things threatening them, most put there by humans. We're the biggest threat of them all."

He raises an eyebrow, and the dimple is back. "That sounds a bit narcissistic. We're not the greatest species, you know."

"I know that, which is why we're here to *protect* them. Come on, you're just being a contrarian for the heck of it." I wrap my hand around his wrist that's resting on his knee. His skin is hot and firm to the touch. He's all bone and muscle. "Tell me you're not having fun."

"Sitting on a sandy beach at midnight," he says. But his eyes have softened around the corners.

My hand stays on his wrist. "Yeah. You could be doing worse things right now. Think of all the legal paperwork you could be filling out at work."

"Mm-hmm."

"All the gavels you could be using."

"I'm not a judge, Eden."

"All the cases you could be arguing in court. Isn't this so much better?"

"Still not what I do most days," he says, "but I take your

point. What about you? Do you miss telling off unruly little kids for running with scissors?"

"That almost never happens."

"Almost isn't never."

"No," I say with a chuckle, "it's not."

Phillip's eyes dip briefly to my lips. My breathing grows shallow, nerves erupting pleasurably in my stomach.

"We could do something to pass the time," I say.

"Hmm. Any ideas?" He's closer than he was when we sat down. Have I moved? Has he?

"Um, there's a lot of sand. We could build a sandcastle?"

"We could," he says. "But I haven't done that in twenty years."

"We'd probably disrupt the turtles, too."

"Yes, and we can't have that," he says.

"No. Conservation is... important."

"Mm-hmm." He's close enough that I feel his warm exhale against my cheek. "Staying put is a safer bet."

"Yes. Much."

There's a second, and then another, of tantalizing closeness. The almost-before-it-becomes-a-certainty, when anticipation is a physical weight in my chest.

Then, our lips touch.

He tastes like fresh coffee and rum, and I close my eyes against the nearness. It's foreign and not quite right, but then he tilts his head, and all of a sudden, we fit. His lips move steadily on mine.

Like he's thought about kissing me before.

Energy runs in a current down my spine, and the sound of waves and other volunteers talking have turned down to mute.

My hand finds his shoulder, right where it meets his neck.

"Come here," he says hoarsely and turns toward me fully. An arm around my waist pulls me in closer, and then we're kissing again. The fit is even better now, with his chest against mine.

He runs a hand along my back, and I shiver at the too-light, teasing touch. My nerves feel electrified, and my skin's too thin, as if I'm feeling the world too strongly.

His tongue brushes over my lower lip, and then he's there, too, the kiss deepening. I can hear my heartbeat drumming in my ears.

Of course, he's good at this.

His hand brushes over my cheek and settles in my hair, holding my face still. And if he's allowed touching, then I am, too, and my hand moves from his neck to his hair.

The short strands are thick and slightly roughened by sea and sun, and I twine my fingers through them. My nails accidentally scrape against his scalp.

He groans against my mouth, and the sound tightens something in my stomach.

"Fuck, Eden," he murmurs against my lips. The hand on my back tugs me closer. "If I'd known…"

I chuckle and press my lips to his again. I'm not done. Not done with the warmth, the closeness, with the not-thinking.

A sharp call nearby makes not-thinking impossible. "It's happening! The first turtles are emerging!"

Excited whoops reach us from the other end of the beach.

"Keep a look out, everyone! No dogs! No mongooses!"

"Mongeese," I whisper against Phillip's lips.

He chuckles quietly and leans back, his eyes meeting mine. The look in them makes my throat dry. "Yeah. It's showtime, Eden."

I get up on shaky legs. He follows suit, standing tall beside me. But he's not as unbothered as he looks. He clears his throat and runs a hand through his hair before he joins me by the closest nest.

A turtle breaks through the percolating sand surface. It's a tiny thing, a perfect miniature replica of the large turtles we'd seen at sea just a few days ago.

A new life begins.

Chapter Fourteen

There were a lot of things I hoped or expected to do on my non-honeymoon. Seeing baby turtles hatch and make their way to the ocean was definitely one of them. But kiss a fellow tourist beneath the stars?

Well, kiss a fellow tourist anywhere, let alone on a moonlit beach. In the three months since Caleb and I broke up, I've not given dating a single thought.

Well, maybe *one* thought, but never two, because it inevitably reminded me of terrible first dates and the dating apps that people use. Life was so much simpler when I reconnected with Caleb over a summer vacation from college.

Not that Phillip and I are dating or anything, or even close to it.

All we've done is kissed. Once.

It had been a hell of a kiss, too. The kind that reminded me why humans kiss at all, why this odd ritual so unique to our species is a thing. Objectively weird and subjectively amazing.

We'd said goodbye back at the hotel, well after midnight. Phillip brushed my hair back, and I stood very, very still, and then we'd gone our separate ways. Me toward the elevators and him toward his private bungalow.

It's the next morning now, and I'm buzzing at the breakfast table. Hummingbirds are native to Barbados, but right now, it feels like all of them are in my stomach, their wings beating rapidly.

He rarely shows, but he *sometimes* does, just to grab a cup of coffee. Maybe today will be the day.

I have my notepad open beside me on the table, my character notes and the plot ideas there to be worked on, but I don't write a single word.

Phillip might behave as if never happened. I don't know how I'll react to that. But there's an even worse alternative, and that is he might *not,* and I really don't know what I'll do, then.

It's not like I'm... ready. Definitely not ready to date anyone. That's not even in the cards here because we're both leaving in a week. But I'm not sure I'm ready to have a wild holiday fling, either.

Becky would be cheering me on to do just that. *Let me live vicariously through you!*

Maybe that's why I don't text her about the last night's kiss on the beach. It exists in its own separate universe, beneath a starlit sky and to the sound of waves. In a place where two people became something very unlike themselves for a glorious few minutes.

I head down to the beach after breakfast. Surprisingly, it's another warm, sunny day, and I can't believe I've already been here for over a week.

I bathe myself in sun lotion and grab a lounge chair that has an umbrella, just to be safe. Then, I google *surfing lessons Barbados* and *best hiking trips* to avoid giving my brain any time at all to linger on the events of the previous night.

Distraction is a great tactic.

I'd employed it heavily right after Caleb and Cindy, where, if I just kept having podcasts playing in my headphones at all times, I could almost drown out the sound of my heart breaking.

Almost.

After a swim, I return to the plot I'm trying to figure out for this resort murder mystery. Why are the main characters so hard for me to find? They're not like side characters. I can't just look around me and get inspired, not when there needs to be great depth to them.

But I know this is the process. It had been the same way when I wrote my first book... the one I actually found a publisher for. It had started out as the best thing that had ever happened to me, which is probably why the fall felt so much harder.

My very first book. My debut. The one I'd written throughout college, the one I'd rewritten, and rewritten again, *and again* until I knew the words of it better than my own name.

Selling a book, not to mention a debut, is nigh-on-impossible. Traditional publishers have a needle-sized hole to pass through... but I'd done it. *One Fatal Step* had sold, and my publisher had been so excited that we'd planned a release party. Roughly six weeks after the launch, the high had started to wear off.

Hard.

They wanted me to market. They wanted me to magically have a social media following over night. And, as it was made very clear to me, they weren't willing to invest more into marketing... because the book hadn't performed.

To this day, it still hasn't earned its advance.

My publisher doesn't want to buy more books from me.

Which means, I write my stories now for an audience of me, myself, and I. No editor to appease and no publisher to bow down to. No readers, either. But, clearly, they weren't there the first time around.

I close my eyes and lean back in the lounge chair. *Think, Eden. Think.* How can I make this story work? What main characters do I want to spend the coming half a year with?

My thinking is interrupted rather rudely a few minutes later by the arrival of a tall man standing next to my chair. I shield my eyes from the sun to see who it is.

It's Phillip.

I can't make out his eyes behind his sunglasses. "Hey," he says.

I struggle to pull myself up into a sitting position and glance down, sneakily, to see that all my bikini pieces are in the right spots. They are. "Um, hi."

"Hungover?"

"A bit this morning, but I'm good now," I respond.

He's fully dressed. Shorts and actual sneakers, and in another button-down. The silence between us stretches out for a beat and *okay, we're going to pretend like yesterday didn't happen,* I think, and that's absolutely the right call. Definitely.

"I was just heading out, but I thought I saw your pink bikini," he says.

"It's purple," I say. "Lilac, really."

Phillip looks down at the said bikini, and my body, and I regret my clarification immediately. But his lips curve just slightly. "Right. My bad. So, I'm heading to the golf course, actually."

"Really?"

"Yeah. I have a tee time in... thirty minutes. It's just ten minutes from here."

"The one we drove by yesterday?"

"Yes, the Winter Resort has a partnership." He shrugs. "I can see that you're busy tanning, but if you want to come, there's a spot."

"To come with?"

"Yes."

"To *golf?*"

"Yeah."

"I don't know how to," I say. "Well, I've played mini golf a few times. That's not really the same thing, right? Although I guess the balls are the same size, though."

There's that curve to his lips again, just barely there. "Yes, I suppose they are."

I swing my legs over the edge of the lounge chair. Golf. With Phillip. He must have been heading out from the bungalow and changed his mind on the spur of the moment when he saw me on the beach.

"As long as you can promise me there'll be no rum, I'm in," I say.

"No rum? You had your fill yesterday?"

"Yes. I think I need *at least* a few more hours before I may want another rum sour."

He snorts. "Look at you, the picture of moderation."

"That's me. Okay, I'm in. But I just brought a cover-up to the beach. Can I go change quickly?"

He glances down at my bikini again but looks away just as fast. "Yeah. I'll be in the lobby."

"Inside it? Or right outside?" I ask.

I can't see him roll his eyes, but I can practically feel it. "*Inside.* Now go."

"I'm on it. Back soon!"

Digging through my suitcase a few minutes later, I face an imminent problem. What do you wear to golf? The question is pretty irrelevant at any length, because whatever the answer is, the likelihood of me having accidentally packed it was zero.

I pull on a tank top and a jeans skirt that ends halfway down my thighs. It looks vaguely tennis-y, and I have a notion that people who play tennis and golf usually wear similar things.

I only brought sandals and flip-flops, though, so my sandals will have to do.

Phillip is indeed waiting in the lobby. I catch sight of him with his back toward me, hands in his pockets. For a second, I want to retreat to my room. Last night had made things real, somehow. The cotton candy cloud of embracing the unknown, being vacation me, and the *why not?* attitude I've tried hard to live on and with for the past week are all shaking beneath me.

But then, he turns.

His eyes take in my clothes and stop at my shoes. That half smile edges his lips, and the cloud beneath me stabilizes. I float the rest of the way forward.

"What do you think?" I ask. "Proper golfing attire?"

"Not in the least. I like the shoes, though."

"They're nice, aren't they?" I hold out my foot and twirl it around, like a moron. We both look down at my sandal and the coral color of my toenails. I give my ankle one last rotation before putting my foot down.

The silence stretches on.

Ignore it, I think. *Just like we're ignoring last night.*

"Anyway, I don't think I'll do very well, so my footwear probably won't matter. Won't I be slowing you down?"

"Maybe," he says with a shrug. He pulls a navy cap down low on his head, and we start walking out into the warm midday sun. "But I'm not playing to set any new records."

"Are we getting there by golf cart?" I ask, seeing the white vehicle parked outside the lobby. The Winter Resort's name and logo are proudly emblazoned on the side.

"Yeah. Robert will take us."

Robert does indeed take us. He's pleasantly chatty on the way there, reminding us to take a couple of water bottles out on the course.

There's someone waiting for us by the club house when we get there. A man in appropriate golf attire that looks almost nothing like my clothes. He greets us with a wide smile and gets us kitted out.

I nod and smile and accept all the clubs handed to me. They have names I vaguely recognize, like putter and driver, but also names like wedge and iron.

Phillip looks over at me from time to time, amusement a faint flicker in his eyes. He can probably spot my fake enthusiasm a mile away.

"So," he says when we're finally all loaded up in our own

golf cart, equipped with pegs and balls and other things that have vaguely sex-related names. "Feeling excited?"

"More like intimidated. You know I've never done this before. Ever, right?"

"I know," he says and gets in the driver's seat. "But there's thirty minutes between our tee time and the next group's. I asked."

"Oh. Is that good?"

"Yes. We have plenty of time. Now come on, get in."

I climb onto the seat next to him. Our bags, with all the clubs I'm going to swing very, very soon, are in the back.

He drives along the trail toward the first hole. I look at him out of the corner of my eye. His shoulders are relaxed, his face unreadable.

"Do you golf often?" I ask.

"Often enough. It's a good way to spend time with clients and coworkers."

"Do you try to win when you play with your coworkers, but deliberately lose against clients?"

He snorts. "Something like that."

We come to a stop near the first hole. The tension between us is slowly melting away, returning to what it had been before last night. Before the rum and the turtles and the ill-advised kissing complicated a good thing.

"This is the teeing area," he says and puts the cart in park. "You'll want your driver. We'll want to hit as far out as we can on this one. See the flag down there? That's the hole we're aiming for. Try getting it on the green."

I nod, like that makes perfect sense, and look at the assortment of clubs in my bag. It should be the one shaped for the greatest impact. My hand grazes over one made of steel, another that has a club-like head, to stop over one with a slanted metal edge.

I pull it out of the bag. "Got it."

"Awesome. Do you want me to go first?" Phillip is crouching, putting a peg in the manicured grass. Atop it, he rests a ball very much like the ones in mini golf.

"Sure. Show me how it's done."

He chuckles. "Okay. You want to stand like this. See my stance?"

I do. I try to copy it, watching his tall body bend slightly, arms and back straight.

He hits his ball. It flies through the air, soaring in an arc before it lands somewhere very far away. I see it bouncing and rolling before it comes to a stop, about twenty feet from the first flag.

"Oh," I say. "You're very, very good."

His smile slants into a crooked thing. "That wasn't very far."

"It looks super far."

"A trick of the light. Feel ready to try?"

I walk up to the spot he'd started at. "Yes. Okay, so, I need one of those peg things, right?"

Phillip chuckles again. "Yes, but you need the right club first."

"Oh. It isn't this one?"

"No. The driver is the one with the…. Here. It looks like this." He pulls the club with the giant head out of my bag.

"Oh. Really?"

"Yeah."

"That club looks crazy."

"It does, but it has a great swing to it. Okay, try this. Grip it like this… no, have your hand slightly… yes." He curves his hand around mine and shifts it higher on my club. It's warm around mine.

"That's it," he murmurs.

"Okay. Now I need to bend my knees, right? Just slightly?"

"Yes. But try the swing first without hitting the ball, just to get the hang of it."

I feel ridiculous, standing there beneath his scrutiny, but I swing the club.

He nods, eyebrows drawn together. "Again."

I do it one more time, and then another.

"Good, but you need to make it slightly more fluid." He takes a step closer, a hand half-extended to me. "Can I show you?"

I nod and hand him the club. But he shakes his head and comes to stand behind me instead. *Oh.*

His arms reach around and grip the club over my hands. He's warm against me, and the scent of shampoo and of man brushes against my senses.

"This okay?" he murmurs.

I nod. Speaking feels like too much.

He shuffles closer until his body is curved around mine entirely, and the cotton candy cloud beneath me evaporates. *Poof.* Goosebumps rise along my forearms despite the warm temperature and the shining sun.

This feels real.

"Like this," he says and pulls both of our arms up. He takes the club in a full arc over my head, before whooshing back down and connecting with an imaginary ball. "Keep the arc going," he says and completes the swing with both of our arms up by our heads again. Opposite side this time.

He's warm. Warmer than me, at any rate, and my lips tingle with the memory of his kisses from last night.

It's been a long time since a man hugged me like this. Even if it's not an actual hug—just "help"—and it's only his front pressing against my back. But it still counts.

"Eden," he says. His voice is a murmur in my hair.

"Yes?"

"Think you can try swinging again?"

"Oh. Yes, yeah, so… I'm supposed to do this?" I'm the one carrying the weight of our arms this time, moving the club in a slow arc.

"Yes, that's it. You've got it." His hands brush over mine

in a lingering touch before he steps back, putting some healthy distance between us.

My entire body feels electrified by the contact.

Phillip clears his throat and takes another step back. "All right," he says. "Okay. So, want to give it a try?"

"Yeah, okay." I get into position and look down at the tiny white ball, so innocent looking against the green. I still feel too-light, and a bit charged, as if I have more energy than I need.

I look over at him. "Are you going to watch?"

He cracks a full smile for the first time today. "I was planning to, unless you don't perform under pressure."

"I don't think this will be much of a performance."

He crosses his arms over his chest, that smile still there. "Just take a swing."

"Okay. Maybe you should take another few steps back," I say. "And get some protective gear. Did you pack a helmet?"

"I'll be fine," he says, amusement in his voice.

"Okay," I say again. I'm gripping the club tight. Bending my knees. My eyes are on the ball and I'm not going to let it escape. "Here goes nothing."

I make the swing, putting force behind it, and feel my club connect with the ball. It flies a full three feet away, and wildly to the left.

"Shit."

"That's okay," he says and walks past me. He bends over and picks it up. The shorts highlight the muscles in his thighs.

"Um, are you allowed to move my ball?"

"Yes," he says and puts it back down in front of me. "Try again."

"I'm almost positive this is against the rules."

"Isn't this your first time playing?" he says and takes a few steps back. "How would you know the rules?"

I turn to him with my most withering glare. "Yes, but I know some things. Like hand-on-ball is verboten in most games."

"Eden," he says, eyes steady on mine. "We'll make our own rules."

"Oh. Okay. I'll try again, then."

I do. It goes better this time, and while the ball doesn't soar in a straight arc like his, it ambles down the hill halfway to his.

"That was excellent."

I chuckle, leaning against my club. "Liar."

"For your second-ever attempt, it was pretty damn good." He climbs back into the golf cart, taking the passenger seat. "Come on, why don't you try driving the cart, too."

I get in the driver's seat, unable to stop my grin. "Really?"

He pulls his cap further down and leans back, stretching his long legs as much as there's room. "Nothing like being chauffeured."

I laugh and press down on the accelerator pedal. Golf, it turns out, might not be such a boring sport after all, and in this beautiful location? I might even find myself enjoying it.

We make it to hole seven before disaster truly strikes. He's two points under par, and I'm about fourteen thousand over. But I'm soldiering on, and Phillip doesn't show any signs of being frustrated by my frequent mishaps.

It's surprising. Somehow, he'd struck me as the kind of person that wouldn't be described as patient. After all, his pacing while talking on the phone, his constant emailing, his clear passion for his job… His own self-proclaimed desire to win in every facet of life.

But here, he doesn't let out a single disparaging comment.

Until I manage to hit my ball into the sand trap. It rolls beautifully off the green and into the sandy depths of a large bunker.

"Oh no," I say. "That one hasn't happened, yet."

I'd hit a ball into a tree—twice—and accidentally thrown my club—once. But no bunkers.

"It's a fun one," Phillip says beside me.

"You sound sarcastic. Are you being sarcastic?"

"I would never."

"Okay, so you are. What club should I use?"

"If you want, you could just lift it out."

I narrow my eyes at him. He gazes serenely back at me, face calm and eyes hidden behind the dark sunglasses.

"Those aren't the proper rules," I say.

He lifts a single shoulder in a shrug. "We haven't really adhered to them so far."

"You have."

"Well, I've done this before."

"I'll hit it and get it out," I say, rolling my neck. "It's not a problem."

"We have more balls."

"I know, but mine is there. I've grown attached to it. Leave no man behind and all that."

"You know, it will never reciprocate those feelings." He pulls out one of my clubs, examines it, and hands it to me. "Here. This one should work for the sand trap, if you insist."

"I do. I'm *learning,* you know, so this is a great opportunity."

"Mm-hmm." He stands beside the pit and watches me clamber into the sand trap. For a second, I get the absurd thought that it might be quicksand, like in a children's book. It's not.

But it is very hot from the baking sun and burns where it hits the tops of my feet.

Sandals were indeed *not* the right choice.

"You look great," Phillip calls down.

"Thanks!"

My ball lies innocently in the center of the pit, like it didn't do most of the rolling to end up there.

I square my shoulders and my hips, and swing.

My first five attempts fail.

Three times, I miss the ball and a plume of sand flies up instead. Twice, I hit the ball, but it doesn't fly high enough to clear the wall of the bunker and rolls back, the devil.

Phillip's shoulders are shaking with restrained laughter.

"It's all good!" I call, giving him a nod. "This one will do it!"

He crosses his arms, a smile across his face. "I bet."

Maybe it's the smirk he's wearing or my own amusement, but I do get it over. The ball soars and lands a few feet away from where Phillip's own ball rests, on the green.

"Yes! Nailed it!"

Phillip crosses the distance to the sand pit. He stands on the edge, reaching down an arm to me. "Very good."

"I think I'm the next Tiger Woods."

"I hope for your sake that you're not."

That makes me chuckle. I tuck my club under my arm and find purchase on the sandy slope, reaching up to grasp his hand.

It's not particularly graceful. I scramble for a foothold while he's pulling, and then I make it up, colliding with his chest, and lose a sandal.

It falls along the sandy slope and lands on the spot my ball had previously occupied.

"Oh no," I say.

Phillip is still holding my hand. It's trapped between our chests. His chin brushes my forehead as he turns his head. "Your shoe."

"It didn't survive the pit."

"No," he says, "it didn't. I'll get it."

"I can do—"

He hands me his club and steps into the pit, doing it more gracefully than I did. He scoops up the sandal and turns it upside down, getting the sand out.

"This is like Cinderella," I say. The words just come out. Maybe it's the sun, maybe it's the scent of his sunscreen still lingering from our close contact.

He looks up at me for a long moment, and then he chuckles. "Yes, strikingly similar. Do you want me to put it on you, too? See if it fits?"

Something tightens in my stomach, and all I can do is shake my head.

He climbs to the edge of the sand pit. I reach out my hand, and he looks at it with obvious suspicion.

"I can do it. I'm strong," I say.

"Right," he says. "Here, take your shoe."

I grab it and toss it aside on the grass before extending my hand to him again. "Come on. Trust me, I've been working out. I lift a ton of weights."

"You're less convincing the more you talk."

"Then, I'll shut up," I say and wiggle my fingers. "I dare you."

Phillip mutters something like *you dare me?* and shakes his head, but he accepts my hand.

And then, it all goes awry. My single sandal slips against the cut grass, as I get pulled by Phillip's weight, and my bare heel digs into the ground. The edge of the pit falters and breaks, and I tumble down. Phillip first, and then me, falling into the depths of the bunker.

I end up half-on-top of him, sprawled on the sand.

It takes me a second to catch my breath. "Oh my God," I say. "It really *is* quicksand."

Under me, Phillip is silent. He's lying on his back, and I watch him blink rapidly up at the clear, blue sky. "It's what?" he asks.

"Nothing." I lift myself off him but keep a hand on his chest. "Are you okay? Did you break anything?"

"Not as far as I'm aware," he says and turns his head slightly to look at me. "I might be in shock."

The sand is warm and soft beneath me, and probably all kinds of dirty. I prop my head up on an arm. "You don't take tumbles regularly?"

"No, can't say that I do."

"This is my… third in a week. You get used to it."

He lets out a surprised chuckle. It grows, until he's half

laughing, half groaning. "Jesus. You really couldn't pull me out."

"I could!"

"Eden," he says.

"My sandal slipped against the grass. I didn't have the proper traction. That's why."

"Traction," he repeats, and there's bone-deep skepticism there. But there's also humor laced through his voice. He stretches out his arms and turns his head back toward the heavens, like he's relaxing on a sandy beach. "Shit, I don't even like golf."

My eyebrows shoot up. "What? You don't."

"No, not really."

"But you're so good at it."

"I'm decent," he says, still speaking to God Almighty up in the clouds. "It's a slow game and occasionally very dull."

I shake my head at him. "Why did you decide to do it on your honeymoon, then?"

He takes off his sunglasses and turns his head, dark-blue eyes meeting mine. "I don't have the faintest idea."

That makes me smile. "You don't?"

"No. We were discussing activities with our travel planner, and she mentioned the resort had access to a top-tier golf course…" he shrugs. "My ex stated that I golf. It was suggested. I thought, why not? Might be nice to get some alone time."

Some alone time, I think. *On his honeymoon?*

My fingers curl over the sand, past the hot layer on top. "Why did you ever start, if you don't like it?"

"I think it was because of work. Golf is often on the agenda at retreats, conferences, and occasionally meetings…" He nods, his mouth tightening. "That's it. I had a client, years ago now. He only conducted his meetings on the course."

"That sounds ridiculous."

"Well, he was ridiculously wealthy, and his company was

undergoing one of the biggest mergers of the year. So, I learned to golf."

"Did you… win the case?"

A smile flits across his lips. "After a fashion, yes."

"Oh. It wasn't really a case."

"No, I was a legal adviser and drew up contracts."

I push up into seating. I'm still missing a shoe, and the sun is devastating, and I can feel a tiny trickle of sweat down my spine. Phillip is still lying on his back and doesn't look like he has a care in the world.

His hair is mussed now, and there's a calmness about him that wasn't there the past week.

I smile. "So, why are we out here then?"

He turns his head. "Golfing?"

"Yes."

"It's a nice day," he says, "and you wanted to learn."

"Right, blame it on me. I've been making you suffer out here, watching me hit the ball at literal trees."

He smiles again. This time it's crooked, and true, and it makes my own smile falter. "I'll tell you one thing, Eden. Golfing with you is definitely not dull."

I dig my teeth into my bottom lip. "Is that your way of saying you're enjoying yourself?"

"I've never ended up on my back in a sand bunker before," he says. "So… yes."

Voices reach us, drifting on the wind. It's a language I don't understand. German, perhaps, or Dutch. And then, a group of gray-haired men looks down at us from the edge of the sand pit. They're in the epitome of golf attire.

"*Ach,*" one of them says, frowning deeply. "*Das sind die Clowns, die den Kurs aufhalten.*"

"Sorry!" I call and get to my feet. "We'll get out of your way!"

"Speak for yourself," Phillip mutters. He's still lying on his back. "I'm having a grand time."

I aim a kick at his shoe, but I can't stop myself from giggling. "Come on."

"If you insist," he says and gracefully unfurls himself into standing. He brushes off his shorts and then reaches out, a hand ghosting over my hair. "Sand," he murmurs. "Let's go then, Eden, and see where you'll hit the ball next."

Chapter Fifteen

My hair is still faintly damp from my shower when I leave the hotel room that same evening. It had taken a lot of scrubbing to get the sand out. Can't say it was the most pleasant experience, considering my shoulders have burned just a tad, but now I'm clean and smelling of perfume and soap.

I glance at my phone. Only five minutes late.

The green sundress I'm wearing has a deep sweetheart neckline that *might* say I'm going on a date, but it's also casual enough for a friendly dinner with a fellow tourist.

Not that I know what I'm hoping for between those two options. But at least my dress can navigate them both for me.

Phillip is the one who suggested dinner after golf. He'd said it casually. *We both have to eat, don't we?*

There was undeniable logic to those words.

I get in the elevator, heading down to the hotel lobby. The middle-aged couple already inside smiles at me in unison. "Good evening," the woman says to me. She's wearing a red top with a rhinestone collar.

I nod back. "Good evening."

Her smile turns conspiratorial. "This is just the most beautiful resort, isn't it?"

"Truly the best. It's stunning here," I say.

The man puts a hand on his wife's shoulder. "We're on our second honeymoon," he says. Their accent sounds midwestern, but it's hard to place for sure.

His wife nods, her eyes sparkling. "Renewed our vows just last week."

God, they're everywhere.

But I just smile at them. "Congratulations!"

I can't blame any of the honeymooners anymore, really. This is one of the best resorts to travel to after tying the knot. Hadn't that been what I'd wanted to do myself?

Phillip is already at the restaurant when I arrive, leaning against one of the columns that frame the entrance. He still hasn't shaved, and the five o'clock shadow darkens his already-tanned face. But he's changed into a button-down linen shirt. Sadly, it gives me no clue as to the date or the non-dateness of our dinner because, as typical, it's either that or a polo with him. Is the man allergic to non-collared shirts?

The kiss from last night is still unacknowledged. It's hovered in the air around us all day, a memory unspoken.

"Hey," Phillip says. His eyes dip down in a sweep of my dress, and my skin flushes under his gaze. "Let's grab a seat."

A server shows us to our table, lets us order drinks, and then we're quiet as we read our separate menus. The table is close to the ocean, next to the waves breaking against the boardwalk, just like our first dinner.

My heart is beating fast. He's not a stranger now, not like he'd been in this very restaurant on that first night.

"I'm having fish tonight," he says. The drinks have arrived, standing between us like sentinels. "Just letting you know."

I meet his amused gaze over the edge of my menu. "I kinda berated you for getting the steak when we met, didn't I?"

"Yes," he says, but it sounds like he's enjoying the memory. "You did."

"I'm so easygoing."

"You know, that's the first adjective I'd use to describe you."

"Hmm. And what's the second?"

He drums his fingers against the table for a long couple of beats. "Curious."

I bite the inside of my lip to keep from smiling. "That wasn't your immediate choice, though."

His eyes meet mine. "No," he admits. "It wasn't."

"What's the real answer?"

"I don't think I'm going to tell you that."

"Keeping secrets, Meyer? From your new wife?"

He chuckles. "Only ones she's not ready to hear, yeah."

Something flips over in my stomach. Like a school of fish being hunted by a shark. "I can handle a full class of unruly five-year-olds," I say. "Think I can't handle this?"

He reaches for his glass of wine. "Oh, I think you can. I'm just not ready to play that card, yet."

"Play that card?" I ask. Something's tightening in my chest. Anticipation. Expectation. "You're not the only one with aces up your sleeve."

I don't even know what we're talking about. And still, I do, and my body certainly does. My heart is beating fast again.

His eyes briefly drop to my dress. It's a quick glance, there and gone again. "Oh, you definitely have some, too," he says.

"Flustered, Mr. Meyer?"

"Frustrated, Ms. Richards?"

"Never."

"Not even after three whole months," he says.

My mouth opens. Closes again. But then, I just go for it. "I have an excellent vibrator."

Phillip's expression goes blank, without a hint of emotion on it. "Ah," he says.

And then, nothing else.

"Did I blow your mind?"

"Yes," he says. "Give me a moment."

I'm my vacation self, and she says things like this to men she's just become friends with. She orders a fancy drink from the menu without agonizing over the price. She might even kiss this handsome stranger one more time.

He raises an eyebrow. "At least a vibrator is guaranteed to last longer than five minutes."

"Yes," I say as heat consumes my cheeks. I *had* admitted to that little tidbit about my sex life with Caleb. "If I've charged the batteries."

"Mmm. Hate it when they run out halfway through," he says, focusing on his sleeves. He's rolling them up his forearms with methodical precision.

"Yes."

"You know, a man with actual stamina would solve both problems."

"Yes, but then there are all the other things involved," I say. "A vibrator won't overstay its welcome or use too much tongue."

He chuckles. "I think it's a given you'll get no tongue at all with a vibrator."

"Yes," I say. Then, I shake my head. "That's a sentence I never thought I'd hear."

"I never suspected I'd say it," he retorts.

"What a historic moment," I agree. "We should toast to it."

He holds up his glass, and I touch it with my own.

"So," he says like we're not having the most outlandish conversation of my life, "was the too much tongue comment a hint?"

My cheeks flame. "Oh."

"Yes," he says, again so matter-of-factly. "If you've got constructive criticism, I can take it."

"I've never met a man whose ego can handle constructive criticism."

He chuckles. "Then, you've met too many insecure men."

"Probably, yes." I look down at my drink. "At any rate, the

comment wasn't about you. Your, um, amount of tongue was excellent."

Around us, the night tightens its hold.

"Excellent?" he asks.

"Mh-hmm. No complaints."

"Right. Well, I enjoyed kissing you."

My throat goes dry. "Yeah. Well… I did too."

He smiles and looks back down at his menu. The air between us feels charged. I try to focus on the list of food in front of me but find my eyes glossing over the text.

I look out at the other guests instead, past the tables of happy diners. My gaze snags on a woman, weaving her way through the restaurant. I can only see her from the side… but she looks distinctly familiar. The auburn hair. The confident walk.

"Oh my God," I whisper. "I think someone I know just walked in."

Phillip lowers his menu. "They did?"

"Yes. My ex's cousin is here."

"And by ex, you mean…?"

"Yeah, my non-husband, if you will."

Phillip lifts keen eyes over to the crowd. "Who is it?"

"Auburn-haired. Five o'clock. God, why the hell is she in Barbados? And at the Winter Resort?"

He frowns. "Do you think she's here to talk to you?"

I shake my head. "I've only met her a handful of times. Oh, God, she's going to report back to Caleb that she's seen me here. Oh. She's going to the bar." I duck my head, focusing on the menu as if my life depends on it. "Everyone at home thought I was crazy for wanting to go on my honeymoon alone," I say. My voice sounds high-pitched. She's going to say that she saw me. *Oh, she looked so brave, the poor soul.*

Phillip is frowning. "Well, you look relaxed and happy."

"Thank you," I murmur. I'm still ducking my head as much as I can.

"She's ordering at the bar now, so she's got her back to you."

"Good." I wrap my hands around my nape, head still bowed. *Please, don't recognize me.*

"So," Phillip says. The gravity in the single syllable makes me look up. He's watching me with unreadable eyes. "She knew your honeymoon would have been here?"

"Yes, Kaelie works for a travel agency and online travel magazine, so she helped me a bit with the planning. Maybe she's here because of her job?"

"Maybe." Phillip gives me a crooked grin. Something an awful lot like determination sparks in his eyes. He leans forward, bracing an arm on the table. "What would be the worst thing your ex could hear? That you've found someone to replace him?"

My heart speeds up from the implication. "But…you… why…yes."

He rests his hand next to mine. "Look up. Let her see you."

I take a deep breath. "You mean we pretend…?"

"Yes," he says. "That's exactly what I mean."

I look down at his hand. Only an inch away from mine. And he's staring at me like… well.

Like he means what he says.

I think of Caleb, his sometimes mean jokes, and his smug smiles when his football team won. I think of that time he asked me to make food for him and his friends for a football game but never said thank you. I don't know why right now, in this very moment, that rankles me more than knowing he'd snuck around with one of my best friends for months. But damn it, I spent hours marinating the meat and making sides and the queso he liked so much. And he'd never said thank you!

So I look over at Phillip like he makes me the happiest woman in the world. My hand slides to his, and he flips it over, twining our fingers together.

A shiver runs down my back.

"That's it," he murmurs. "She's spotted us… It's clear she doesn't know what to think."

"You're enjoying this," I whisper. I can't tell how close she is, so I focus on the dark-blue of his eyes instead.

His hand squeezes mine. "Showtime, Eden."

Then, she's upon us.

Kaelie's auburn hair is up in a high ponytail, and she's wearing a blue dress. She looks lovely, as always, and cautious, like never. Every time I've met her, she's been a gusher.

"Eden?" she says. "Hi! Wow, I'm so sorry to bother you like this. I just can't believe I found you here."

"Kaelie!" I say. "I didn't know you'd be here."

"Oh, I know, isn't it just the craziest? I should have texted you and let you know, but I wasn't sure… well." She waves a hand. "You know. The whole thing is odd."

"Right," I say. "Odd."

She glances at Phillip. He's looking at her with an expression that makes it clear she's interrupting. It's the unfriendliest I've ever seen him look.

His hand is still on mine.

I clear my throat. "Sorry. Phillip, this is Kaelie. We know one another from back home."

He extends his free hand. "Phillip."

"Kaelie," she says and shakes his hand over the glass of wine on the table. "Pleasure. How's the trip been, Eden? Having fun?"

I smile wide. "Yes. The island is stunning and so's the resort. You're here for work?"

She nods. "Yes, my boss wanted a feature on the Caribbean, and I'm here to scoop out the Winter Resort. Apparently, the Winter Corporation is looking to open more locations like this worldwide."

"Oh, I hadn't heard."

She nods again. Shifts from one foot to the other and

smiles. "Well, I don't want to interrupt your guys's dinner. I'll be around on the island for a few more days before I need to head to St. Lucia. How about we grab a drink before I leave?"

"Yes," I hear myself say. "Sure. You've got my number?"

"Sure do," she says. Her eyes flick down to my hand intertwined with Phillip's, and I know she's burning with curiosity. "See you later, Eden. It was nice meeting you."

Phillip nods, the tiniest dip of his head.

She heads back in the direction of the bar.

"Oh my God," I mutter.

"That was painfully polite."

"Yes, but I'll get the Spanish Inquisition if we meet for drinks. And when she knows about us, whatever our pretend *us* is, everyone back home will, as well."

His hand tightens briefly around mine. He's looking at something over my shoulder. "She's still glancing over at us every so often."

"What are the odds that her agency sends her to Barbados at the exact same time as I'm here?"

"Slim to none," he says. "If I argued that in court, the jury would draw their own conclusion."

"But you don't go to court."

He smiles. "No, I don't. Because I'm good at my job… and also because I'm a corporate lawyer."

"So humble," I tease.

"False modesty is a sin."

"Thank you," I say, tapping my finger against the back of his hand. They're still intertwined. "For this."

Serious eyes meet mine. There's something about being enveloped in his focus. It makes me feel seen and heard on a level I don't think I ever been before.

Like whatever I have to say is interesting.

"How did your families handle the breakup?"

"Not well," I say. "My mother used to knit him a new sweater every Christmas."

He grimaces. "Ouch."

"Yeah. I mean, I'm an only child, you know? My parents thought of him as a son." I give a half chuckle. "My mother had her own breakup with him."

"I have to hear that story."

Thinking about it makes me smile a bit. "Well, she went to his house and told him that she was disappointed in him, that he had hurt her, too. And then, she dramatically unraveled the arm of the sweater she'd already knitted him for next Christmas."

Phillip's eyes widen. "No way."

"Oh yes. My mom's awesome and crazy like that. My dad, well, he turned into the exterminator."

"Punched the dipshit?"

"Oh God, no, he would never. No, he made sure to scrub our entire lives of any mention of Caleb. From one day to the next, my father had removed all pictures of him from the photo albums and had thrown out the air fryer Caleb bought them for their thirtieth wedding anniversary."

"Poor air fryer," Phillip says. "Civilian causalities."

"It really was a war crime. It made incredible fries."

His fingers tighten around mine. "So what do your parents do?"

"My mom's the chattiest librarian you'll ever meet, and my dad's the detail-oriented accountant," I say. "They're great people."

"They sound like it," he says. "She *really* unraveled her knitting in front of him?"

"On his very doorstep," I say. "My mother could have been an actress in another life."

"How about Caleb's family?" He nods his head toward the bar. "His... parents and cousins?"

I sigh. "I haven't had a lot of contact with them since the breakup. I sort of... well."

The weeks right after I had found out aren't ones I really want to remember. Being sad is one thing, but feeling like a foolish idiot on top of it makes for a powerful cocktail.

"I get it," he says quietly.

I take a deep breath. "Anyway, I don't know what Caleb told Kaelie, or his parents, or any of his siblings, actually. Maybe I should have spoken to them, but I had zero interest in that at the time."

"Of course, not."

I rest my other arm against the table. "What about your parents?"

His eyebrows narrow. "Mine?"

"Yes. How did they handle your sudden non-wedding?"

Phillip looks out at the ocean. "Well," he says, "once the shock settled, they seemed pleased."

"Pleased?"

His jaw tenses, his expression shifts into that of a man who decided he's just overshared. "Yes."

"You know," I say, "if you were a witness on the stand, you'd be a difficult one to cross-examine."

He looks back at me. "Yeah. I've been training for this very moment."

"How about you? After the breakup, what did you feel?"

He looks at me for a long time. "We spoke about this before. Anger. Mostly at myself. And then…"

My curiosity is like a burning thing inside my chest. I wonder what happened to make Phillip and his ex call it off.

"And then?"

"Relief," he says quietly. "That's what I feel now, most of all."

My mouth opens in soft surprise. Oh. That stage is hard to get to. "That's good," I say, nodding. "Isn't it?"

"Mm-hmm. I've always been more of a clean break kind of person. When it's over, it's over."

"No contact?"

"None, when it's possible," he says. He looks down at our hands, where he is still holding mine. "That's really why I went on this trip."

"To… have a clean break?"

"Yeah. She needed to move her things out of my apartment. Sticking around wasn't very appealing."

Everything makes sense, now. The already planned out vacation days, the expensive trip. None of that had really been his main reason.

I look down at our hands, too. The back of his is tanned and broad, all of his fingers ringless. Just like mine. "So that's what'll happen to us, then? After our fictional breakup? A clean break."

"Hmm. I wouldn't mind a dramatic breakup scene with unraveled knitting, but I'll take what I can get."

"I'll see what sort of drama I can come up with."

"I have full confidence that you'll think of something," he says. "Maybe fall into the pool this time?"

"Very funny."

He leans in closer. "She's still watching us."

It takes me a second to remember what *she* he's referring to. "Oh. Darn."

"Means I'll have to up my act a bit." He extends his free hand, the one not holding mine, and tips my head back. "You liked kissing me, you said."

"I did say that," I whisper. "Wouldn't mind doing it again in service of a cause."

A quick smile flashes across his lips, there and gone. "Such pillow talk."

Then, he presses his lips to mine again, and all thoughts of called-off weddings, of Kaelie and Caleb, and Phillip's mysterious ex-fiancée, disappear.

I'm my vacation self. And my vacation self is kissing a handsome man in candlelight, next to the softly rolling waves. Tomorrow can wait…

I'm enjoying the present.

Chapter Sixteen

I'm back in the resort's giant lobby, standing by the plush sofas and waiting for Phillip to arrive. The space is quickly becoming familiar after all the times I've lingered here. I'm usually never this early. Never early anywhere, really, always arriving with my breath too fast and my car keys in hand.

But today I'd woken up earlier than usual, and I'd braided my hair and been fully dressed more than fifteen minutes before I needed to head down to meet him.

All of that, of course, is because of *it*. The kiss that has now turned into two kisses, neither of which we've talked about in any detail. Maybe kisses don't need to be discussed, but I'm not sure of that, either. It's been seven years since I kissed anyone but my ex.

Phillip had kissed me long and deep in the restaurant last night, in front of *everyone*. Kaelie, and the servers, and the happy honeymooners. And when he'd pulled back, his eyes had been slightly glassy. *Still good?* he'd murmured, and the only thing I could do was nod.

Yes. Very, very, *very*.

My phone buzzes in my pocket, and I pull it out to see Becky's name.

I can't believe Kaelie is there, or that you kissed the hot stranger again… to make her report back to Caleb that you're having a rebound?

Reading it back makes it sound absurd. Lurid. It definitely sounds like it's something that's happening to another person. Not me.

Yes. I can't believe it either, but yes.

The three dots appear, and I can imagine Becky furiously typing.

What are the damn ODDS that Kaelie shows up?? She has to be there to spy on you? But why?

I don't know. I'm having dinner with her tonight. We'll see…

Exciting. I have to say, I'm loving your rebound guy's attitude. Making out with you to make sure K had something to gossip about. That's the kind of energy we need!

I chuckle and glance around, but no one is paying attention to me and my phone conversation.

Maybe, but it's messing with my head. I'm meeting him again now. We're going on a hike.

OMG. Just the two of you?

Yes.

Okay, so he likes you.

I look down at her text for a long few seconds. I don't know how to answer that. I don't even know if I want him to.

That's a lie. *I do.* But I don't know if I'm ready for the things that come with that or for going on an actual date, or seeing if he wants to do *more* than kissing… Or going home and facing the cold weather and my familiar life and *not* have any more nights with him in paradise. The whole thing is overwhelming.

Maybe. Or maybe he was just being nice.

Eden.

Men do not kiss women to "be nice." It's literally never happened. Not once.

I chuckle. Maybe not.

"Eden?"

My phone slips out of my hands and falls to the hard stone floor of the lobby. It lands with a decisive sound, and my heart drops.

"Shit, sorry." Phillip bends in front of me to pick it up. His hair is dark and thick, and damp again as if he's just had a shower. He grabs my phone and flips it over. "Unbroken."

"Thank you," I say and take it from his outstretched hand. The screen's mercifully gone dark; Becky's last text is hidden from view.

He straightens. "Ready?"

"Yep. Let's go."

We leave the hotel lobby and walk toward the waiting car. Phillip and I booked it last night, after dinner and after the discussion of what other secrets were hidden in my annotated guidebook. I mentioned hiking, and he'd agreed to it immediately.

So here we are.

Phillip opens the car door for me and I get in. Somehow, this feels even stranger than after our previous kiss. I don't know what to say or what to think, and the easygoing rapport between us feels strained.

The driver puts the car in drive and we head away from the resort. Phillip apologizes for being distracted as he answers emails on his phone. I send a glance his way and he smiles in return. It's the crooked one that warms his entire face. "I promise, I won't touch my phone on the hike," he says.

"I'm going to hold you to that promise."

"I know you will," he says. "And I don't want to be put in a time-out."

We drive past fields of sugarcane, small villages and bright yellow Moringa flowers, and through groves of palm trees and dense tropical foliage. The road turns from straight to crooked, with sharp twists that have my hand permanently glued to the seat in front of me for support.

Phillip puts his phone down with a loud sigh.

"Work?" I ask.

"Yes," he says. "But it was just a few emails. I've told everyone that I'm unavailable for the rest of the day."

I look at him for a long few moments, and he rolls his eyes. "I am capable of that, you know?"

"I am now," I say, and he shakes his head. But he looks amused.

The car turns onto a gravel road, and around us, the view changes. We pull to a stop at the trailhead. Mountains rise from the green-covered landscape on either side of us, thick forest spilling down toward the deep-blue sea. White froth dots the ocean, forced to the surface by waves far stronger on the island's east coast than back at the resort.

"This is incredible!" I dig out my phone and grab a few pictures of the sight.

"And we haven't even started our hike yet," Phillip says and slings a backpack onto his shoulders. He's wearing shorts and a T-shirt, the laces on his sneakers tied with double knots. Phillip's shoes look infinitely more sensible than my sandals.

He stretches, hands high above his head, and his shirt rides up. I catch a sliver of the tanned, taut stomach and the happy trail that disappears into his shorts.

I look away.

I've seen him in swim trunks several times already, but something about this moment felt intimate.

Because you've kissed him now, my mind whispers. *And you want to do it again.*

By the trailhead is a thick wooden sign that indicates the starting point and a map. Below, someone has drawn a smiling sun and scribbled the words "Have a good hike!"

We start up the dusty gravel path that winds its way along the mountain. Soon enough we need to duck beneath low-hanging tree branches, and Phillip gets a smile on his face.

"My dad used to do this with me when I was young," he says.

"Really?"

"Yeah. Not in Barbados, though."

"Hiking, fishing... you were an outdoorsy kid."

"At times," he says.

The trail turns too narrow to walk side by side, and he steps ahead of me, doing most of the work to hold back the branches or shrubs that hang in our way.

I watch his broad shoulders and narrow waist, and the muscles shifting beneath his T-shirt and backpack. He's so stupidly attractive. Far more than he has any right to be.

Tearing my eyes away, I focus on putting one foot in front of the other. "What did you want to be then? Growing up?" I ask.

He looks over his shoulder, his eyes amused. "You don't think I grew up dreaming of being a corporate lawyer?"

"Something tells me no."

He chuckles and keeps walking, trudging up the hill on legs that are longer and probably stronger than mine. I'm glad he can't see me panting.

"An astronaut," he says.

"Wow, really?"

"Yeah. My mom made the ceiling in my room into a planetarium." Then, he shrugs and looks back at me again. "What about you?"

"I wanted to be an author growing up."

"An author?"

"Yeah."

"How come you ended up teaching instead?"

That makes me laugh. "Well, it's not exactly easy to land a publishing deal. And, well, I loved school and enjoyed tutoring. It was something I did part-time in high school and in my freshman year of college."

"You were good at it?"

"Yeah," I say. "So, I'm a teacher now."

"Do you write in your spare time?"

"Some," I say. There's no point in admitting the rest of it. Because it really is hard to get a publishing deal... but I had, five years ago, on my debut novel. And that book sold terribly.

And now the publishing house has no interest in buying another from me.

Phillip walks on ahead of me. "So what do you write?"

"All kinds of things, really. Whatever I feel like," I say with a shrug, my cheeks heating up.

"Something Eden doesn't like talking about?"

"It's a shocker, I know." I duck under a branch and run my hand over the leaves. They have sharp edges and are crisp to the touch.

"That's it?" he asks. "That's all I'll get? What happened to the Eden who loves to ramble?"

"Very funny," I say. "Don't you have emails to answer?"

"No, I'm all done for the day. But, you can still become an author, right? There's no time limit on that dream."

"No, I suppose not," I say. Except I'd already tried and failed, and opening myself up again to the same kind of disappointment appeals as much as jumping into one of the thorny shrubs we walk past.

"The enthusiasm," Phillip says. "It's overwhelming."

I roll my eyes, not that he can see it. "I don't think I'm ready. But I do write in my spare time, yeah. I have… well, I have stories that I've finished."

"That's incredible," he says, and there's not a trace of sarcasm or judgment in his tone. "Is that why you listen to all that true crime? You write crime stories?"

"Maybe," I say, drawing out the word.

He holds up a branch to let me pass under it. It brings me close to him, and his interested gaze.

"Is all of this research?" he asks.

"Depends," I say. "Do you want to get murdered and give me a story?"

His eyes widen, and then he smiles. It lights up his tanned face. "By you? Any day."

I laugh to hide the blush creeping up my cheeks. Stupid conversation. *Stupid man.* "Watch out, then."

I take the lead for the next part of the hike. It's steep now, and I have to stop twice to catch my breath.

After a twist in the path, we emerge at a spot where the trees open up, and the landscape unfurls in front of us. The lush green terrain stretches as far as my eyes can see, dotted by palm trees swaying in the breeze. The sun has come out from behind a cloud, its rays almost too bright on my face.

Inhaling deeply, I savor the beauty of it all.

"Oh," Phillip says. "It looks like it might rain."

"No, it doesn't."

"That cloud right there?" he says, coming up next to me. His arm points toward the sky. "That's full of rain."

I look up at the sky, and sure enough, clouds seem to be moving in quickly. I hear the distant roll of thunder, and it sends a thrill through me. The tropical rain we'd experienced by the pool had been almost magical.

"You're such a cynic," I say, but my voice is soft with wonder as I take it all in. His shoulder brushes against mine, and I feel the contact intimately, almost as if it's his lips on mine again.

Phillip shrugs like he doesn't care much one way or the other, but I catch his gaze lingering on me for a moment before looking away. We turn to keep walking along the path, the pace slower now. I'm tired and thirsty, and I've never felt more alive.

"Have you heard from your ex's cousin since last night?" he asks. The path is wide enough here for both of us to walk side by side.

"A bit, yeah. We texted last night."

"Did we fool her?"

I keep my focus squarely on my next steps. "Well, I think so. She wrote that... well, that I looked like I was enjoying my holiday."

Phillip chuckles darkly. "Good."

"So, thank you for that. For your efforts."

"It was my pleasure," he says, and it sounds like he means it.

I glance at him from the corner of my eye. He looks back at me, catching me in the act. I look away, but there's no hiding the smile on my face.

He clears his throat. "Think you'll be seeing her again?"

"We're having dinner tonight," I say. "It was her suggestion, and maybe it'll... I don't know. Clear the air a bit."

I still want to know why exactly she's here when she knew I'd be, too. If it has anything to do with Caleb, I want to nip it in the bud.

Warm, humid air surrounds us as we walk. The closer we get to the top of a mountain, however, the lighter my heart feels. It's as if I'm lifted higher with each step until nothing else exists except us, this moment, and the beautiful forest around us. With the clouds in the sky, it's not too hot, either.

We're hiking up a stony patch when the first drops begin to fall. It drizzles for two or three seconds, and then immediately shifts into a downpour. It's tropical rain as I've never experienced before.

Everything around us is drenched in moments. Phillip grabs my arm, pulling me under the shelter of a huge bearded fig tree. The thick branches block most of the heavy rain, leaving only errant droplets to make it to us.

"Oh my God." I brush a wet tendril of hair back from my face. "The sky just split in two!"

"Who's the cynic, huh?"

"Fine," I say, grinning. "You're a realist."

"Thank you."

I dig through the pocket of my thin cotton shorts for my phone. "We should keep valuables dry," I tell him and slip it inside my sports bra. It's the classic move I've done a hundred times at the gym or when I'm walking around at home, listening to a podcast, and my shorts don't have pockets.

His eyes linger on my chest for a heartbeat before he looks away. "Good idea," he murmurs.

I watch as he does the same, tucking his phone into the inside pocket of his backpack. His hands move slowly, solidly, looking large against his bag.

The tree's foliage provides shelter from the rain, but only right next to the trunk, forcing us to stand close. *Men don't kiss women as favors,* I think.

My heart is beating fast, and I need to do something, to be something, to avoid this clawing feeling inside. I pull my phone out and hand it to him.

"Keep this safe, too."

He takes it with a frown. "Where are you going?"

"Into the rain," I say and back away from the tree. It only takes a few steps for the few drops to turn into to turn into a deluge. The ground beneath my feet is dark and spongy from rainwater.

"Eden!" he calls.

I tip my head back at the sky and close my eyes. It's rare to be able to do this, to stand in the warm rain and not be worried about ruining your makeup or your clothes, or your electronics. The rain hitting the ground and leaves around us is a steady beat. It sounds like hands on a drum.

"You're really staying out there?"

"Yes!" I shout. "This is my next crazy thing. You said you wanted to keep me around for that, right?"

I hear him curse, and I laugh, spinning around. My hair is soaked and the T-shirt I'm wearing feels plastered to my skin. It's magical. The air smells earthy—wet and fresh, with a hint of sea salt. It's warm against my face and tastes like the promise of a kiss.

I feel alive.

A firm arm wraps around my waist. I blink my eyes open to see Phillip's face. His hair looks darker in the rain.

"You'll get cold," he says.

"No, the rain is warm."

"But after it's over, you'll be soaked."

I nod at his own clothes. His T-shirt is sticking to his chest and molds to his shoulders. "So will you."

He shakes his head, his lips tilting up at the corners. His arm is still around my waist and I lean into the contact.

"I watched you by the pool," he says. "One of the early days after we met. You were smiling at the tropical rain when everyone else was scrambling."

Water sluices down my body but I can barely feel it. His eyes are on mine, and I can't look away. I don't think anything in this world could make me.

"It's so rare," I murmur.

He reaches up with his free hand and brushes a lock of my hair back from where it stuck to my cheek. I can feel the heat from his hand, even in the rain.

"Yes," he says. "It is."

He leans in and pauses for a second, just long enough for me to know that he's savoring the moment before his lips touch mine.

His kiss is shockingly warm against the rainfall, gentle and strong at the same time. I rest my hand against his chest and melt into his touch, into the arm around me, and the lips that move with determination.

He tips my head back, long fingers curving down toward my neck. It sends a shiver through me that has nothing to do with the storm around us.

I'm the one who deepens the kiss.

My tongue brushes his lower lip, and he groans. It's a rumble through his chest and into mine, and he pulls me tighter against his body.

Around us, the rain continues its frenzy. The droplets turn into a curtain of water that blocks out the real world. I wrap my hands around Phillip's neck and press my body against his, drowning in the moment. His fingers burn trails on my skin, along my arms, across my back. Each promises more.

I feel on fire.

He lifts his head an inch. "I should be getting you out of the rain," he murmurs. His voice sounds hoarse.

I shake my head and draw him back to me. "I'm perfectly fine."

"Oh?" He kisses my lips gently before tracing the edge of my jaw. "I didn't expect this, Eden. I didn't expect you."

A shiver runs through me again, and it's not because I'm cold. Pressed against him, our clothes soaked and bodies molded to one another, I've never felt warmer.

"Me either," I say. "You were a complete surprise."

He rests his forehead against mine. We're both breathing hard. And there's no one here watching, no one we're performing for.

"What are we doing?" I whisper.

"I have no idea," he says. "I don't know what I've been doing this entire trip."

"Vacation self," I murmur.

He runs his fingers over my wet hair before coming to rest

on the bare skin of my neck. "Maybe," he says quietly. "Or maybe it's just me, and it's just you."

I feel unmoored, like holding on to him is the only real thing left. "Kiss me again?"

He smiles crookedly and lowers his head. Our lips meet, and around us, the rain keeps pouring down.

Chapter Seventeen

When we finally get back to the resort, I have exactly forty-eight minutes to get ready before I'm meeting Kaelie. My clothes are half-dry and my hair is frizzy from the rain and humidity. I throw myself into the shower to try to put it to right.

The water is warm, just like the rain had been. But there are no lips pressed against mine this time.

Phillip had kissed me until the downpour lessened, until the heavy drops turned into a soft drizzle, and the sun made its triumphant return. I'd tipped my head back and whispered that I could get used to this.

He'd paused, lips at my neck, and a splinter of fear cut through the feelings of pleasure. I hadn't meant to hint at the future. It didn't exist, not yet, not here.

But then, he'd continued to kiss me as if I hadn't spoken, and that had been that.

After the shower, I quickly put on some makeup and slip into a sundress. My hair will have to be damp. At least it's clean, and it'll dry fast in the tropical heat.

Kaelie is waiting for me when I arrive at the hotel bar.

Nerves twist in my stomach for the first time today. I hadn't spent much time thinking about this meeting. About her being here or what she might tell Caleb about me.

It feels like I'm heading into a battle where the weapon of choice is delicately phrased small talk.

"Eden," she says and gets out of her chair for a hug. "I'm so glad we could do this."

"Me, too," I say, but I don't really mean it. My voice doesn't betray that, though. It's polite and upbeat.

"Did you have a good day?"

"Yes. I went for a hike, actually," I say. "It's truly a stunning place. Have you gotten to see much of the island?"

She nods and uses the straw to stir her drink. "I've been with the photographer today, shooting a few key spots for work. You didn't hike alone, did you? That sounds dangerous."

"No, I was with my… friend."

"Oh, your friend from last night?" Her voice is carefully neutral.

"Yes, him."

"That's so exciting," she says and lifts the drink to her lips. Her eyes widen like she's expecting me to spill all the deets.

I order a rum punch instead.

An uneasy silence falls between us, and I shift in my seat. Consider my opponent. We've always been friendly, even if we'd only met a dozen or so times. Those occasions were usually brief, taking place at family barbecues or during the summer stays at Caleb's parents' lake cabin. I'd liked Kaelie and even reached out to her with a few questions about this trip, but now it feels like a trench has opened up across the table.

"What are you going to write about the island and the resort?" I ask. "For your agency?"

She smiles, and we spend a solid ten minutes talking about things very far from either of us and miles away from the man we have in common.

I finally ask her the one thing I need to know, despite my rapidly beating heart. "And they just happened to send you here?" I ask. "At the same time I'm on my… trip?"

Kaelie looks down at her drink. "Yes, but I did ask for it, too. This is part of a big Caribbean project we're working on, and I requested Barbados for these dates. I won't be here long, Eden. I'm flying out to St. Lucia tomorrow."

So, she'd specifically timed it. "Why didn't you tell me about it?"

"I considered texting you before the trip, but..." Kaelie shakes her head. "I wasn't sure how you'd react. I knew I wanted to see you, though."

"Yeah. You and I have always been friendly," I say. "That doesn't have to change just because of what happened with Caleb and me."

She gives me a genuine smile. "I'm so happy to hear that. Honestly, Eden, that's kinda what I wanted to talk to you about."

"Oh?"

"Yes, what happened between you and Caleb. He's been... well, he hasn't been himself since you broke off your engagement."

Something sour strikes my throat, like the rum punch is finally delivering on the second word of its name. "Since *we* broke up, you mean."

"Mm-hmm. The rest of us are kind of at a loss about the whole thing. He won't talk to us about it, except to say you changed your mind." Her smile is tentative, and her words are careful. "Eden, as you know, his parents put in the non-refundable deposit on the venue."

I close my eyes. The tide of emotions swelling inside me feels like a wave too great to surf. I'd spent months trying to get over the whole thing. Caleb. Cindy. Every well-meaning relative on my side who asked questions.

I don't have to feel bad for his parents, too, I think, even if they're nice people. There's a limit to what I can handle, and Caleb has to carry his share of the responsibility.

"Kaelie—" I start.

"Wait, just hear me out," she urges. "Caleb is really sorry.

He said you won't answer his texts or calls, and that you've blocked him entirely. You two were together for *seven* years. Do you think that's really fair? Eden, whatever happened, please know he's sorry for it. He wants you back."

The turmoil inside me is replaced with ice. It burns, it's so cold. "He said that?"

She nods. "Yes, just a week or two ago."

"And you two spoke before you came here... did he *ask* you to do this? Schedule your work trip so you'd meet up with me?"

"Well..." She shrugs, a sheepish smile on her face. "Yes. He's my favorite cousin, Eden. You know that."

I close my eyes. "Oh my God, I can't believe his fucking nerve."

There's a shocked silence across the table. "Eden..."

"No, he doesn't get to do this. Send a message like this," I say. My voice is strong enough to surprise us both. "It was nice to see you, Kaelie, but I don't want to hear anything from him. I don't want to talk about him, or what happened, and I... just really don't want to do this." I rummage through my bag for my wallet and pull out the money to pay for my drink. "Have a nice time on the island."

There's a genuine shock in her voice. "All I wanted was—"

"He was sleeping with my best friend. For *months*," I say. "With Cindy. You remember her, don't you?"

She blinks at me. "Oh. Yes, I do."

"Well, they were having an affair. Feel free to tell the rest of your family about that, including Caleb's parents. I'm really sorry for their lost deposit, but... but honestly, that's on Caleb. I'm done with him. Forever." My chest is rising fast, and I can't count the bills quickly enough. There should be enough money here. Five dollars, one, a few coins...

"Eden," she says. "God, Eden, please sit down."

I shake my head. There's something in my throat, and I

don't know if it's tears or a scream, but I don't want to be here when it erupts.

"I had no idea. I'm sorry... Holy shit. That's why he's been so moody." Kaelie runs a hand over her face, the pleasant, extroverted demeanor gone. Now she just looks tired. "I shouldn't have come here like this. I see that now. Damn Caleb and his screwed-up requests."

"Yeah. Can't trust him."

"At least you can cut him out of your life," she mutters and half laughs.

A surprised chuckle slips out of me, too. I finally find the correct amount of money and put it down on the table. A debt paid. "Yeah."

"Sorry, Eden," she says again. "I'll make sure the rest of the family knows."

I shrug. "It's up to you. I'm done with him."

She raises her glass to me. "Enjoy the rest of your vacation, Eden. The guy last night looked hot."

I laugh again. "Yeah. Um, thanks."

With quick steps, I leave the restaurant and find myself in the resort's garden. A blooming flower next to me spreads its soft scent in the evening air, calm and serene. It's a sharp contrast to the burning feeling inside of me. I feel like I've just survived a battle.

Adrenaline pumps through my veins.

Caleb wants me back.

I press a hand to my mouth, laughter bubbling up. He must be delusional to think I'd ever consider that.

Or maybe the old me gave off those vibes... made him think I was the kind of woman who'd only needed a few weeks to cool down before forgiving the biggest betrayal of her life.

The word *never* isn't strong enough.

I tilt my head back and look up at the star-studded sky, here on an island that's so far, far from where I've lived my entire life. The air is warm, and the gentle wind feels pleasant against my skin, making the plants around me rustle in the breeze.

"You okay?" a voice asks. It's familiar now after days spent together.

I smile. "You followed me?"

"No," he says. "Well, yes, I suppose, but not in a creepy way."

I turn around. He's leaning against one of the columns, eyes intent on me. He looks so like he did that very first night, when he'd been a stranger stealing my table. The only change is the tan overtaking his skin and the stubble growing more prominent by the day.

"Did you have dinner in there?" I ask.

"Yes. Far away from you and Kaelie, though." He shrugs, a look of uncertainty on his face. "I figured… well, you might have needed a backup again."

"Thank you," I say.

He looks at me like he can feel the odd mood I'm in. "Did it go all right?" he asks. "Do you want to be alone?"

"No, I really don't."

He nods, a small smile curving his lips. "All right, then."

We walk through the garden, now lit with intricately placed outdoor lights. The air is thick with humidity, but a comforting warmth envelops us.

"How was it?" he repeats. "Really?"

"With Kaelie?" I ask. Not that I need the clarification, but I ask anyway, the moment stretching between us. With every step, I get further and further away from the memory of the past.

"Yes," he says.

"She told me some stuff I wasn't happy to hear." Apparently, my ex hasn't told anyone in his family why we ended our engagement."

Phillip gives a slow shake of his head. "Can't own up to his mistakes."

"No, it doesn't seem like it."

"You're better off without him."

I look at Phillip. He's walking steadily beside me, his hands in his pockets. He notices my glance. "Not that it makes it okay, you know," he adds. "What he did."

"Thank you. I think I'm better off, too."

"Good riddance," he murmurs and pulls out the key card from his pocket.

We end up back on the patio of his bungalow. There's a fire in my stomach, put there by the rum punch. The island seems to run on them, and for as long as I'm here, so do I. It's been an excellent fuel so far.

I toss my sandals on the stony path and sink down onto one of his outdoor chairs. "Imagine if life could be like this every day," I say quietly. "No major worries or concerns. No drama or sadness. Just beautiful weather and the ocean close by."

"You'd get bored after a week," he says. "Want something to drink?"

"Yes."

I listen to the familiar shuffle as he opens the sliding patio door into his bungalow. The stirring of ice and uncorking of bottles from his minibar.

I look up at the stars while I wait. This trip has been more challenging than I expected it to be, and in none of the ways I'd anticipated. I've felt different here, yet also more myself than I've ever felt before. Maybe that's what happens on a vacation. You leave all your stuff behind, all the baggage, and for a short period of time, you can forge an entirely new identity. Keeping only the best parts of yourself and adding new facets, like trying on a costume for size.

Caleb is in the past. Kaelie being here had dragged it up again, but sitting in this beautiful backyard with the starlit sky overhead and the ocean nearby, I force myself to consign the memories back into the past.

Where they belong. Where *he* belongs.

"Tell me something you've written," Phillip calls.

"Nope."

"Not a single thing?"

"No."

"Damn," he mutters and returns to my side. He hands me a chilled glass. "A rum sour for the lady. I'm having brandy. I think I've had enough of rum for a while."

"Really? I still love it." I take a long sip of my drink as he sits down on a patio chair across from me. But he's not doing the same. He's just watching me. "What?" I ask.

"This is the wrong time to go mute," he says, running a hand over his jaw. There's speculation in his eyes. "Tell me why you won't talk about it? About your writing?"

I look back up at the night sky. "No."

"Oh, if only I could get you on the stand."

"I'd perjure myself," I say. "But it wouldn't happen. You don't go to court."

"I can still use the expression," he says. "You're making me think the absolute worst right now."

His curiosity feels like a gift. It's been a long time since I've been this interesting to anyone. Since someone cared and wanted to get to know me. Since secret-sharing was a thing.

And then, I spot a way to leverage it to my own advantage. "Well," I say slowly. "Maybe there's something you can barter for that information."

His lips twitch. "You're thinking like an attorney."

"From you, that's the highest of compliments."

"Yes," he says. "So let's negotiate."

My heart feels heady in my chest, beating like the bass in a club. "Why do you want to know what I write?"

"Is that one of your questions?"

"We're counting them now?"

"There's a limited amount of time allowed for a deposition. Choosing the right questions to ask is paramount."

I clear my throat and look at him like he's on trial for murder. "Okay, then. A question for a question. If we veto we have to drink."

"All right." He glances down at his drink like he's already thinking of all the lovely times he'll just drink instead of answering any of my questions.

"Wait a second," I say. "We can't veto all the time. Let's say we can only pass every... third question."

"Mmm. Good stipulation." He sets the glass down on the small table between our chairs and folds his forearms over his chest. "Does your family know about your writing?"

"Yes," I say.

He utters a low humming sound as if that's an interesting nugget of information. It makes his voice sound deeper.

"Right. My turn." I roll my tumbler slowly between my palms; the glass is cool from the ice.

"Well, you know me," he says. "I'm an open book."

I laugh, and satisfaction flashes in his eyes. He likes making me laugh. The knowledge settles like a hot stone in my stomach. "You might be the least forthcoming person I've ever met," I say. "All right, here's one. Tell me more about your sister."

"Really?"

I make a keep-going motion with my hand, and he sighs like I'm subjecting him to waterboarding. "She's younger than me," he says.

"Are you two close?"

"Is that your next question?"

There's a towel hanging over the back of my chair. I grab it and lob it toward him. He catches it with a chuckle, that half smile on his lips threatening to break out in full force. "Fine. She lives in Chicago, too. We grab lunch every now and then."

"You said she's a dentist?"

"Yes, so I see her regularly at my check-ups, too. I think she makes them extra painful just for me."

That makes me smile. "What's her name?"

"Tess."

"Did she get along with your ex-fiancée?"

"That," he says, "definitely qualifies as another question."

"Damn it," I say. "Can't fool a lawyer."

"Best not to even try," he agrees. Studying eyes meet mine. "So tell me about your writing."

"You're persistent," I say, lowering my eyes to my own drink. "I wrote a book a few years ago and had it published by a publishing house. But... well, it didn't sell as much as they'd hoped. Since then I mostly just write for myself."

"And you write crime stories? Tell me the plot of one of them."

"That," I say, "is another question. And it's my turn now."

He sighs. "You're going to ask the last question again, aren't you?"

"Yes."

"No, Tess didn't really get along with my ex-fiancée."

"Oh?"

"They were civil," he says, "but it was a fairly cold civility. They had very different interests. As I said... Tess was happy to say 'I told you so' the other day. Apparently, she was never a fan of my relationship."

"Mmm."

He narrows his eyes at me. "I can see you coming up with ten more questions now."

"I'm curious! You know so much about Caleb, the disastrous end of my relationship, and why I'm here alone. I, on the other hand, know almost nothing about you and yours."

"Not true," he says. "You know we used an excellent travel planner for the honeymoon."

I roll my eyes. "Yes, that's very useful knowledge, thank you. Please send me her details for when I book my next honeymoon."

"Sarcasm," Phillip says, "doesn't work if what you're joking about is pretty darn likely."

"Oh, it isn't likely," I say. "I'm done with the whole wedding business."

He laughs and reaches for his drink. "*Right*."

"No, it's true. I am! At least for a couple of years."

"Mm-hmm." He takes a long sip of his drink. "'At least a couple of years.' Tell me you don't already have men lining up to date you at home."

I stare at him. "Um, I *really* don't have any men lining up for me at home."

"Or you're just not very good at spotting them," he says.

There's intensity and something else—a challenge?—in his gaze. "My next question. How did the single men around you react when you told them you called off your wedding?"

"I don't know." I dig my teeth into my lower lip. What a question. "It's not like I regularly hang out with a dozen single men of my age, you know. I don't have a harem of them on speed dial."

"Still," he says. "Humor me. Friends of your friends, maybe."

"Nope."

"Guys at work?"

"Oh. Well..."

"Bingo," he says and leans back. There's satisfaction written all over his face. "You're going to be married within five years."

"What kind of prediction is that?"

"So there is a guy at work? Tell me about him," Phillip says. There's a silky undertone to his steady voice, a persuasive note, and I wonder if this is what he sounds like when he negotiates.

"Andrew," I say, frowning. "He teaches math to fourth graders. We're coworkers and friends."

"And as a friend," Phillip says, "how did he react when you told him you dumped the dipshit?"

I shift on the patio chair. "Like a concerned friend. He asked what happened and told me that he'd be there if... damn it, Phillip, now I'm questioning what he meant by those words!"

There's a smirk on his lips. "All I'm saying is, if I refer you to the travel agent, you'll get a solid discount. You and Andrew could use them for your next honeymoon."

"Thank you," I say sweetly. "Please email me the details. Also, when you need a best man—um, woman, for *your* next wedding, let me know. Because I don't believe for a minute that you don't have a list of phone numbers to attractive twentysomethings at the ready."

Both of Phillip's eyebrows rise. He leans forward again, elbows on his knees, and settles his gaze on me like he's trying to decipher the Rosetta Stone. "You said something the other day. I want you to explain what you meant."

"Wow. Okay."

"You said I wouldn't have looked at you twice if we were Stateside," he says. "What did that mean exactly?"

My mouth goes dry. I chuckle, trying to find my equilibrium. "Well. That was a joke."

Kinda.

"Okay. And what was the punchline?"

I look at my glass of rum sour. I've answered two questions before. I'm allowed a sip.

"Don't," he mutters, "or I'm going to ask the most absurdly invasive question as my next one, and you'll wish you'd answered this one instead."

That makes me smile. "Maybe I'll prefer the absurdly invasive one to this one."

He grows still. "That bad?"

"No. It was just a bit of self-deprecating humor." Rip off the Band-Aid, Eden. "I don't know what your ex-fiancée looked like, but I'm sure it wasn't anything like me. I'm normal, and I like being normal. But *normal* doesn't usually end up getting invited to the most expensive bungalows or onto private sailboats, you know?"

"Hmm." He runs a hand along his jaw. "In this scenario, I'm not considered normal, am I?"

"Well, yes and no. There's nothing weird about you.

You're just above the average?" I say, but when I hear the words out loud, I cringe. "Did I just say that?"

"Yes, I think you did," he says. "But don't worry. I'm comfortable hearing it."

"I bet you are."

"Eden," he says. "Ask me your next question. And don't make it about either of our exes, will you?"

I swallow. The air feels headier at night. "What's your vacation self?"

"My vacation self," he repeats slowly. "Well, it's seemingly someone who does things he had no intention of ever doing."

"Like protecting innocent baby sea turtles from vicious mongeese."

"Yes, exactly," he says. "Or getting increasingly attracted to a fellow tourist at the resort. The last one's a bit of a problem."

The rum sour is like liquid fire as it slides down my throat, heating my already burning insides. My skin feels too hot, my cheeks are flushed.

For seven years I haven't flirted with a man. And here I am, sitting beneath the star-speckled sky on a tiny Caribbean island, and a man is looking at me like *that*. His intense gaze remains unwavering, piercing, and my mouth suddenly feels dry.

"A problem," I say. "And why is that?"

"Well, my impression is that she's here to get away from men," he says. "She's also great company."

The compliment magnifies in my mind, mixing with his previous words. I curl my toes into the groove between two stone plates. "Maybe she *is* here to get over a man," I say, my words slow but my breathing quick. "But what if she was open to getting some help with that? What would you do about it?"

Phillip keeps his gaze one mine. And then, he reaches for his brandy and slowly, deliberately, takes a long pull of his drink.

Something tightens in my stomach. It's the possibility and nerves, and I hear Becky's voice in my head as clearly as if she's standing next to me. *The rest of your life starts now,* she'd said after Caleb and Cindy's grand revelation.

"Oh," I breathe.

His eyes burn. "I think it's pretty clear what I'm willing to do."

"Yeah."

"Eden," he says, and there's a murmured warmth in the words. My heart is pounding a rapid beat against my ribs; pulse thumping in my fingertips, down to the very soles of my bare feet. I haven't done this in so long.

And then I reach for the hem of my dress with hands that only shake a little.

Phillip watches the movement. "Eden?"

"I'm going for a swim," I say, "in this lovely, conveniently located little pool of yours."

I let my dress drop to the chair. I've started wearing bikinis all day round here, and I'm grateful for that now. I'm also grateful for the shadows as I stand before him. "Want to join me?"

Phillip starts to undo the buttons on his shirt, one at a time. "You want to swim laps," he says. "Now?"

"I think laps would be pretty difficult here." I slip my legs beneath the lukewarm surface of the water. "But maybe cooling down is a good idea."

He looks at me. "Yeah. All right."

I slip into the water and swim across the pool. It only takes three strokes to cross the distance. The water is like a warm embrace, and I lean against the pool's edge, watching as he gets in at the other end. The muscles of his shoulders ripple with his motions across his tanned skin.

"Well," he says. Across the water, his voice sounds deeper. "You didn't drink once. I should've asked harder questions."

"Did you have any harder ones to ask?"

"There's more I want to know, yeah."

"Ask me now, then."

He leans against the side of the pool and rests his arms on the edge. "I'll ask the one you avoided earlier. Tell me the plot of one of your books."

I swim toward him. His hair is pushed back off his forehead. I know what it feels like now, from running it between my fingers while we kissed. Thick strands that are surprisingly soft. "I'll have to drink," I say, "for that question. When I get out of the pool."

"Eden," he murmurs. "Tell me."

I shake my head. "My turn. I want you to tell me the answer to the question you avoided by taking a drink."

"What I'd do," he says slowly, "if you were interested in me, too? Hypothetically."

"Yes."

"Eden, you told us to cool off."

"Well, we're doing it together." I reach through the water and put my hands on his shoulders. His skin is warm above the surface, and firm, and my fingers curve over the slope of his muscles.

"Thanks for kissing me yesterday. In front of Kaelie."

"Happy to help," he says. His eyes have turned molten, the blue is as liquid as the water around us. His hands slide around my waist. Bare skin on bare skin, pulling me closer, his movements effortless in the water. "So," he says. "Are you avoiding men? Was I right?"

"If I am, I'm doing a terrible job of it right now."

His lips twist into a half smile. The sight of it sends a jolt of heat through me, like a shot of fire whiskey in the middle of Washington winter.

"You sure are," he says.

My hands tighten around his neck, and his breath ghosts across my lips. The waiting is excruciatingly delicious.

"This is my favorite part," I whisper.

He pauses, lips an inch from mine. "The seconds right before?"

"Yes." I slide my fingers into his hair, curling them at his nape.

The world starts and ends in this tiny pool, and with him.

It has collapsed into this warm and real place, with Phillip holding me beneath the surface.

He closes the distance between us.

Soft lips against mine, tasting faintly of alcohol and then of nothing else but him, insistent and steady at the same time. He was a good kisser on the beach and in the forest. Here, pressed close together, he's excellent. Shivers race across my skin.

His long fingers curve over my hips and dig into my skin. I nip at his lower lip, and he groans, the sound reverberating into me. Our bodies align. My chest against his, our hips pushed together. The kisses are so much headier in our almost-nakedness.

Making out in a bikini is like skipping directly to go *and* collecting the two hundred dollars on the way. Unearned, but very enjoyable.

"Eden," he murmurs and tips my head back to reach my neck. The brush of kisses across the sensitive skin is my undoing.

Neck kisses always are.

Above us, the night sky is alight with stars. *I'm so far away from home,* I think. So far away from the real Eden. Or maybe I am the real one, here, embracing adventure and the unknown.

Phillip's hands return to my waist and squeeze into a tight grip. Almost like he's forcing them to stay put.

But I don't have the same qualms. I slide mine down his shoulders, over the muscles honed by all the laps he swims, and down his chest. There's a smattering of dark hair here. I trace it with my fingernail.

He groans softly.

I smile. "Didn't know guys had sensitive pecs."

"We don't," he says. "Well, I don't. But the way you're looking at me…"

I kiss him again. This time, I press myself against him, my breasts flattening to his chest. He moves immediately. Like a switch has been flipped, his hands lose their statue-like grip and slide down over my hips. Settle on my thighs and lift me up.

I wrap them around his waist and kiss him again, molding our lips together. With Phillip holding me, I feel weightless in the water.

I notice the water moving around us, but not what it means. Not until my back softly hits the opposite wall of the pool.

His arms settle against the edge on either side of me, and he devotes himself to kissing me like it's a career, a job, a vocation. Like I'm an altar. It's slow, and yet there's no mistaking the fervor behind it, his lips taunting mine, his tongue there in occasional slow strokes.

It takes my breath away.

There's fire spreading through my limbs. It's unhurried and heady, but it burns all the same, battling with the nerves in my stomach.

I'm the one who takes his hand and moves it to my waist, and then higher up, to the left cup of my bikini top.

Phillip groans and steps in closer, our hips molding together beneath the water. His hand closes around my breast, but it's not the salvation I was looking for. It just makes me need him *more*.

"Eden," he says, but I don't wait to hear what else he has to say. I reach up to undo the halter top. The straps fall to the water's surface, and then his hand is there, behind my back, tugging at the second strap.

My bikini top floats away, a strip of blue fabric.

"Jesus," he mutters, eyes downcast between us. The pained look on his face sends my heartbeat racing. Excitement and adrenaline push through my veins with every pulse.

He uses his hands, and I let my head fall forward, my forehead on his, as his fingers tug and tease. It's been a long time since a man's hands were on me. His touch makes me more aware of my body, too. It's as if I've come alive under his admiration. Like I'm existing more in this moment than I have been for months.

He pulls me tighter against him, my breasts crushing against his chest, and kisses my neck. "You're so beautiful." He murmurs the words into my wet skin.

I relax into his embrace. "Am I?"

"Yes." His hands slide down my body. "Your body, your smile, your dark eyes, your hair… it's been driving me crazy. The long, light-brown mass of it. And these curves?"

His hands tighten around my hips, his eyes on mine appear a darker blue. There's a hungry question in them.

"It's been a long time," I murmur, "since I did… any of this."

He smiles. "You're doing great."

"Oh, am I?"

"Yes. Faultless, really."

"Top of my class?"

"Definitely."

I tighten my legs around him, locking them together behind his back. He gives a low groan as our bodies come in even closer contact. "See?" he mutters. "You're acing it."

"I always was a teacher's pet."

"I knew it," he murmurs and kisses me again. Warm lips and even warmer hands grip my ass and pull me tight against him. We kiss for a very long time. We kiss until I feel like I'm one with the water around me and so ready for more that it's an almost painful ache inside of me.

I wonder if he knows that, if that's his goal, if my little *it's been a long time* had made him do this.

Kiss me like he'd be content to do this forever.

"God, Eden," he whispers, mouth at my jaw. "The way you're grinding against me…"

My hips stop their movement, and a blush races up my cheeks. "Oh."

"Don't stop," he mutters, and there's a bit of roughness in

the tone, too. "I just don't want to… rush things here."

"Good," I moan. It's been seven years of sex with the same person, and my nerves are like a tight bundle in the pit of the stomach, competing with the desire.

"Good?" he asks.

"Mm-hmm."

His hands slide down, and then move further, hovering at the waistline of my bikini bottoms. "Let me take care of you."

The words spiral through me, spreading heat that sears me along its path.

"I want to focus on you," he says, stroking over the fabric of my bottoms.

"Okay," I whisper. My body is pushing down against his hand. Needing. The pressure, even the hint of friction…

He pats my thigh. "As much as I like you here, you're going to have to release me, baby."

I unhook my legs and slide down his body. Warm water rushes in between our bodies, and then his hand follows, sliding down my bare stomach and finding the waistband of my bottoms.

I can't look at him. I can't—I can't—and then he kisses me as if he knows that, and I'm back in the moment, needing his touch so badly—

He slides his big, warm hand down and cups me completely. I catch my breath at the sensation, and he gives me back my air, his lips moving to my neck.

I grip his shoulders and hold on as he explores me—gently, then more insistently, his fingers parting and curling and circling within the tight confines of my bikini bottoms. He teases me until I'm arching up against his hand, until the only sound between us is my constricted breathing and his low groans of appreciation.

"Fuck," he says and pulls his hand away.

"No," I say. "Please—"

"I'm not stopping," he says and curses again. "But I need to… come here."

He grips my thighs and hoists me up, out of the water. He puts me on the edge of the pool and steps in between my splayed legs, his head now at the perfect height…

"Phillip," I whisper, my hand finding his thick hair. I don't know if I'm scared or excited or on the very edge of ecstasy, or if it's all three emotions at once, and the only solution is release.

"Beautiful," he mutters again and runs his hands up my thighs. He tugs me closer to the edge. I let go of the nerves and sink into the darkness of the night and the soothing rhythm of the waves against the beach and the sensation of his hands tugging my bikini bottoms to the side.

His breath is shockingly warm against me, but it's nothing compared to the heat of his tongue and mouth. He's skilled, and maybe it's his enthusiasm and the newness of it, or the star-studded sky above us and the warm air against my wet skin, but I don't feel self-conscious at all. I'm entirely in the moment.

"Fuck," he mutters again, muffled against me, and I look down at his dark-haired head between my thighs. He pushes one of my legs up and over his shoulder, giving him better access. And then a finger is added, and I'm not going to survive this.

"You okay?" I whisper. I want to hear him say it, to confirm that I'm not alone with my racing heart. He lifts his head, eyes that are nearly black look back at me.

"I'm fucking fantastic," he says, and pushes my left thigh further to the side. "Tell me what you like. What you need."

"This," I whisper. "Just more of it."

He smiles, and it's equal parts wolfish and victorious. It makes me think of how he said that there are winners in sex. How it was the only game he played where he wanted both parties to win.

"Trust me, I never want to stop." He lowers his head back down.

And I find myself relaxing on the hard stone deck that

surrounds the pool. My leg lifted over his shoulder and the other floating in the water. And Phillip Meyer between my thighs as pleasure races up my body.

It's hard to breathe. I look at the full moon above us as the pleasure grows and grows and grows, and I must be making noise because Phillip grunts against me and reaches up, his right hand finding my hip, my waist, and then teasing one of my nipples.

I break apart.

The strength of it surprises me. A wave sweeps me under, and it takes a very long time before I resurface from the sensations exploding across my skin.

My knees are clamped around his shoulders, and he's kissing my inner thighs, looking up at me. The hair at his temples has started to dry in small curls, and there's fierce color staining his high cheekbones. But it's the intensity in his eyes that makes it impossible to look away.

"Hi," I whisper.

He smiles, and it's a wondrous thing. "You're glorious."

And I surprise myself by believing it.

Chapter Nineteen

I have the beautiful turquoise sea in front of me. There's warm sand beneath me, so lovely I had to slip off my sandals and bury my feet, just because. And there's a piña colada with a purple umbrella on the table next to my lounge chair.

And I can't quite concentrate on any of it because of the man sitting next to me. He's fully stretched out on the lounger, his body tanned and muscled, and his hair shockingly dark against the white towel.

Phillip walked over a little before noon, and seeing me here, had chosen the chair next to mine. *Good morning,* he'd said; the tone of his voice not hiding what happened between us last night. It brought a blush to my cheeks.

We hadn't spoken about yesterday yet. I'm unsure if there's much to say, or if daytime Eden can talk about what Eden of the night did.

I glance at him out of the corner of my eye. He's reading something on his phone that has absorbed his attention for the past ten minutes, but he still looks relaxed. And handsome. For some reason, he hadn't let me reciprocate last night.

I look back out at the open ocean.

"This," I say, "is the life."

Phillip makes a non-committal sound.

"I'll probably never stay at a resort this good again." I stretch out my bare legs. They're finally shifting from pink to a light tan now.

"Mm-hmm," he says. Then he puts his phone down on the side table between us and looks over at me. "Why?"

"Because this place cost me a month's salary," I say. "But if there is a travel bug, it's bitten me pretty much everywhere. I can't imagine *not* traveling abroad again after this trip."

"You should. You're great at making the most of wherever you are."

"Is that a sly way of mocking my guidebook?"

He runs a hand along his jaw to hide his smile. "No. It was a genuine compliment."

"See, when someone uses sarcasm as much as you, it's very hard to take you seriously."

"I've been told that before," he says, and there's such seriousness in his voice that I roll my eyes.

"See? It's when you do *that*."

"But I bring joy to all those around me. Are you asking me to stop?"

"You're impossible," I say and turn on my side to face him fully. "You know, if I'd never—"

The phone between us starts to ring.

Phillip stares at it without making a move to answer. His hair is usually brushed back, but it's messy now, dark and ruffled in the ocean breeze.

"You're ignoring it?"

"Thinking about ignoring it, at least," he says. "I already know it's an attorney at my firm. He's an idiot."

"Doesn't he know you're on vacation?"

"Oh, he sure does."

I reach for the phone, pausing with my hand over it. "Can I?"

Dark-blue eyes meet mine, and there's that dimple again, flashing briefly as he smiles. "Go right ahead. His name is Briggs."

"You won't regret it," I say and answer the call. "This is Phillip Meyer's phone," I say in my brightest, most teacher-y voice.

"Who's this?" a frazzled male voice asks on the other end. "Is he around?"

"My name is Eden, and yes, he is," I say sweetly.

"Well, can you put him on?"

I look across at Phillip. He's resting his head on his hand and watching me, amusement shining in his blue eyes.

"No, I can't," I say. "He's on vacation."

The man on the line sighs. "Yeah, I know, but he's needed. Put him on."

"You're Briggs. Right?"

There's a pause. "Yes."

"Well, Mr. Meyer is a hardworking member of the team and is, at present time, enjoying two weeks of his earned vacation. All we ask is that these days are respected. And Briggs? He's spoken highly of you and your work ethic. I have every confidence that you're fully equipped to handle whatever crisis has just occurred. You have the voice of a competent man."

Phillip is grinning now.

"Um, thanks. Right. Well… I'll send him an email, then."

"Don't," I say, "unless someone is dying. Is someone dying, Briggs?"

"No."

"Then, he'll be back in the office in due time. Have a great day!" I say and hang up. My hand is shaking when I put the phone back down on the table. "Oh my God, that was an adrenaline rush!"

"You have," Phillip parodies, *"the voice of a competent man?"*

I chuckle. "A little flattery never hurts?"

He grins. "You really are wild."

"That's two superlatives in one week. Am I really that crazy?"

"You just never react the way I expect you to. Hell," he says and chuckles darkly, "that probably made my year."

"I wasn't too harsh?" I reach for my piña colada and take a long, calming sip.

"He's a corporate lawyer," Phillip says. "That phone call with you was probably the nicest he's had all day."

"Wow."

He chuckles again. "You're answering all of my phone calls from now on. I have a few other people you're welcome to give the same treatment to."

"I think you're fully capable of saying that to them yourself. But you don't." I lift my eyebrows. "Maybe you secretly like working twenty-four-seven?"

The amusement on his face fades like dissipating ripples on water. "Yeah. I've heard that before. Good thing you're here, then. Can't work when you're around."

"You can't?"

"No," he says. "I don't want to miss whatever stunt you'll pull next. Plenty of things to fall into around here."

I hold up my drink. "Well, for my next trick, I'm going to make this piña colada disappear. Please observe."

He watches me lock my lips around the straw, face oddly serious. Like he's studying me doing it. Something flips over in my stomach.

"I'm watching," he murmurs. Then, he clears his throat and takes the sunglasses off his head, resting them on the table between us. "I'm going in the water."

"Need to cool down?"

"Something like that," he mutters and heads toward the sea. I watch as he wades out until the waves reach his hips and then dives in, his broad shoulders emerging again in a crawl.

He swims back and forth along the shore, far enough out that he's not bothered by any of the other tourists swimming in the shallower waters.

He returns a long time later and stretches out beside me, droplets drying on his skin.

I flip the next page in my novel. I'm nearly at the climax, at the point where the story tips from the predictable to chaotic, and I have a few theories about what'll happen. Finding out if I'm correct is the best part of every reading experience. It's like I'm solving a puzzle along with the characters.

"What are you reading?" he asks without opening his eyes.

I curl my fingers around the top of the book, keeping my place. "A cozy mystery."

"A *cozy* mystery?"

"Yes."

"What's that?"

"It's a bit like... Agatha Christie. Murders and feel-good vibes."

"Right, I almost forgot you were obsessed with true crime."

"This isn't really true crime. The crime is kind of incidental."

"Tell me about the plot."

So I do, lying there beneath our umbrella. I tell him about the lead detective and how she'd moved back to her hometown only to discover that her ex had been keeping secrets, and that the boy who'd teased her in high school had become her shut-in but attractive neighbor, and then a teen disappears, and—

Phillip interrupts me. "Is that the kind of stories you write?"

"I knew you would try to get that information out of me."

"I'll find out before we leave the island," he says, putting his hands behind his head. "What are you in the mood to write next?"

I flip the book closed, committing the worst of all acts. Dog-earing. Maybe talking about it with him won't be that hard. He's been supportive so far, and... well, he'll be a stranger again in just a few days. "I'm actually planning to write something inspired by this resort."

His eyes light up. "Really?"

"Yes."

"Interesting. Tell me about it."

So I do. I talk about the people I'd seen—the arguing sisters, the rich couple on the beach, and all the theories I have for them. Phillip laughs at several of them and gives suggestions for others.

I don't tell him about the mysterious businessman character, though.

"Is this the one?" he asks. "Will you try submitting it to a publisher again?"

I look down at the book in my hand, at the tiny name of the publisher on the spine. It's easier to face than him. At least while I speak these words. "Probably not. I told you I failed at the publishing part. Now... now I'm not really sure it's worth doing again."

It feels easier to say out loud than I'd expected.

"Well," he says. "People fail all the time."

"They do?"

"Yes. That's part of the game. You lose at times. But that doesn't mean you stop playing. You go out again and again, and maybe next time, you win. And if you don't, well... then, the game isn't over, yet." He turns to look at me. "How many publishers are there in the world?"

"I don't know. Thousands? Tens of thousands?"

"Right. And are they all identical? Do they all have the exact same understanding of the publishing industry?"

I sigh. "No, you know they don't."

"Right. So another publisher might love your next book or the one after that. They might package them differently, market and sell them better."

"They might, yeah."

"Don't let some stuffy editor who didn't know how to sell

your first book be the arbiter of whether or not you've got talent." He leans back in the chair, head tilted up. His stubble has thickened into the beginnings of a decent beard. It makes him look older, somehow, and gruffer. But more relaxed, too. "If you decide a career as an author isn't for you, that's fine. But let it be because *you* decide it. Not someone else."

I look at him for a long few moments. "You're right. I mean, my first publisher doesn't know everything. They never put any advertising dollars behind it, either."

"No wonder it didn't perform."

"I also think I'm a better writer now." I look down at the book I'm reading. It was a great quick read, and halfway through, it had given me that feeling. *I think I could do this. I think I* want *to do this.* "Maybe I should try again."

"Of course you should," he says. "You've got more time on your hands now, too. You don't have a wedding to plan."

"Well, that's definitely true."

"Until you get married for real the next time. To the math teacher at your school, right?"

I use the paperback to smack him on the shoulder. He laughs, raising an arm in defense, and the sound makes me smile. "I should never have confessed that."

"Think you'll go out with him when you get back to Washington?"

"No, of course, not." I shake my head and lean back in the lounge chair, stretching out my legs. "I don't want to date someone at work. Can you imagine how awkward that could be?"

"Yes," he says. "I can."

That makes me look over. "Sounds like you've got a story."

"Not particularly."

"Phillip."

He sighs. "During one of my early years as a legal intern, I dated another intern."

"Oh no."

"Yeah. Didn't go great when she decided she was more interested in her roommate than me."

"Her roommate?"

"Yes. He was steady, dependable. Didn't work too much and always answered the phone."

I frown. "What, as opposed to you?"

"Yeah. I haven't always been the best partner, Eden." He runs a hand through his hair and adjusts his sunglasses. With them on, I can't see his eyes. I can only read his expression from the movement of his jaw. "None of my exes were okay with my work days occasionally running to midnight."

"But that goes in phases, right? Like when you're deep into a mergers and acquisitions negotiation. It doesn't happen on a normal Tuesday, right?"

He turns to me. "You remembered what I work with?"

"Yes," I say. I had googled *m&a* the other night while in bed. Read up on the firm he worked for, too. I'd even googled his name. *Phillip Meyer.* But I hadn't found much. Seems like social media isn't his thing. "It sounds interesting."

"You mean that?" he asks.

"Yeah, I do. Even if you never go to court."

"Rarely," he agrees. "I mean, I definitely have."

"I bet you were the hottest lawyer that day."

He chuckles, just like I'd hoped, and runs a hand through his hair again. It seems like he does that a lot when he's flustered or taken by surprise. "I couldn't say."

"Don't be modest," I coo. I lean back in my lounge chair and open up my book again, still smiling.

Beside me, Phillip flicks some sand off his forearm. "So?"

"So, what?"

"Are you planning on dating when you get back home? Math teacher or someone else."

"Oh," I say. "I might. It's not really something I've thought about. People seem to use a lot of apps these days, and that's not really something I'm keen on."

He makes a deep humming noise and falls silent again. I

look over at the sky and the quickly moving clouds. Our conversations are always like that. They take unexpected routes and always end up in places I never anticipate.

"Will you?" I ask.

"I don't know," he says quietly. "I don't really have any plans to."

"Same as me, then."

He hums again. It's become a familiar sound these days. An answer that's neither yes nor no, just a deep rumble in his throat.

"I'm not looking forward to going home," I say. The wind sweeps in gently from the ocean, like a warm caress. I close my eyes at the sensations—the breeze, the sound of waves, and the sand beneath my left foot.

"Not many days left," he says.

The words send a shiver of anticipation through me. I don't look at him, but I'm aware of him nonetheless, just a few feet beside me. "Only a few."

"Yes," he says. "Wonder what you'll get up to."

"Who knows? I could do anything at all," I say. "I heard those fancy bungalows have private pools. Might go skinny-dipping."

His breath hitches. "Really?"

"Mm-hmm."

"Funny, that. I have a bungalow."

"No, you do?"

"Yes."

I bite my lower lip to hide my smile. Flirting is fun. I can't remember ever doing it like this before, relishing the deepening attraction. With Caleb, it had been over and done with quickly. Both of us fell into a comfortable twoness on the second date.

I reach for my sunscreen and sit up. "I'm thinking of flipping over," I say. "Would you mind?"

Phillip holds out a hand. "I can do it."

I turn my back to him and sit still. This is the second time we're doing this, but on the first, we'd still been cautious—two strangers, not knowing the limits of the other.

His hands sweep over my back in warm strokes. They linger at my waist, my lower back, and skim the edge of my bikini bottoms.

"You're thorough," I murmur.

His voice is a whisper against my right ear, and against my neck, his newly grown beard tickles. "I always am, Eden."

"Yes… I know."

His hands glide along the sides of my chest one final time. "How are you feeling?" he murmurs, and I know he's asking about yesterday. Words dance on the tip of my tongue.

On the beach, someone claps loudly.

We both turn to see an employee from the hotel, wearing the Winter Resort uniform, standing on the beach with a big smile on his face.

"Sorry to bother everyone!" he says. "But this week's Winter Olympics is about to begin in the courtyard garden. We have a spot left, so if there's a couple interested in competing against other guests, we'd love to have you. We start in ten minutes!"

He smiles again and heads back up the beach, toward the main building.

I chuckle. "The Winter Olympics?"

"It's clever, you have to give them that," Phillip says. His hands have fallen off my shoulders, but he's still sitting close behind me.

"Should we go?" I ask.

Just then, a couple stops in front of our lounge chairs. I recognize them as the middle-aged people I've met in the elevator the other day, the ones who renewed their vows.

"Hi, you two," the woman says, throwing a special smile at me. "Sorry, but I couldn't help but overhear. We took part in the games last week, and it was a blast. You two should join in!"

"Maybe we will," I say, returning her friendly smile.

She takes a step closer. Beside her, her husband has sunglasses on and doesn't look particularly interested in talking to us. "Are you two married?"

I glance from her to Phillip, and back. "Here on our honeymoon," I say.

He huffs a quiet laugh beside me and nudges my knee with his own. I nudge right him back.

"How wonderful," she says. "It's the most beautiful place, isn't it?"

"Yes, it definitely is."

She pushes her sunglasses up on her head and looks between us. "Where are you two from, then?"

"Chicago," I say immediately. "I just love the Windy City. Can't get enough of the skyscrapers and those lovely breezes."

Beside me, Phillip sighs, and I have to bite my tongue to keep from laughing. I don't know who I am, joking around like this. But it feels good.

"Oh, that's an exciting city," the lady says. "We're from Detroit ourselves. We're all escaping the winter here together!"

"Sure are!" I say and lean against Phillip's shoulder. "How long have you and your husband been married?"

"Twenty years, this year. That's why we renewed our vows. What about you two? Where did you tie the knot?"

"On top of a skyscraper," Phillip says. His voice is matter-of-fact. Believable. "It was a small ceremony."

She shifts her focus to him, her eyes widening. "You did? That's so unique! Did it have any special significance for you two?"

"It's where we met, actually," he says.

I glance at him out of the corner of my eye. There's a stiffness in his jaw that makes me think he's trying very hard not to smile, either.

I nod. "I was with friends, just admiring the view. And he

was performing at a corporate event that was taking place up there."

Phillip goes very still at my side.

"Oh, is that true? That's incredible!" The woman says. "Frank, did you hear that? They met on top of a *skyscraper*!"

He grunts and looks down at the book in his grasp. Based on the cover, it seems like it might be a thriller. A sibling of the true crime genre. Respect.

"What instruments do you play? Or do you sing?" she asks Phillip.

"I'm not musical at all," he says. "I was a juggler."

I have to bite the inside of my cheek to keep from bursting into laughter.

"Wow. I didn't expect that," the lady says and chuckles. "But then, what does a juggler look like? They could be anyone!"

"We are a pretty universal bunch," he says. "I only dabbled for a while, really."

"Oh honey," I say. "Don't sell yourself short. You were the best in Chicago."

He shrugs, the picture of modesty. "You're biased, Eden."

"I'm just your biggest fan," I say.

"Oh, you two are adorable!" the woman beams. "You just have to come and join the games."

"It does sound like fun," I say. "We're in. Aren't we, Phillip?"

He looks at me like I've lost my mind.

"Perfect. Frank, we've got our work cut out for us now!" she says with a laugh. "They look like excellent sack racers!"

"What are you doing," my own lovely husband mutters at my side.

"There are *games*." I bat my eyelashes at him like a besotted honeymooner. "And I know how much you love to win."

He blinks twice before answering. "Fine. But I'm not getting into any sacks."

He gets into a sack.

Not right away, of course. No, when we arrive at the courtyard garden for the resort-sponsored games, there are various supplies laid out on the lawn in front of the same smiling hotel employee.

About eight couples are milling around, some are chitchatting with others, but a few partners are keeping to themselves. One of the couples, both dressed in matching blue, can't keep their hands off one another.

"Juggling," I whisper to Phillip. "Why on earth did you choose that?"

"That's payback for you saying you like the *wind* in Chicago. That was outrageous."

"Worse than getting married on the roof of a skyscraper?"

"Yes," he says. "That actually happens. I think."

"And you don't think women can fall in love with jugglers?" I ask. "You'd probably break hearts left, right, and center if you grabbed a couple of balls."

His eyes widen, and a smile starts at the corner of his mouth. "Eden, I—"

"Don't," I say. "I heard how that sounded, too."

He grins. "That's all that counts," he says. "This seems like an awful way to spend an afternoon."

"Does that mean you want to leave?" I ask. "Because we totally can. I mean, I'm down. As long as you know it means we're losing on walkover to all the other guests, half of whom are probably insufferable honeymooners."

"I hate you," he says, but it doesn't sound like he means it at all.

"Thanks, sweetie pie."

He frowns. "No."

"My lucky charm?"

"Absolutely not."

"My honey nut," I say, and then grimace. "No."

"Yes," he says, amusement dancing in his eyes. "That one for sure. But why the cereal theme?"

"Because they're—"

"Welcome everyone!" The hotel employee—and the apparent emcee for this event—calls out. "Ready to get started? We have some awesome activities lined up for you!"

What follows might be the most chaotic half an hour of my life. I go head-to-head with eight other women in the noble sport of racing with an egg on a spoon being held in my mouth. And I watch Phillip struggle to shoot darts at the water-filled balloons after spinning around a stick.

By the time we're grabbing the sacks, he's forgotten about his promise. We're doing a relay race.

He rushes across the lawn in his burlap sack, neck and neck with the man in a pink polo shirt who seems determined to win in every single game. In my mind, I've deemed him Phillip's nemesis.

Phillip returns to the start line and quickly kicks the sack off his legs before holding it out for me to step into it. "Come on, Eden," he urges.

I pull the burlap sack up to my waist and leap, but I get too much momentum too fast. Three hops forward, and I take a fall. Straight onto the green grass beneath the blue Caribbean sky, and I can't help but laugh, lying there on my back. Everything is so silly. This, me, us. I don't think I've laughed this hard in weeks.

Phillip's face comes into view. "Eden!" he says. "Come on, we're losing."

That only makes me laugh even harder. But I hold up my hands, and he takes them, pulling me up into standing.

"Eden," he says. His skin is flushed from his own race.

I put a hand on his cheek. "We're racing in sacks," I tell him and laugh again.

His mouth cracks into a reluctant smile beneath my palm. "It's ridiculous."

"Yes. But I'll be damned if we lose to the couple in blue over there."

I race the rest of the course and all the way back amid the frantic cheers of the others. Beside me, the other competitors struggle to do the same and, somewhere among all the voices, I make out Phillip's.

"Come on, fruit loop!" he yells. "You got this!"

I fall across the finish line. But Phillip is there to catch me. All around us, the other participants are cheering on their partners. I'm struggling to laugh through my heavy breathing. The jasmine-laden air is thick with heat and humidity, and beneath my bare feet, I can feel the softness of trampled grass.

"That," I say, "was so much harder than I thought it would be!"

Phillip's hands wrap around my hips. "You looked very graceful."

"Liar."

"No, it's the truth. Like a ballerina."

I hit his chest. My hand stays there, fingers curling over the collar of shirt. "Did we at least win?"

"They're tallying the 'scores now," he says, "but we beat "PDA One" and "Two" over there."

I peer over his shoulder at the couple in blue. They seem to have given up on the contest all together. Still hovering around the finish line, they've got their arms wrapped around one another, lips locked in a display that should really only take place behind closed doors.

"Amateurs," I say.

"Can't keep their eyes on the price."

I nod, something tightening in my stomach. It's not desire. It's something else, something much more dangerous, and I know that saying goodbye to this little fling won't be as easy as I once thought.

Beside us, the woman from earlier loudly clears her throat. She's stepping out of her sack and smiling at us. "You two are just the cutest," she says. "Aren't they, Frank? And to think, you're a professional juggler!"

I lean my head onto Phillip's chest to hide my laughter. Above me, I hear his deep voice, laced with amusement. "If only that had been one of the games," he says.

Chapter Twenty

Today, I'm the one in charge of choosing our activity. *But it can't involve hotel games,* Phillip had said the night before. *It needs to be something from that guidebook of yours.*

The concierge at the Winter Resort had been somewhat surprised when I asked her about the best rental car company. Apparently, most tourists either stay at the resort or go on pre-planned excursions, but she obliged.

Phillip drives. It turns out he's driven on the left side of the road before, while he was in England for work, and I gladly let him take the wheel.

"But you're responsible for the map," he tells me, steering the vehicle out of the car rental agency's parking lot and onto the trafficked main street of Holetown.

"You know," I say as we pause at an intersection, "this might be the wildest thing we've done during this whole trip."

He raps his fingers softly against the steering wheel. The car is larger than we needed, but it was the only one with an automatic transmission they had at the rental company. Driving stick *and* on the left side of the road was more gambling than Phillip was willing to do.

"I'd say going to an abandoned beach to watch turtles

hatch in the middle of the night was moderately wild," he says. "Not to mention that van ride to the fish market."

I glance over at Phillip, wondering if he's remembering the same thing I am. Me, sitting on his lap. He glances my way, and a slow smile spreads across his face.

"Well, it was good in some ways," I say.

"Definitely. I have no complaints."

I trace my fingers along my bare thigh. My sundress of choice is pretty short today; a light-blue thing with ruffled sleeves.

We haven't kissed since the pool two days ago. It's like he gave me all the pleasure and decided to take none for himself, and I can't quite work out why.

Phillip clears his throat. "Wildlife center first?"

"Yes. Should only be a twenty-minute drive."

"Awesome."

I rest my head against the seat and watch the landscape unfurl around us. It doesn't take long for the scenery to turn into a golf course and then fields of sugarcane. The winding road takes us through villages in quick succession. The island really is small, and beautiful, and so different from anywhere I've ever been.

I cross my ankles in the roomy passenger space. "Let's play a fun facts game."

"Let's not," Phillip says.

"My students love this one."

"I'm sure they do, but we're not five."

"Are you telling me you're not a fun facts person? Because I don't believe you. I think you watch a lot of documentaries and movies about wars and dead presidents in your spare time. Don't you?"

He taps his fingers along the steering wheel again. "I might have watched a documentary or two about JFK."

"Which means you love useless facts."

"The history of our political establishment is not useless."

I grin in triumph. "And now you're defending your

useless facts, which means you think they're fun. See? I knew this would appeal to you. It's the right amount of brainy and silly."

He shakes his head but relents. "Fine. Hit me with your first one."

"All right," I say and cross my arms over my chest. This needs to be a good one to start the game off strong. I run through all kinds of possibilities.

"Well?" he asks.

"I'm thinking! I have to make the first one really good."

"You do?"

"Yes, if I'm going to win."

"You can win at this game?" he asks. "Now I'm interested."

"I knew you would be. Okay, did you know that forty-eight different piglets played the role of Babe in the movie?"

There's complete silence from the driver's seat.

"Come on," I say. "The movie about the little pig who herds sheep?"

"I remember it. Vaguely. I think my sister and I watched that like two decades ago," he says and shakes his head. "Forty-eight piglets? That seems… excessive."

"Well, the piglets grew so fast they were too big for the role after like a week."

He snorts. "Wow."

"Yeah. Your turn."

"I don't have random pig facts up my sleeve," says the thirty-two-year-old serious lawyer from Chicago. "Just so you know."

"I promise I'll hide my disappointment."

"Thank you," he says. "Fine. So, you know the moon landing?"

"I have heard of it," I say.

"Glad to hear our education system didn't fail you. Right, well, two men went down to the moon. The third stayed in orbit."

"Michael Collins?"

Phillip shoots me a look. "Yeah, that's right. You know this?"

"Maybe? But keep going. Also, you're definitely a science documentary nerd."

"He spent hours alone in orbit. And every time he flew around the far side of the moon, his radio contact with Earth was cut off. He couldn't even *see* it. He was later called the 'loneliest man in history' because for forty-seven minutes of each lunar rotation, he was the farthest person from Earth and more alone than anyone who has ever lived. It was just him and outer space."

I shiver. "Wow."

"Yeah."

"Do you think about that a lot?"

"What's a lot?" Phillip asks with a half laugh. "That level of complete solitude sounds appealing, sometimes."

"I can't even picture it."

"Very few of us can, I think. Your turn."

"Well… the King of England owns all swans in the country."

"He does?"

"Technically speaking, yeah. So if you ever thought of poaching one, look out."

"There go my summer plans."

"I know, it's a real bummer."

He slows down at an intersection, and I have to remember to guide us. It's a solid five minutes before the game can resume, with the course corrected.

"I've noticed," he says, "that all your facts are animal-related."

"Well, we're headed to a wildlife center, so it's fitting."

"I should step it up. So… okay. You asked for random facts, right?"

"Hit me."

"A duck's dick is shaped like a corkscrew," he says.

"What? No way."

"It's a hundred percent true."

"How the hell do you know that?"

"It was a go-to fun fact for a friend of mine in college. He pulled it out at parties all the time."

"The fact, I hope?"

Phillip laughs. "Yes, the fact."

I chuckle, too. "He must have been wildly popular."

"Oh, he was a real crowd-pleaser," Phillip says.

"A corkscrew. Oh my God, I can't even..." I shiver again, in discomfort this time. "Poor female ducks."

"Might not be so bad if it's all you know," he says. Then, he laughs again. It's a full laugh, and it fills the car up, warming the air between us. "I can't fucking believe the conversations I have with you."

"You were the one who brought up the intimate anatomy of a duck," I say, but I'm grinning, too.

"Yeah, and I stand by it because I want to win the game."

"I feel like my Babe fact was killer, though."

He reaches across the center console and pats my bare leg. "It was, I'll admit. Let's call it a tie."

My entire body hums at the contact of skin against skin, and the memory of his fingers sliding even further up. "Okay," I murmur.

His hand lingers a second too long before he puts it back on the steering wheel. Then, he clears his throat again. "Fuck."

"What?"

"It's hard to be around you now," he says. "After the other night."

"It is?" The words come out soft. We haven't spoken about it, not in the bright light of day.

"I know too much now," he says, glancing over at me. "It's killing me to not do it again. Right now. All the time."

My chest constricts, making it hard to take in a full breath. "Well, right now would be pretty unsafe."

"Yes, but that doesn't stop me from wanting to do just that. Your short dress doesn't exactly help."

I stretch out my legs again and watch the fabric ride up an inch. "Good thing you're a self-controlled lawyer with the discipline of steel."

He glances down at my legs. "I used to be," he mutters. "Now, I'm someone who competes in sack racing."

That makes me laugh, and it breaks the tension rising in the car.

"Hey, is this the place?"

"Shoot, yes," I say, looking out the window. "Turn in here to the left."

He pulls the car to a stop in a gravel parking lot, right in front of the giant gates.

The wildlife center is exactly what the guidebook said it would be. Small and family-run, with palm trees and foliage all around. It's inhabited by the green-tailed monkeys that live on the island. They run wild all over the countryside, but here they're more numerous, jumping from tree to tree and watching us with big eyes.

Phillip takes pictures of me next to the monkeys, and I pester him into taking a picture with me, too. A fellow tourist snaps the shot of us.

"To remember the trip by," I tell him.

He rolls his eyes. "It's not memorable enough? You fell off a boat, Eden."

I elbow his side, and he reaches for me, tickling until I finally end up tucked beneath his arm. He drapes it around my shoulders and keeps it there for the rest of our tour around the little center.

After our visit, we drive on. Our route takes us from spot to spot, all the way to a cove on the north end of the island. We eat lunch there, high above the crashing waves of the Atlantic, and I make him tell me about his childhood, and his experiences in law school and the late nights he spent in the library.

In return, he quizzes me about my books, and I finally tell him the name of my first one, the flop, and he listens attentively. Like he truly cares.

Our last stop of the day is at a deserted beach mentioned in the guidebook. We make our way to it using a combination of GPS and a very friendly man who points us in the right direction. The sun is hanging midway down the sky, the afternoon fading. I sit down on the sand, and Phillip sinks beside me. The deep-blue waves beat softly against the shore.

"I can't believe we're here," I say. "That this is my life right now."

"It could be your life more often. You know, if you wanted it to," he says. "There are ways to incorporate traveling into your reality."

I rest my head on my knees. "Yes. I used to be kinda jealous of Kaelie, actually. She gets to travel so much for work. But now, I don't know if I want that."

"No?"

"I like it like this, when it's rare and special. And I like that I've been here long enough to become someone else." I turn to look at the man beside me. Strong profile. Arms outstretched behind him, propping him up. "I don't want to lose this entirely when I go back home."

His blue eyes shift to me. "Lose what?"

"My vacation self."

"Ah. Well, you can carry her with you pretty easily."

"I'll try. Because the person I am right now… it's such an upgrade from who I've been the past few months."

His lips tip into the frown similar to one he'd worn during our first days of vacationing together. "Because of the dipshit?"

"Yeah," I say. "Sorry. We don't need to talk about our exes."

"We can talk about whatever you'd like," he says. "I believe I'm the one who brought up avian genitalia earlier, so you have a free pass for eternity."

I brush my shoulder against his. "I'll never let you live that down."

"I expect nothing less from you. But you can tell me. It was rough after you found out about…?"

"Yes. All our friends knew, my entire family. It took me a few weeks before I felt ready to have all of the conversations, you know. Anyway. I like who I've become here, on this island. Free-spirited and adventurous, and not so hung up on the past."

"Mm-hmm," he says. "You are probably more like this than you realize when you're back home."

"You think?"

Phillip's eyes slide from the ocean to me. "Yes. You're a planner and a hopeless optimist. You like talking to strangers and you're curious. You strive to do a good job, and you're a little afraid of messing up."

"That's… a pretty good assessment."

"I pay attention," he says.

The sea is rougher on this side of the island. Without the natural buffer provided by the island from the open Atlantic Ocean, the waves on this coast are higher, and the water looks darker.

It's beautiful.

"Do you still love him?" Phillip asks.

The words hang between us in the warm afternoon air. I take my time answering because I know this is important. Getting this right.

"I don't think so," I say. "But who knows when love really fades, you know? It's not like a switch. Right now, I still hate him a bit for what he did. And hate is not the opposite of love. That's indifference, and I'm not indifferent to him. Not yet."

"I wonder if you ever will be," Phillip says, "considering what he did."

I wrap my arms around my knees. "I'm almost angrier over him doing it with my best friend. Because he chose someone who'd otherwise be my friend for life. Him… well. We weren't always the most compatible. I loved the idea of us more than those differences, but now they seem pretty stark."

"Yeah, I can empathize."

I turn to look at him. "Do you still love her?"

He sighs and looks back out toward the waves. "You're going to judge me."

"I really don't think I will, Phillip. I'm not sure I can anymore."

"Hmm. Well, I don't think I ever really loved her."

My eyes widen. "Oh."

He sits up straighter, brows drawn together. "Not that I didn't care for her. Of course, I did. I *thought* I loved her. Otherwise, I wouldn't have proposed."

"Sensible," I say, and he shoots me a look that's amused and dry in equal measure.

"Yeah. But we didn't have a lot in common, and I've realized since the… non-wedding, as you called it once, that we never really spoke. Not properly, not deeply. Not about everything and anything."

"That's important," I say softly. I'm finding the exact same thing was true for Caleb and me.

"It is." He runs a hand over the back of his neck. "We had similar goals in life, and I think we both saw the other as fitting into those goals. In a way, it was almost more of a relationship of convenience."

I dig my teeth into my lower lip. "Did you enjoy it? When you were in it?"

"I thought I did. It was fitting." He looks down, dark lashes fanning over a tanned cheek. "She cheated about a year ago."

My eyebrows shoot up. "Really?"

"Yeah, with an ex-boyfriend who was back in town one weekend. And you know, I wasn't hurt as much as annoyed. She apologized, promised it wouldn't happen again, and I… accepted that."

"That was very generous of you."

"Maybe. But now, I think my lack of care was probably a big red flag. For myself, I mean. I'm more irate at your dipshit of an ex for cheating on you than I am at my own."

"Yeah. I don't know if I'll ever be okay with it. I mean, I'm pretty sure I wouldn't."

"Which is probably the right reaction." He runs a hand along his jaw. "I worked too much before this trip."

"Mm-hmm. I suspected."

"I really like my job, though. But if I had a relationship that truly matters, that's right… I don't think I'd make the same prioritization."

I can't look away from his eyes. "That's probably true."

He leans back, locking his hands behind his head, and looks up at the sky. "That was a damn long answer."

I chuckle and lie down beside him. The sand is warm beneath me, and I'm sure it's getting in my hair and my clothes, but I don't care one bit. "Yeah. But it was a good one."

We lie there for a long time. I savor his words and let them linger in my mind.

After a while, he turns onto his side. I look over and meet his gaze.

"Hi," he says.

I smile. "Hello."

"About the other day."

Heat passes through me and settles in my stomach. "You mean our drinks by the beach?" I ask.

He grins. "No."

"The phone call from your colleague that I answered?"

"Not that, either," he says. "The thing I'm referring to happened in a certain pool."

"Ah," I say. "That."

"Yes, that."

"What about it?"

His hand stretches out, lands on my hipbone. It's a warm

weight over a thin sundress. "Do you want to come over tonight?"

Nerves flutter beneath his hand. Perhaps he senses that in the brief silence because his voice softens. "No pressure," he says. "I just have a painfully well-stocked minibar and too much cash to burn."

I turn toward him. He kisses me, a slow touch of his lips against mine.

"I would," I say, "but I have plans."

"Don't tell me you've met another man who is honeymooning alone."

I playfully push on his shoulder but leave my hand pressed to his skin. "No. I actually booked myself a massage. It's a gift from my parents and best friend. They told me to choose something from the spa menu."

His eyes warm. "That's nice of them."

"It really is. But after that, though, I'm free. I could... come by. We could order room service?"

He leans in and kisses me again, letting me know exactly what he thinks of that plan.

Chapter Twenty-one

With my body pleasurably sore from the massage, and butterflies dancing in my stomach, I knock on the door of bungalow twelve. Phillip opens the door. He's in a pair of shorts, feet bare, and another one of his linen button-downs. It's only buttoned halfway up, and his hair is ruffled.

"Eden," he says.

"Hey, I'm sorry my massage appointment ran so late."

"No problem." He takes a step back, inviting me across the threshold. "Want to come in?"

I step inside his bungalow. I've only seen it from the deck and the comfort of the pool through the glass patio doors. Just a hint of a king bed and an armchair.

Now I'm getting the full tour.

The tiled floors are a soft sandy color, and the walls are painted in the same hue. The furniture is mostly rattan, woven into intricate patterns. Cream-colored throw pillows adorn the sofa and armchair. Off to one side is a small kitchenette with a wooden countertop and cabinets stained rich mahogany.

I pause halfway through the living room. "This is all for one person?"

"I think the bungalow technically accommodates four, so

it works for families. You're not supposed to be enjoying it alone."

I peek into the giant bathroom, and that's the real highlight. The walls and floors are covered in marble, and the vanity is outfitted with gold-plated fixtures. A deep soaking tub sits in the corner. And as a finishing touch, there is a walk-in shower, complete with a rainfall shower head and an array of oils and shampoos to choose from.

Everything about this place screams luxury.

"That shower is the size of my entire bathroom at home," I say.

Phillip chuckles behind me. "Yeah, it's larger than it needs to be."

"Fits a family of four, too." I walk through to the spacious master bedroom. This is the room I've seen while peeking through the sliding doors. They're half-open now and let in the familiar sound of Bajan nightlife. Chirps and serenading insects.

His bed is larger than the one in my room. A continental king. It's neatly made, the pillows stacked into an inviting headrest. The TV is on, but the program is paused.

I read the caption on the screen. "No way."

There's a sigh beside me. "It's good."

"You're watching a sports documentary?"

"Yes."

"No JFK assassination tonight?"

"No, I'm saving that for tomorrow." He steps past me to the minibar. It's beautifully built into the mahogany cabinetry that combines the master bedroom with the living room, in an open floor plan. "Want a drink?"

"Yes, please."

He sets to work with the array of small bottles and mixers he has in the fridge. I spot a plate of beautifully arranged fruit hidden in there.

Oh, to be staying in a bungalow.

There's a suitcase in the corner next to a walk-in closet. His shirts hang neatly in a row on the left side of the rod.

I want to snoop and I can't. Turning, I catch sight of a bundle of papers next to a beautiful arrangement of tropical flowers on a table.

The top page has the word *itinerary* printed on it.

"Oh," I say. "I've found it!"

Phillip glances over from the drink-making. "Did you bring your guidebook so you could compare notes?"

"No, but I should've." I pick it up and start reading. There are names at the top. *Honeymoon in Barbados for Mr. and Mrs. Meyer.* Below is a detailed itinerary. Pickup at 06:00 from 113 Row Street, Chicago. Takeoff from O'Hare at 09:00, arrival in Bridgetown at 17:45.

"She wrote it using military time?" I ask.

Phillip adds ice into two glasses. "I requested it," he says. "It's more accurate. No risk of confusion."

I smile down at the itinerary. "I thought you said you weren't involved in the planning."

"Not much."

"But you requested the fishing trip."

"Yeah, I did."

I flip through the papers. Day by day, activities are laid out. Some of them, I know for a fact, he hasn't done. Fruit carving with resort staff?

"You planned to scuba dive?"

He shakes his head. "I was never going to do it. She was interested in trying."

"Why aren't you?"

"I've spent my entire life swimming at the surface. I like that," he says. "Not interested in trying to breathe underwater."

My eyes snag on a note next to day eight. *Lauren, the massage is booked for 10:00 at the bungalow.*

So that's her name.

Phillip comes to stand beside me. His forearm rests

against mine, his breath fanning the hair at my temple. "So?" he says. "Care to finally admit that my travel planner knew her job?"

I flip to the end of the trip. To the day fourteen where his flight is listed. A stopover in Miami, and then to O'Hare. Airport transfer back to 113 Row Street.

And back to his normal life.

"You stayed in the same place," I say.

"Eden?"

"After the two of you broke up, I mean. How was that?"

He shrugs. "Okay. She'd moved in two years ago, and now she's packing up all of her stuff." He takes the itinerary out of my hands and puts it back on the table. "Here," he says and hands me my drink. "How did you and the dipshit do it?"

"We both moved out. Our place was too expensive for one person."

Not to mention I hadn't wanted to stay another night, never mind weeks, in the space where we'd lived together.

He nods and sits down on the edge of his bed. Behind him is the documentary, still paused, a basketball player is poised to make a beautiful layup shot.

"You've been relaxing," I say.

"Yeah, and catching up on some emails." His gaze drifts down, over my bare arms. "How was the massage?"

"You're not allowed to work, I've told you."

Phillip half-grins. "Yeah. But you weren't here to see me."

"Good thing I dropped by, then."

"Yes," he says and takes a long sip of his drink. "It is. So?"

"The massage was good. Great, even. There was soft music playing and… and… well. I almost fell asleep."

"Is that a good thing?"

That makes me chuckle. "I think so, yeah. Best present ever. But I didn't stop by my room to shower, though." I hold up one of my arms, and it glistens in the dimmed lights of his bungalow. "She used a lot of oil."

"Right," Phillip says. He gets up off the bed and comes closer, his eyes on me. "That's fine."

"Is it?"

"Mm-hmm."

"I still think I should shower," I whisper. "Plus, we were lying on the beach today for such a long time."

"You can shower here," he says. "Use all the weird soaps you want."

"Thank you. Will you save my drink for me?"

"Yes," he says and clears his throat. "I can order room service for later. What do you want? I feel like having a burger."

"Oh, I'll have that, too."

"Okay," he says. "Well, make yourself at home."

I do.

There are tons of big, fluffy towels in his bathroom, and the rainfall shower is every inch as perfect as it looks. I stand beneath the steady stream and let it wash everything away, leaving only nerves and excitement in its wake. The combination of hot water, steam, and luxurious oils creates an aromatic escape from reality.

And *he's* right out there.

I haven't had sex with anyone but Caleb. Ever. And I knew this day would come, hoped it would, but I never expected it to be here. On a vacation, on my *honeymoon,* with a man who couldn't be more different from me or my ex.

Maybe I shower too long. Maybe getting into a shower at his place was weird, too. Or maybe I should have invited him in.

I let go of all my second-guessing as I step out and wrap myself in a giant fluffy towel. I wring the water out of my hair and take a deep breath.

And then I look in the mirror.

"Oh my God," I say and shift, turning so I can see my back and shoulders. I push my long, light-brown hair out of the way to assess the damage. "That's going to hurt so bad."

"Eden?" Phillip's voice comes from the other side of the bathroom door. "You okay?"

"Yeah, just a bit sunburned."

"Really?"

"Yeah." I drop the towel a bit, giving it a cowl neck in the back. The outlines of the straps from the sundress I'd worn today are clearly visible across my shoulder blades. They're white lines in the surrounding redness.

"There's after-sun lotion on the counter," he says.

"Oh, awesome! You don't mind?"

"No," he says. There's silence for a long moment "Need any help?"

I meet my own dark-brown gaze in the mirror. My hair is wet around me, and I look rosy from the hot shower steam. My eyes are wide and excited.

"Yes," I say and walk across the sandy-colored tiles toward the bathroom door. I crack it open a few inches. "Come on in."

Phillip's eyes are cautious as if he's expecting me to be naked. But then they drop to my shoulders and widen. "Fuck, Eden."

"Yeah, it's bad, isn't it?"

"Your poor skin."

"I must have missed this whole area this morning when I put on sunscreen." I turn and let the towel drop further along my back, holding it tight against my front. "Remember when we ate lunch today?"

"Yes," he murmurs and grabs the lotion.

"I was sitting with my back to the sun, and it was hot, so I put up my hair."

"Yeah. This'll feel cold."

"It's okay. I'm—oh, damn."

He runs a steady hand with cool after-sun over my back, and I let my head fall forward. My skin feels taut and too hot beneath his palm.

"Mmm. At least I had fun today."

His hand continues its smooth sweeping motion over my shoulder blades. "I didn't know today would be the day I finally learned how many pigs were cast in Babe."

I smile down at my toes. "I'm glad to have enlightened you," I say. "You're finally an educated man. How do you feel?"

"Nervous," he says. "There's so much pressure to use this knowledge responsibly."

"With great power, you know," I say. Our conversations are banal. Sometimes serious, often not, and never predictable.

"Mm-hmm." His hand glides down the small of my back, his fingers trace along the edge of the towel. I'm not burned there, but I feel hot all the same.

"Your shower was really nice."

"Oh? Good," he says. Then he tuts and bends, and I feel the touch of a cool hand along the back of my knee. "You're burned here, too."

"I burn easily," I say and reach out to grab a hold of the marble counter for support. His hand strokes up my leg, along my calf, the back of my thigh, until he reaches the edge of my towel.

"Maybe," he mutters, "but you have beautiful skin."

"Oh."

His hand moves up, just a few inches, along my inner thigh, and my breath whooshes out of me in a sharp exhale. Anticipation tightens in my stomach.

"Eden," he says and stands up. "I want to make sure—"

I turn around and meet his gaze, and his words falter. We look at each other, and the large bathroom suddenly feels very small, and very warm thanks to the steam from the shower.

Maybe my old self wouldn't say this now. Wouldn't be so open with it. But my vacation self doesn't have the same restraints.

"I am sure," I whisper. "It's just, I've only slept with one person."

His mouth parts. "Ah."

"We started dating when I was in college, you know."

"Makes sense." Phillip's eyebrows draw into two dark lines over his eyes. I can see unasked questions swimming in them. "The last thing I want is to pressure—"

I drop the towel before I lose my nerve.

It falls to the floor, a heap between our feet, leaving me in nothing but an uneven tan.

Phillip's words die for the second time. His eyes drink me in, and it's not the comforting darkness of the night that surrounds us now, but the spotlights in this exclusive bathroom.

"Fuck, you're gorgeous," he mutters, almost like he hates that it's true, like it pains him. He lifts a hand and traces his fingertips down my collarbone, down to where the tan disappears and the white outline of my bikini top starts. He traces the line across my skin, following the curve around my breast. "It's like these are no-go zones."

His hand brushes down, over my tanned stomach and to the pale white triangle where my bottoms have shielded me for the past week and a half. "So pretty," he says.

He's still fully clothed, and this might be the most turned-on I've ever been in my life, in this moment, having him watch me with burning eyes.

Words rise to my lips. "I don't want you to compare me to… anyone. Compare this. I want us to leave the past behind, both of us, with this."

His eyes return to mine. They blaze. "Eden, I can't think about anyone else right now. I can't even think about tomorrow."

I laugh, half-embarrassed and half-pleased.

He must think I don't believe him because he pulls my hand tight against his body. His erection is a hard length beneath my palm, and even through the fabric, he's hot. "It's true," he says and kisses me.

The kiss is hungry yet slow at the same time, like he's savoring it, savoring me.

And I get what he means. Because I can't think of tomorrow, either, never mind our exes. There's no room for anything but *this*.

He fills his hands with my ass and pulls me tight against him—me naked and him fully clothed. I'm about to protest that fact when he spins me around.

We stand in front of the mirror, him at my back. In the reflection, his eyes are heated. "Look," he mutters, and wraps an arm around my bare waist. "You're so unbelievably hot."

I look.

And I don't laugh it off, not as his hands skim the indent at my waist and the flare of my hips, or as he traces the outsides of my thighs. There's nothing funny at all about the intensity in his eyes or his hand pushing my legs apart so he can reach between them, just like he did in the pool, touching me like he already knows all of my secrets.

I lean my head back against his shoulder. "Did you order that room service?"

"Hmm?" he says, eyes focused on the two of us in the mirror. He's pressing the heel of his hand against my clit.

My breathing speeds up. "You're usually so articulate."

"Yes," he says.

"What did I just say?"

He forces his eyes to meet to mine. The dark-blue looks almost black. "I have no fucking clue."

I laugh, and then he's smiling, too, bending to kiss my neck. "Was it important?"

"It really, really wasn't."

"Good," he says, and his hand delves deeper. His middle finger pushes inside of me. "Because I have work to do."

"And you really like your job."

"That's right," he says. His hand circles and parts and

speeds up as we both watch. Maybe it's the watching, or the fact that it's so bright in here, or the strong feel of his arm around my waist and his free hand gripping my breast, but I'm at the edge quicker than I expected.

I squirm against his hand. "Why are you still wearing your clothes?" I ask, the need inside of me growing. "This is just like last time… I…need…"

His arm around me tightens, and I can see it flex in the mirror. His dark hair is a smudge against my neck as he kisses me. "Stay still," he says.

"Okay. But I'm… oh."

The fidgety restlessness, the pleasure-pain, all of it breaks into an orgasm. I come around his hand, and my legs threaten to give out, or maybe they do, but he supports me through it all. And when it's over, I feel him hard against my backside, and I know this isn't going to be a repeat of the pool.

Not again.

I turn in his arms and kiss him, my hands move between our bodies to make quick work of his shirt. His skin is warm to the touch, his chest hair a soft scrape against my fingertips.

"Eden," he mutters with a groan when I find the button of his shorts.

"You didn't let me last time."

"I didn't have a condom last time," he says and looks down between our bodies.

The word flashes through my brain. *Condom.* "Oh. I didn't even think about that."

"No, I noticed," he says. "But we stopped at a mini-mart today."

"That's what you bought? I thought you needed a new phone charger."

"Well, I needed that too," he says. *"Eden."*

I pull down his zipper, going achingly slow. There needs to be payback for all the taunting he's done. The bulge beneath my hand is big, growing larger with every slow inch unzipped.

The sharp, loud sound of a doorbell rings out.

Phillip takes a ragged breath. "Damn."

"What is it?"

"Room service." He takes a step back, his face drawn in pained lines, and pulls his zipper back up. "Stay in here."

"Yeah."

He pushes the bathroom door shut behind him, and then I hear a loud *fuck, where's my wallet?*

Five minutes later the hotel attendant has left, none the wiser, and the scent of fresh french fries spreads through the bungalow.

Phillip locks the front door and walks across the room to me. "I thought I told you to stay in the bathroom."

"You did," I say and walk backward toward the bedroom. "But I don't like doing what I'm told."

He wraps his arms around me, kissing me, his hands roaming over my body. The gentleness of when he put after-sun lotion on me is gone.

I shove at his shorts, impatient with the zipper, and he helps me push his shorts down. His cock springs free, and I reach for it, wrapping my hand around him.

If I'd thought he was warm before, he's burning hot now.

Phillip's breath catches when I stroke, clumsily and at a weird angle, but he doesn't seem to mind.

"I want to taste you," I say. I mean it, too. Every part of this man is sculpted and handsome. I feel high from my orgasm in front of the mirror and powerful, standing here with his arousal in my hand.

But he halts me on my way down his body. "Eden," he says harshly. "I really want that, trust me. But I'm too fucking turned-on for that right now."

Oh.

His words spread warmth through me, and I wonder if I've ever been this wanted before.

He kisses me deeply and disappears for a second to get the condoms he'd bought. I trace my fingers along my lips and marvel at the aching feeling inside me. I need him. Can't wait for the feeling of being filled.

Phillip returns and rolls the condom on with one hand. My stomach tightens at the sight, and the nerves that had crept in disappear in a blink, singed away by the heat in his eyes.

I crawl backward up the bed, propping myself on my elbows.

"No," he says. "Your back. It'll hurt you."

"Oh. I can prob—"

He grabs my hips and flips us over, pulling me on top of him. My thighs fall astride him, and I'm sitting right there, above the thick length of his cock. As I look down, it twitches against his stomach.

"Eden," he mutters, his hands digging into my hips. He lifts me up, and the muscles in his arms flex. "I need to fuck you now."

God, do I need that, too.

I brace my palms on his chest and tilt my hips into position. He grips his cock and aligns us, right at my core.

Being on top was never my favorite position. I enjoyed it, but Caleb complained that I went too slow. I think about that now, about how I need to speed up my tempo, but then I'm sinking onto Phillip, and there's no thinking at all.

His eyes are locked on my body, on the place where he's disappearing inch by inch inside of me.

The stretch is total, and I breathe a sigh of relief when I'm finally down, taking all of him in.

His face is etched in lines of pleasure-pain. The hands locked on my hips tighten their grip, his thumbs dig into the hollow above my hipbones.

"God, you feel good," he mutters.

I roll my hips, testing the limits. He groans, so I do it again, and then again, rocking my hips against him in a slow but steady rhythm. It stokes the fire inside, and I can't believe it, but I might be able to come again.

This never happened before.

I look at him, stretched out beneath me—long torso, wide shoulders, and tanned skin. His jaw is tense and his eyes are locked on mine.

He doesn't look like he needs me to speed up. He looks like he's enjoying every single moment.

Phillip's hands slide over my body. My thighs, my hips, my arms. He cups my tits and teases the nipples, his breath audible.

And when his hand returns between my legs, rubbing circles? My hips stutter in their movement, and then falter entirely; my body riveted on the pleasure radiating from his touch.

"Let go," he says. "That's it, let me feel it, how you'll—oh my God."

I come, and my hips lose all their rhythm. My fingers turn into claws on his chest, and I can't breathe, can't focus, can't think.

His arms are an iron grip around my lower back. He's breathing fast, and there's something unrestrained about his body beneath mine, like he's a hairsbreadth away from losing control.

"Phillip?"

"Mmm," he says harshly. "Fuck, I'm close. You were squeezing me so tight."

"I was?"

"Yes."

"Flip me over, then," I say. "If you want to, you know. Go hard."

His fingers brush my burned upper back, surprisingly gentle compared to the tight grip his right hand has on my thigh. "Not tonight," he says. "Stay like this. Hold on to my shoulders… that's it."

His hands slide down my body until they grip my ass. He tilts me forward, and then he's thrusting into me from below.

It's sudden and powerful, and I collapse on top of him, my forehead bracing against his chest.

He fucks me like that, with the heat of his body against mine and my legs splayed on either side of him, and his groans in my ear.

It's the hottest thing I've ever experienced.

"Tell me when you're close," I say against his neck. I want to hear it when it happens, to savor it.

His voice is rough in my ear. "I'm close now. So fucking close."

"Yeah?"

"Yes. God, you take me so good."

My exhale turns into a shudder. I can't come a third time, but still, my exhausted body makes a valiant effort. I dig my nails into his shoulders instead.

This is a vacation me, vacation self, and I have no inhibitions. They were behind in Pinecrest, checked at the gate, and never picked up at baggage claim.

"I want to feel you when you come," I say. I'm too turned-on to be embarrassed. Dirty talk is new to me.

"You will," he grunts and lifts a hand to slap my ass. His hips jerk, his thrusts still powerful but irregular, and then he comes. His body turns tight beneath mine, his arms nearly crushing as he holds me close. His groan is a broken, harsh sound in my ear, and I can feel him pulsing deep inside.

It takes both of us a long time to come back down to earth after that.

He finally tilts my hips up and eases out of me, and I shift onto my stomach on his bed.

I watch him get up and throw away the condom. He moves confidently through the room. Being naked doesn't seem to bother him at all.

"Are you getting our food?" I ask.

"Yes. Want your drink?"

"Yes, please." I grab a pillow to rest my head on. My body

feels molten, and my hair is a damp weight on my burned shoulders and back.

Phillip returns. He's put on a pair of shorts and is now setting the tray down in the middle of the bed. His hair is mussed, and there's a sharp color staining his cheekbones.

His eyes dance as they travel over my naked body. "Hey," he says.

I reach out and take a french fry. It's still crunchy, even if it's no longer warm. "Hi," I say. "So… it wasn't a corkscrew."

He looks at me for a surprised moment before he breaks into laughter.

It's the best sound I've ever heard.

Chapter Twenty-two

I draw my knees up on the lounge chair and rest my head on them, looking over at Phillip. He's reading on my phone. There's a frown between his eyebrows.

I feel like I've jumped off the deep end.

He makes a humming sound, and his thumb flicks as he scrolls through the contract. His patio umbrella casts a shadow across us both, and that's good because the midday sun is scorching.

"Okay," he says. "So the royalty clause seems pretty standard, but I'm not an expert in the publishing field."

"Right."

"The rights clause though… They own the rights in perpetuity. There is no time limit set for renegotiation."

I sigh. "Yeah, they do. That's pretty airtight, right?"

He nods, and the last shred of hope I had in showing him the contract for *One Fatal Step* melts away.

Phillip looks up at me. "But, and this isn't a legal advice, you could probably buy back the copyright."

"I could?"

"Yes. Do you know how much the book is selling for now?"

It takes me a second to answer. "Practically nothing. It hasn't earned back its advance."

"All right," he says. "Well, then you can make them an offer. Something they can't refuse. Let's say you offer to pay back half of your advance in exchange for getting the rights back."

"Half of the advance?"

"As an opening offer," he says. The beard on his face is thicker now, and his hair isn't brushed back the way it was the first day I'd met him.

He looks like he's on vacation.

"You can always up the offer later on," he continues. "If you want the rights back, I'm sure there's something you can do. Just don't leave them with the impression that you're hungry for it. That'll give them the advantage."

"Right." I dig my teeth into my lower lip and consider my next words. It's not something I've spoken out loud. "I might decide to give it another shot... at some point."

"Getting published?"

"Sort of." This was the part Caleb never understood, and Becky wanted to, but her advice was always *do what makes you happy,* and I'm not sure if this will. I could fail again. "Not through a publisher. I've been reading a bit about self-publishing. And... you know I've kept writing."

"How many books do you have finished?"

"Two, but they need editing."

His eyebrows rise. "Really?"

"Yes. I mean, they're just on my hard drive because the publishing house wasn't interested in anymore. And the last book, well, it didn't sell, so I'm not exactly sure if my others would."

"They might," he says. "As I said, publishers have different preferences. But self-publishing might be another avenue. If you've already written the books, you don't have anything to lose."

I sigh. *Just my self-confidence,* I think. "Yeah, you're probably right."

He puts my phone down. "Either way, though, I want you

to ask a lawyer to read through any future contract before you sign it. Did you have help with this one?"

"A friend who went to law school read it over," I say. "Is it bad?"

He shrugs, but it looks careful. "It's not *bad,* but it could have been better. There are definitely clauses I would have put in that could have protected you. Maybe the publisher would have rejected them, but I would have at least tried."

I smile. "If only I could afford your hourly fee."

He snorts. "I'll give you a deep discount."

"Oh?"

"Of course. I'd also expect to read the book."

I groan. "Why do people always want to do that?"

"Because they're interested," he says. "Because I've never met a writer before. You know, I'm going to find *One Fatal Step* at my local bookshop."

"Oh God."

He leans back in his deck chair, eyes on me. There's something different in them today. Something that wasn't there yesterday when we were driving around the island. It speaks of last night.

I didn't spend the night in the bungalow. After sex and food, he walked me to the lobby. He said I was more than welcome to stay, of course, but there was something so intimate about the idea. I wasn't ready to face the reality of waking up together and not having any of my own things. I needed the freedom of my own hotel bed, clean underwear, and my toothbrush.

But here I am, back at his bungalow, anyway. We've ended up here after spending most of the day on the beach. I look down at the hem of my cover-up and tug at a stray piece of thread.

If I think too much about last night, I'm not going to make it through a normal conversation with him.

"Eden?"

I look up. "Sorry?"

He smiles. "So, you're writing something inspired by this vacation."

"Oh, yes. I'm still at the plotting stage, though, but I'll start the actual writing when I get back home."

"You're taking real-life inspiration?"

"Yeah, definitely. The resort is stunning, and so is the beach, nature, all of it. I'm going to use as much as I can."

He raises an eyebrow. "And for characters?"

That makes me smile. "You want to know if a version of you is in it?"

"Maybe," he says. "Is there an annoying, table-stealing jerk?"

"No table stealing as of yet," I say, looking very serious. "But I do have an overworked character who's brought his laptop with him on a vacation. He's going to be a mysterious background character and the main suspect in the murder investigation."

"The *main* suspect?"

"Yes."

Phillip shakes his head. "I would never be the main suspect."

"Come on, you're pretty mysterious."

"But I'm a lawyer," he protests. "I would know how to conduct myself in order *not* be a suspect."

"I thought you never worked on criminal cases."

"I'm a mergers and acquisitions lawyer *now*. But I did parts of my internship at a courthouse, and I've read hundreds and hundreds of pages of criminal cases in law school."

"Really?"

"I knew that would excite you."

"You're like the ultimate true crime fan. That's what a lawyer is, you know."

He shakes his head, but he's laughing. "You're unbelievable."

I sit up straighter. "But it's true! You guys were the first-ever fans. Some of the cases I've followed, you must be an expert in."

"I'm an expert in all things," he says.

"Right, of course, but like *an actual* expert." My eyes widen. "Hey, on second thought, don't read any of my books. Ever."

"Why not?"

"Because I'm sure I've made every mistake in the book when it comes to legalese."

"Don't you want that pointed out?"

"Not *after* the book is finished!"

He stands, stretching. His body should be familiar to me now, after yesterday, but the long planes of his frame, and the muscles of his stomach and chest still beckon me to explore.

"You'll have to use me before it's finished, then," he says.

"You'd take time out of your precious schedule for that?"

Phillip crosses the distance to me. He leans a hand on each armrest. "I think I'd find the time," he says. "Especially if it would mean reading about a version of myself."

"Your fictional vacation self," I say.

"Exactly."

I uncurl my legs and lie flat on the lounge chair. "What is your hourly rate, anyway?"

He leans down. "Why do you want to know?"

I shrug, trying to look nonchalant. "Maybe I'm just curious to know what last night would've cost me."

His eyes widen, and then he chuckles. The sound is dark. "Baby, I would never have charged you."

"Mmm." I spread my legs a little and arch my back. "You weren't exactly giving legal advice, either."

"Not a lick of it," he murmurs and kisses me.

It starts slow and deep. Skin warm from the sun where I drag my hands over his arms. His knee comes to rest between my thighs, and I tug at him to get closer. He lowers, bracing over me on the lounger.

It creaks us.

"Worth the risk," I say.

His mouth is at my collarbone. "What risk?"

"Doesn't matter," I murmur and pull my knees up to grip his hips. *Good thing we're not on the public beach.*

His kisses are lazy. He's taking the scenic route over my skin, and I drag my hands over the broad muscles of his back, not in a hurry, either.

This man was made to be savored.

"I want to keep you here for the rest of our stay," he mutters, his hand coming up to cup my breast over my bikini top. "You know, if you don't want any tan lines…"

"Oh, that's so helpful of you."

His smile is crooked. "It's pure selflessness."

I lock my hands behind his neck and pull him down to kiss him. I don't think I'll get enough of that before this trip comes to an end. I'd forgotten how good it feels to just kiss a man and be kissed in return. I could do this for hours.

Against my thigh, I feel him—already hard—and the anticipation makes my stomach tighten.

He tugs the bikini top to the side.

"Whoops," I whisper.

He gives a wolfish smile and bends to take my nipple in his mouth. I sigh, digging my fingers into his hair.

Best decision ever, I think. *Going on this vacation.*

The sound of his ringing phone cuts through the moment. I chuckle against him. I'm not really capable of movement right now, my arms and legs are locked around him.

The ringing persists.

"Phillip," I murmur.

He shakes his head once, fingers still teasing my nipple. "Let it ring," he murmurs. "I'm with an attractive twentysomething-year-old."

I laugh again. "That's not what I meant the other day."

My mind had pictured women in beautiful dresses and heels, sipping drinks with him in hotel bars in Chicago. Young professionals with similar life trajectories.

The phone stops ringing.

"Yeah, of course you didn't," he says. It sounds like sarcasm. The realization that he meant what he said seeps through me like warm honey. Compliment-starved. Maybe that's what I am.

His mouth closes around my right nipple, and I sigh at the sensation. The tug of his teeth and the lap of his tongue, and the hard, solid weight of his body on top of mine.

"My vacation self," I murmur, "is very pleased with herself right now."

He chuckles darkly and trails kisses over the curve of my other breast, yanking the bikini top clean off. Warmth pools in my stomach and spreads out through my limbs.

His phone starts to ring again.

Phillip doesn't react and doesn't change the tight grip of his hands or the press of his body against mine.

"Another one of your colleagues?" I murmur, weaving my fingers into his hair. "Do I need to tell Briggs off again?"

Phillip chuckles. There's a flush on his face, staining his skin beneath the tan, and the eyes on mine are all pupils. "I wouldn't want to be in his shoes."

I grin and push against his chest. He gives a low groan of disappointment, and I laugh, wriggling out from beneath him.

"Eden," he says.

I walk backward towards his phone, smiling. Adrenaline pumps through me. "You're on vacation!" I say. "They should learn."

I reach for his phone and hit reply. "Phillip Meyer's phone," I say sweetly. "Is this an emergency?"

There's silence on the other end. I wait for a response and watch Phillip pull himself into sitting. There's a carefully neutral expression on his face.

A woman's voice comes through the phone. "Who is this?"

"A friend of Phillip's," I say. "He's on vacation."

"Yeah, I know," she says. Her voice is hard now. "Tell him to call me back, will you? Whoever you are. It's important."

"His office was notified that he would be on vacation," I say, "but I'll let him know all the same. And who should I say is calling?"

"His fiancée," she says. And then she hangs up.

I take a moment before I lower the phone. Phillip is beside me now and he takes it from me. "Eden."

I cross my arms over my bare chest. "I shouldn't have answered that."

"It's fine," he says. "You okay?"

I nod. "Yeah. Maybe I should find my bikini top..."

He stops me with a hand on my shoulder. There's a furrow between his brows again, drawing them together into an angry line. "What did she say? Eden?"

"You knew who it was?"

"I suspected," he says and runs a hand through his hair.

Staring at the devastatingly serious expression on his face, I hear the word fiancée echo through my mind.

I push past him toward my chair. My bikini top is lying across one of the armrests, and I snap it up.

"Eden," he says again. "I'm sorry I let you answer that."

"No, no, I was the one who insisted," I say, standing with my back to him and tie up my bikini top. Shame and something else, something painful, burns in my stomach.

I knew he'd been about to get married just weeks before coming here. That was nothing new. So why does it hurt so bad to be reminded of that fact?

"She's been a nuisance this whole week," he says. "Calls with thin excuses about logistics, only to start with apologies or to pick fights. I've started to ignore her."

"Yeah," I say, nodding so fast my vision goes blurry. I turn and reach for my cover-up. After quickly pulling it over my bikini, I stick my feet into my sandals.

Fiancée. The word feels heavy with possibility. Could they have decided to take time apart, instead of breaking up fully?

Maybe they're still planning to figure things out. But he had said he didn't love her… My brain fractures, spiraling in ten different directions at once.

Besides, that should be okay. Because he's only a distraction from my own pain, isn't he?

"Eden," he murmurs, hand landing on my shoulder again.

"She said she was your fiancée." I shift from one foot to the other.

"Well, she's not."

"Not even a little bit?"

"In no possible way," he says, voice hard. "Zero."

"What happened between you?"

He looks at me for a long moment. Beneath the beard, his jaw is tense.

I sigh. "Look, I'm sorry. I should not have answered. I shouldn't have… thanks for today."

"She left me at the altar."

My breath whooshes out of me. "Oh. You never told me."

"Yeah, because it's pretty fucking humiliating."

I chuckle. It's half astonishment, half shock. "Phillip, my fiancé *cheated* on me for months with one of my best friends. That's embarrassing as hell, too."

"No," he says. "That just proves he's a dipshit."

"I'm sorry," I say. "That… I'm sorry. It must have sucked."

Because despite it all, I'm glad I found out before I ever had to put on my wedding dress, and before the venue filled with all of our relatives.

He hadn't gotten that courtesy.

Phillip looks over my shoulder, at some spot in the distance. "It is what it is. Honestly, I'm… relieved."

"Relieved?"

"Yeah. I was pissed off at first, but now I'm pretty sure it was for the best. She and I are better off apart."

"Why did she call herself your fiancée?"

"Probably because you picked up, and she wanted to stir up shit," he says, voice dripping with annoyance. "In her last phone call, she hinted that we could continue as before, too."

"Oh."

"Which just means she probably realized how expensive rent is in the area where she wants to live. Eden, none of this has anything to do with you. Or with what just happened." He inclines his head toward the lounge chair like it's the scene of a crime.

"No, I know."

"You do? Then why do you look like you're about to race out of here like you just found out I'm a convicted mass murderer?"

I laugh, but it's a bit strained. "It's just a lot. All of it. Your past, and my own, and what just happened..."

It sinks in, as I look at him, that we're each other's rebounds. That this ends in a few short days, and I'll never see him again, and that probably doesn't bother him at all. This truly *is* a vacation fling for him, but it's starting to feel like something else for me, and I can't have that. Not again.

"Okay," he says. "I get it."

I shift back on my heels and take a step toward the gate. "Thanks for today. Sorry again for the... well. Is it okay if I take a rain check on dinner tonight? I just need some time to think."

He nods, but his blue eyes are troubled. "You've got nothing to apologize for."

As I close the gate softly behind me, all I can hear is the sound of crashing waves and the rapid beating of my heart.

Chapter Twenty-three

"Oh my God," Becky says on the phone. "If you're making this up, please keep going. I want to live in this fantasy forever."

I chuckle. "You're the one living the fantasy."

"I can't see my feet anymore," she says. "I've officially *lost* my feet, Eden, and I won't find them for another month. If that's anyone's fantasy, they're absolutely off their socks."

"I mean, they could be," I say. "How would they be able to tell?"

She giggles. "Tell me again. What did he say when you asked him about it? The fiancée?"

"He said they're definitely broken up. Like, one hundred percent."

"Isn't that great news?"

"Yes," I say, "but, Becks, he's only been single for like five weeks."

"Well, his relationship couldn't have been that good anyway since he's on his honeymoon alone and in the process of falling for you."

That makes me scoff. I shift my phone to the other ear and stick my feet into my sandals. It's later than I've typically been getting up here, and I'll be cutting my time short with the breakfast buffet, but I needed the extra hours of sleep.

"He's not falling for me," I say. "If anything, it's a rebound fling. We both fly out in two days time."

"And isn't that exactly what you need?" she asks. "Exactly what you deserve?"

I make sure to grab my guidebook and key card. Never forgetting that one again. "Yes. I just didn't expect it to be so complicated."

"So complicated?"

"Yes," I say and close the door behind me. "He's very different from any man I've dated before, and well… I think I might have a crush."

"Oh no," she says.

"Yeah, I know."

"Where's he from again?"

"Chicago. I know, I know, and I was fully prepared for this ending. It's just that I'm a teeny bit afraid I've gotten attached."

On the other end of the line, I hear her sigh. "I'm sure I would, too. The whole casual thing is hard."

"Yeah," I say. Her husband, Patrick, is an accountant with too many dad jokes and a killer instinct when it comes to playing board games. They met six years ago, but even before that, she hadn't been a big dater. "It's not like either of us has a lot of experience with it."

"None," she agrees. "But maybe it's good that whatever happens on the island stays there. You can come back home, rejuvenated, having had a rebound, and all ready to get back out there."

"Thanks for trying to make it sound like a good thing," I say. I'll be returning to a half-decorated house, the one I'd been lucky to get on such short notice after my engagement imploded.

It's a quick drive from the school where I work and fifteen minutes from both my parents' and Becky's houses. On paper, it's perfect, but it doesn't feel like home yet.

"Eden," Becky says. "You don't owe anyone anything. Not

Caleb, not Phillip's ex-fiancée, and not him, either. You do you."

"Yeah. I know, and you're right. The whole thing is just taking me by surprise. I feel like it got real somehow, by hearing his ex's voice."

"Of course it's surprising. You expected to spend two weeks sitting with a book on a beach, and what you got was a non-stop flirtation with a hot-as-hell rich dude."

I laugh in the elevator, and the middle-aged couple beside me gives me a look. I smile apologetically.

"Yeah. Sorry, I'm almost at breakfast. Thanks for the pep talk."

"Anytime. It's not like I envy you or anything, of course," she says. "Having hot makeout sessions in the Caribbean."

I chuckle again. "Bye, Becky."

"Bye."

When I reach the breakfast bar and the overflowing buffet, most tables are empty. The majority of vacationers must have gotten a jump on the day. I have my pick of the place.

I grab a glass of tropical juice, mango this time, and a cup of coffee, and head toward the table that's become mine.

But it's not empty.

Phillip sits in the chair opposite mine. He's reading on a tablet and has a cup of coffee in front of him. His hair looks damp, and it wouldn't surprise me if he was up early and swum his laps in the hotel pool. What a madman.

"Hi," I say.

He looks up. "Good morning, Eden."

I shift from one foot to another, debating setting my glass of juice down on the table.

"Join me?" he asks.

I slowly pull out the chair. "Yeah, thanks. I'm not used to seeing you here."

"I decided to check out the buffet," he says.

I look meaningfully at the lack of a plate before him.

He chuckles. "I had pancakes a while ago."

"You've been waiting for me?"

"I might've been," he admits and puts down the tablet. I catch the headline. He's reading the Chicago news. "You're up later than usual today."

"Yeah, I wanted to sleep in."

He nods. Color rises up his cheeks, but the eyes on mine are as steady as always. "Right. I'll come with you, I want another cup."

We fill up our plates. Mine with pancakes, fruit, a piece of toast, and a little bowl of acai and granola. His, another large cup of coffee and a croissant.

Nerves turn over in my stomach as we sit back down. He's the one who broaches the topic, leaning back in the chair.

"About yesterday," he says.

I shake my head. "Yeah, I shouldn't have answered your phone like that. It was crossing a line. But I'm glad you explained the situation afterward. Thanks for that. For clarifying, I mean."

"Mm-hmm," he says. He hasn't shaved today, either, and the beard is growing in, accentuating his sharp jaw. "Eden, I wasn't trying to hide anything from you."

"No, I get that."

"She's the last person I want to talk about while I'm here," he says. "Especially with you."

"Especially with me?"

"Yes. An attractive woman, fun conversations, and a paradise island. Why would I want to bring up my ex?"

I grimace. "I've spoken a lot about mine."

"Yeah, but I enjoy hearing you talk." He stretches his neck, like he's shared too much. "Anyway. She's not my fiancée anymore, Eden. I'm not like your ex."

"No, I know," I say, nodding again. "I realized that."

"Just wanted to make that clear."

"Mm-hmm." I take a sip of my juice. "Got it. And you're not, by the way. You're super different."

"Super different?"

"Yes. Well, so far, at least. I don't know what you're like outside of fancy resorts and catamaran cruises, you know."

He snorts and reaches for his croissant. The sleeves of his button-down are rolled up, the linen fabric slightly rumpled. Combined with the thickening facial hair and the unstyled strands, he looks even more handsome. Manly and relaxed.

I attack my pancakes to keep from attacking him.

"Perhaps I'm different back home," he says. "But aren't you?"

I consider the question. "Yes. I usually wear more clothes."

He laughs. It breaks the tension between us, resets the score, and I smile down at my food. It feels like a small victory every time I get a laugh out of him.

"What a bummer," he says.

I roll my eyes, but I'm smiling. "Yeah. I bet the men of Pinecrest are real sad about that."

"They should be," he says. He reaches down to his tablet and locks the screen, turning it over.

I take a deep breath. "Yesterday, I reacted pretty strongly by needing time alone. Some of it was that call, but it was also… I got a bit overwhelmed."

His eyes are locked on mine. *Go on,* they say.

"It's been a lot, you know? Meeting you, going on excursions, and… staying in."

"It has," he says.

"I've enjoyed all of it," I say quickly. "A lot. And then, I realized we only have two days left, and the real world is waiting for me when I get back…"

A smile hides in the corner of his mouth. "Right."

"Anyway, I overreacted, and I want to make sure we make the best out of our remaining time here."

"Good," he says. "Because I agree completely."

I smile widely at him. "Awesome."

"So, what are your plans for your last days on the island?"

My hand goes to the guidebook, lying beside my phone on the table. There are a few pages earmarked that I had hoped…

Phillip clocks the motion. "Ah. What does the holy book say?"

"There's tons to do here," I say. "As I'm sure your fabulous travel planner told you."

He nods. "There's an appendix to my itinerary with a history of the island."

"No way?"

"Yes."

"Can I see it?"

His eyes dance. "Maybe later. Come on, tell me what magical place you have bookmarked in the guidebook. I can see the Post-it notes from here."

"Well, we saw most of the things during our drive. I'm really glad we did that. But there's a spot on the south coast that's supposed to have a lot of surfing and a really nice restaurant. I know we've already—"

"We could go there," he says. "Make sure you get to see the entire island."

"Yes. But in all fairness, it's not terribly large."

"It's about one-sixth of Rhode Island," Phillip says and reaches for my guidebook. He raps it twice with his knuckles. "Should we rent a car again? To make sure we check it off your list."

"Yeah. Sure. Yes, that would work."

He nods and takes another bite of his croissant. Dark hair falls over his smooth forehead. No furrow this time, like it was always a foregone conclusion that we'd spend the day together.

I find myself smiling at him. For all of his complicated past, he's great at making this—us—wonderfully uncomplicated.

"What?" he asks.

I shake my head, still smiling. "Nothing. Just that I'm glad you were on your honeymoon alone at the same time as me."

He runs a hand over his mouth, hiding his own grin. "Yeah. Come on, eat your pancakes, Eden. The island awaits."

"Admit it," I say. "You're having more fun here than you expected."

Phillip reaches over and flicks me across the nose. It's something my older cousin used to do, but I don't think anyone has since I was twelve.

"I admit it," he says. "Now, come on. I want to hear more about the plot for your next book. Have you decided on the murder victim yet?"

I smile at my juice. Two days left.

But I'm not going to waste another minute of them.

Chapter Twenty-four

The book on my lap is the third and final one I brought on the trip. I thought I'd have them all read in the first week, with having so much time to myself, but the days have been fuller than I expected.

It has a lot to do with the man lying in the chair beside mine.

After our conversation at the breakfast buffet yesterday, we'd spent the entire day together. The evening, too, which had been room service and sex in his bungalow. A pretty great combination, I'm coming to learn.

Phillip had been at the breakfast buffet again this morning, sitting at my table and reading the newspaper on his tablet. Drinking a cup of black coffee. Half-eaten pancake on his plate.

Good morning, he'd said, eyes glittering. *Sleep well?*

Over breakfast, we'd decided the previous day's car rental was enough excitement, and our last full day should be spent at the resort. On the beach, in fact, with our feet in the sand and faces to the sun.

I glance at him, resting beside me. Last night had been just as good as the night before. We've slept together several times now, and each time has been better than the last.

It has to reach a zenith at some point, but it seems we're not there, yet.

Noon. That's when my flight leaves tomorrow, taking me to Seattle. At 5:45 p.m. the same afternoon, he'll leave, too, and we'll never see each other again.

Phillip glances at me. "You're thinking about something."

I smile. "Well, I always am."

He pushes into sitting and looks out at the ocean, shading his eyes from the bright light. "It looks like it might rain."

I glance up at the clear, blue sky. The only cloud in sight is a thin sliver of white, right along the horizon.

"Ah," I say. "You're right."

"I think it's best we head inside or we might get drenched."

"Grab some shelter?"

"Yes," he says, eyes sparkling. "Even though I know just how much you enjoy the rain."

We walk up the sandy beach and past the resort's pool. The backs of our hands brush with every step, and energy buzzes through me.

"You know, I haven't seen your hotel room," he says.

I smile down at my sandals. "Really? It's pretty great. Makes your bungalow look... well, I don't want to say the word, but gauche."

He chuckles. "Gauche?"

"Yeah."

He holds the button for the elevator doors and motions for me to enter. "Well, you have me intrigued now."

"As you should be." I whip out my key card, brandishing it in the air between us like a trophy. "It's a testament to minimalism."

He gives a sage nod. "I see. The Japanese kind or the Scandinavian?"

"A mix." I walk in front of him down the hall, past the vending machine. "Observe," I say.

"Ah, the famous vending machine?" he asks and gives it a brief pat. "To think, it caused so much trouble."

"I give it the finger every time I pass," I say.

"Well, I should thank it," Phillip says. "It meant you ended up in the pool with me at midnight."

I reach my hotel door with a pounding heart and look over my shoulder at him. His eyes are heated, and his hands are in his pockets, and I know exactly what will happen if I let him into my little room with the AC unit in the corner, the beautiful carpeting, and the bright overhead lighting.

I turn the handle.

It's slower this time. We take our time getting undressed, and he kisses every inch of my chest before he lets me take off his shirt.

I bury my hand in his hair and rake my nails over his scalp, and he groans, lips at my hipbone. I'd discovered just how much he enjoyed that yesterday.

"I want to try something," I murmur and push at his shoulders. He lets me tug down his shorts and watches with color on his cheeks as I take him in my mouth.

He curses, eyes never leaving mine, and I feel powerful. I'm my vacation self *and* I'm my regular Pinecrest self at the same time, and I'm watching a man come undone by my touch.

I haven't felt like this in a long, long time.

"Fuck," he says and slides a hand into my hair. "I don't know what I'm gonna—oh."

I've sheathed my teeth and upped the pressure, and he tips his head back, words forgotten. I feel like a goddess.

"You're too good at that," he mutters.

He pulls me up twenty seconds later, his eyes laser-focused on my underwear. He tugs them down, and then I'm on my back, the sunburn faded, watching him roll on a condom with lightning speed. He pushes into me a heartbeat later.

I tighten my legs around him and hold onto his shoulders,

and I don't let myself think that this might be one of the last times we do this.

Getting attached wasn't part of the deal. Not the one I made with him, and definitely not the one I made with myself.

I'm not ready to have these feelings again, and I'm certainly not ready to get hurt again. *Write books. Teach my students. Decorate my new house.*

Pine over Phillip is nowhere on that list.

He slows down and thrusts deeper, his movements like waves crashing against me. He lifts one of my legs, and it takes me no time at all to finish. And I don't know if it's the sex itself, or him. This. The fact that we've been so open about all of it from the start.

A long time later, we amble down the corridor to the elevators. Phillip's hand plays with the tie of my bikini top, hanging out over the back of my sundress.

"I love this one," he mumbles. "The purple one. It looks so good on you."

"Thank you." Warmth blooms in my chest, and I pull him into the elevator. "I have an idea."

He leans in, an arm braced on the elevator wall next to me. "Tell me."

"They sell postcards in the lobby. I've seen them before."

His eyebrows lower. "Not where I thought you were going with this."

I chuckle. "I know, but hear me out. Let's send a postcard to each other."

"To each other?"

"Yes. I've heard of how long it can sometimes take for international mail. We might get them in two weeks, or two months, or never. But if they arrive, it'll be a little reminder of this." I rest my hand on his chest, and through the linen of his shirt, I can feel the beating of his heart.

A reminder of you, I think.

"What would we write?" he asks.

"Anything we want. But it'd be a secret."

"Ah, neither of us would know until we get our card."

"Exactly," I say. "Are you game?"

His mouth tips up into a smile, and his hand brushes over my cheek. "Sure."

We stand on either side of the little display of postcards. Up top is a sign that says the concierge will be happy to postmark and send them on their way. It's a complimentary service, apparently, and if I ever suspected this wasn't a five-star resort, this would have convinced me.

"Which one are you choosing?" I ask Phillip, looking at all the versions of tropical beaches.

"I'm not telling," he says.

"What?"

"The whole thing is supposed to be a surprise, right?"

"Yes."

"Then so will my choice of the card," he says. He holds up a card and an envelope in one hand and steps back. "Don't peek."

"I would never!"

"Right," he says and raises an eyebrow. "Remember, I'm a lawyer. Breaking the rules is a suable offense."

"It absolutely is not."

"That's your last warning," he says with a smile and turns around to the concierge. I'm smiling at his back. He asks for a pen, and I watch as he writes down whatever it is he wants to say to future me.

What do I want to say?

I choose a postcard with a map of the island on it, and with my marker, I draw a little heart around the Oistins Fish Market.

I hesitate for a few seconds before I start writing.

Hello from Barbados,

By the time you read this, you'll be back at your twenty-four-seven job, merging and acquiring. But I don't want you to forget your vacation self. How rarely you shaved, and how you told your coworkers to fend for themselves. Your vacation self was a tough nut to crack in the beginning... but he turned out to be a really great guy. I didn't expect to meet him, but I'm really glad it happened. And I want you to remember it, too. How you were. Don't forget to relax sometime and watch the metaphorical turtles hatch.

And if you ever want to take a trip to Pinecrest, I'd love to be your guide.

Thanks for everything,
Eden.

I finish the tiny scrawl on the postcard. My words don't feel like enough. Not at all. But as I look over at him, standing tall by the concierge and conversing with an employee, I realize he probably isn't writing beautiful poetry or anything, either.

Don't fall off any more boats, perhaps. Some quip about the baby turtles hatching, maybe. A dig at my guidebook, for sure.

Phillip and I exchange addresses. I had his memorized from the itinerary, but I pretend I don't, and write it out on the back of my postcard.

Both of our missives disappear in the hand of a smiling receptionist who assures us they'll be mailed first thing Monday morning.

"Let's see whose makes it home first," Phillip says as we walk out of the lobby.

I nudge his shoulder with mine. "You just have to make everything into a contest, don't you?"

"It's what makes life interesting," he says. But then, he puts an arm around my waist and pulls me into his side, pressing a kiss to my temple. "But I like it best when we're both winning."

I smile against his shoulder. Public displays of affection? This is dangerous for my overworked heart, but I lean into him because I know it's too late regardless. It'll hurt when this ends.

We walk past the arguing sisters I'd spotted those early days on the beach. One of them gives us an irritated glare and then mutters to the other in a British accent. "Look, even more honeymooners. I told you this place was…"

I chuckle. Beside me, Phillip shakes his head. "Those are fighting words."

"Good thing you have your hands full," I say with a smile.

His hand tightens around my waist. "Spend tonight at my place."

"The whole night?"

"Yes," he says. "You'll still be up in plenty of time to enjoy your final taste of the breakfast buffet, I promise."

We step out into the late afternoon sun. The clear sky promises a brilliant sunset, my final one on the island.

"Okay," I say. "One last night."

He kisses my temple again. "One last night."

Chapter Twenty-five

We eat room service on his patio while looking out at the ocean and the setting sun beyond. The insects serenade all around us, and as happy as I am to be flying back home to my own bed and my couch and the familiarity of tomorrow, I know I'll miss this.

Nostalgia is heavy in my chest, and I haven't even left the moment I'm in, yet. But somehow, I know I'll come to miss it long after it's passed.

Phillip sits across from me. He has a serene look on his face, perfectly at ease with himself. No turmoil at all. As if it'll be nothing more than a simple goodbye and *wish you all the best* and *have a safe flight* for him.

He looks over at me. "So, have you decided on an outcome for your mysterious businessman yet?" he asks. "In your story?"

I blink a few times. "Oh. Um, not yet. At first, I was going to have him be involved in the affair, the one the main couple is uncovering, but now, I'm not sure anymore."

"No?"

"No," I say. Yesterday, while I was writing in my notepad before bed, I had the image of him sneaking away with the female main character. Maybe that's the romance story, the one I've been struggling to figure out these past two weeks.

Maybe he's just misunderstood. He's accused of the murder, and my main character has to work to clear his name… while questioning her own judgment.

"Eden?" Phillip prods.

"Sorry." I look up at the beautiful, colorful sky. It looks as vast as the ocean spreading out in front of us. "I think, I would have been so miserable," I say, "if I was that astronaut."

He frowns. "Michael Collins?"

"Yeah." To my horror, my eyes well up. I can feel them betraying me. I blink a few times to try to clear my vision. "Sorry. I'm just thinking about what happens after this."

He grows still. "You are?"

"Yeah. It's stupid. Sorry, I think I'm just being sentimental."

"Sentimental?"

I nod, and a stupid tear slips down my cheek. "Yeah, at the thought of going home tomorrow. Of leaving… the resort."

"I see," he says, but he looks so distressed that I quickly shake my head.

"Don't worry, I'm not… I knew what this was, you know. This has been great. I hope it was just what you needed, too. We both had a rebound, right? A vacation fling."

His frown deepens. "Right."

I force a note of cheer into my voice. "And I broke my one-man-for-life streak! Thank you for helping with that."

He nods and reaches for his drink. But he's silent.

"Anyway, I didn't expect any of this, but I'm grateful for it." I chuckle, and it sounds a bit deranged. "I didn't expect a lot of things that happened during this trip. Like Kaelie swinging by uninvited and dropping bombs."

Phillip's voice is quiet. "What do you mean?"

"Well, she said that Caleb wants me back."

His eyebrows lower. "Did she?"

"Yeah. Not that it'll ever happen or anything."

"And he sent his cousin here to deliver that message to you? That's psychotic."

I laugh again. It sounds a bit more real this time. "You know what, I completely agree."

"You are better off without him."

"Totally," I say. My tears have stopped. I'm almost in full control again, and I hope I haven't freaked him out too much. And that he doesn't think I was crying over him. That I'm upset over losing *this,* whatever it is, and the possibility of it ever becoming anything more.

Even if I am.

"Eden," he says again, and there's roughness in his voice now. "What are you going to do after you get back home?"

"I'm going to take the longest shower known to man. I'm going to develop my photos, and I'm going to write a book and research self-publishing." My glass is almost empty. I set it down beside me and cross the space to him.

He's still sitting very still.

"I'm also going to make sure my vacation self makes an appearance every now and then."

"You are?"

I nod and put my hands on his shoulders. He opens his arms and pulls me down on his lap. He's warm and familiar, even after this short time. My heart constricts.

"I'm going to say yes to more things. To life," I say.

"To seeing more turtles hatch?" he says.

I nod, my hands flat against his chest. His eyes are locked on mine, and there's an intensity there I haven't seen in the past few days.

"To taking chances," I say.

"Hmm."

"Which you should do, too."

He raises an eyebrow. "I should?"

"Yes. Don't forget your vacation self when you're back in Chicago."

He catches a lock of my hair between his fingers and

twists it around, eyes locked on the motion. "It would be very hard to," he says.

My hands find the top button of his linen shirt. I undo it, and then the second, so I can feel the warmth of his chest beneath. "Don't go back to her," I whisper.

He looks up at me sharply. "I won't."

"Good," I murmur. "Because you deserve a lot better than someone who cheats on you."

His hands slide down to my waist and grip me tight, like he would keep me on his lap forever. "So do you, Eden. So do you."

I spent my final night on the island in Phillip's bungalow. Room service, drinks, and the casual banter I'd come to enjoy so much with him. We had sex in his giant, luxurious bed, originally meant for two newlyweds.

He'd kissed me with crushing intensity and I'd dug my nails into his shoulders, closing my eyes and wondered how I will survive with only these memories to remember him by. Afterward, he'd tucked me into the curve of his body, and his deep breathing had lulled me into sleep.

It's the next morning, D-day. Departure day. I use his shower before we head to the breakfast buffet together.

"Have you checked in?" he asks me, and I nod, digging into my pancakes. "Booked a car?"

"No, I'll ask the front desk to call me a taxi."

"Good," he says. "Picked your seat on the airplane?"

I smile at him across the table. His dark-blue eyes are warm, his face so familiar after all the days we've spent together. "Are you a nervous flier?" I ask.

He shakes his head. "I'm a prepared one."

"Well, I have prepared. Remember, I'm the queen of guidebooks. Of research."

"That's right. How colorful is your luggage tag? Does it have glitter on it?"

I stick out my tongue at him.

He blinks in surprise before he chuckles warmly. "So that's a yes."

"Eat your pancake," I say. Singular. Because that's all he's allowed himself. Along with a huge plate of bacon and fruit.

He's smiling as he digs in.

The time for my flight comes too soon. Butterflies chase one another in my stomach, throwing me off-kilter. I feel like there's still a conversation left to be had. But I'm not sure if it's a conversation I can handle, either.

My emotional outburst last night hadn't allowed for it, and today, I've been focused on packing and eating and trying not to cry whenever I look at Phillip.

I request a taxi from the front desk, leave my key card in the designated checkout box, and walk with Phillip out of the lobby. He's silent beside me, carrying my bag. I look at him out of the corner of my eye. He's wearing his shades again, and he looks tall and handsome. I wish I could keep him.

I wish there was some way to make this last, even if we're several states apart and leading two very different lives.

We come to a stop at the curb.

"So," I say.

He takes off his sunglasses. "So."

"I'm really glad you were here, too."

His lips lift in one corner. "Yeah, me, too. Even if the circumstances that led us here weren't great."

"I've had better years," I agree.

He runs a hand through his hair. "I'll be waiting for your postcard. Back in Chicago."

"I'll be waiting for yours," I say. "If it doesn't get lost in international mail."

He nods again. "Eden… thank you."

"For what?"

He takes a deep breath, and the moment between us

stretches out into silence. But then he speaks. "For being my guide."

"Oh. Well, I enjoyed that. Thanks for sharing so many of your planned activities." I shift from one foot to the other, the unspoken, useless words hovering on the tip of my tongue.

"I enjoyed the company," he says.

My taxi pulls up, and I rock back on my heels. "Well."

"Yeah," he says.

The cab driver rolls down a window. "You're the one going to the airport?" he calls.

"Yeah."

Phillip takes a step closer. "Eden," he says, and there's frustration there. "I wish I could… come here."

He pulls me against him and tips my head back. He kisses me—hard—lips against mine, hands bruising on my hips. I twine my fingers into his hair and *thank you,* I think, *for letting me experience this.*

I don't want to step back. I don't want to get in the car. And most of all, I really don't want him to let me go.

He kisses me like he feels the same way.

"Sorry, you two," the cab driver calls. "There's a minibus coming up behind me. Should I park…?"

Phillip steps back, his eyes heated and mouth set in a grim line. "She's coming," he says, but his eyes never leave mine. "Bye, Eden."

"Bye, Phillip," I whisper.

He lifts my bag into the trunk of the cab, closing the door behind him. I get into the car, but I can't stop looking at him. I watch him as the taxi pulls away and heads down the Winter Resort driveway toward the main road.

Phillip remains standing by the lobby doors, watching my retreating car. Stoic, imposing, and alone.

I lean my head back against the seat. My heart is beating fast. I don't even have his number. He never offered his digits, and I didn't give him mine.

Maybe this is the way it was always meant to end. Just

two weeks. Two strangers who enjoyed some time together, soothing their hurts… even if it means they aren't strangers at all anymore. Quite the opposite.

We make it ten minutes from the resort before panic sets in. What if my postcard never arrives? What if his never does?

I'll have no way of finding him.

"Can we go back?" I ask the driver. "Please. Just a quick stop. I forgot… something."

"Passport?" he asks.

My heart is pounding. "Yeah, I think so."

"No worries," the driver says and sends me a smile through the rearview mirror. "Small island. I'll still have you at the airport in plenty of time."

"Thank you," I say. "I promise I'll be a really great tipper."

He laughs. "You have the look of one." He turns the car around on a side street and cranks up the volume of the radio, humming along.

Phillip isn't in the lobby when I return. I leave my bag in the cab and take off at a run, racing down to the bungalow area. I weave past The Sandpiper and The Green Monkey and head toward The Hawksbill. I rush past the hedged patio and toward the gate. He has to be here, where else would he be? He *has* to be here.

That's when I hear his voice.

"—yeah, I've just finished it with her. For good."

I freeze, my heels slapping against the stone path.

"No, I won't miss her. Genuinely, Tess. It was good for what it was, but it wasn't meant to last. All I feel now is relief."

He's quiet for a few beats. That's when I recognize the name. Tess. His sister. Are they talking about me? It could be. It might be.

"Right. It was tiring hearing about all the wild ambitions she'll never follow through on, too. Do you know she asked me to read a contract the other day?"

My heart stops.

Just flat-out stops.

It is me. It has to be. So, it was good while it lasted, was it? And I'll never achieve my wild ambitions. Just like Caleb used to say. My fingers tingle, as if I've touched an exposed live wire.

Seems like I've misjudged someone yet again.

"Yeah, I know. I told her to stop—" he continues, but I can't hear anymore. I turn around and race back up the path, toward the lobby and the waiting car.

This time, it doesn't stop on its way to the airport.

Chapter Twenty-six

Three Weeks Later

"Okay," Becky says. She's sitting on my couch, her feet up on the coffee table. Her cup of tea is perched on top of her giant stomach. "So, the two sisters who are always arguing. They are the real killers?"

"Yes!"

"Okay, I love that. I suspected them from the very beginning, you know."

I chuckle. "Of course you did."

She wiggles her toes. "This is great. I haven't seen you this fired up in months."

"It's a great story," I say. Maybe that's just because I'm in the magical phase, only ten thousand words into a new story and a little too in love with my own vision, but I believe it this time. "And you know what? Up until the *very* last moment, everyone will actually suspect the—"

"Businessman," Becky says and winks. "I remember."

"Well, I was thinking of changing him into this foreign banker, maybe in his sixties? He's just made a terrible financial decision and comes to the island to hide."

She frowns. "So he's not going to be our girl's love interest anymore?"

"No, not in that case." I pull up my legs beneath me, sitting like a pretzel on my armchair. Then I reach for a blanket and studiously drape it across my lap.

"Eden," she says.

I sigh. "Yeah, okay, so I can't figure out the businessman character."

"Because he's based on the real person," she says.

It's not a question, but I nod anyway. "Yeah, inspired by one, anyway. It would have been awesome if I could still… If I could separate my own experience from the inspiration."

"Maybe you can use your own experience."

"Yeah," I say. "It's just… if I write him as the mysterious businessman my main character initially suspects, and then falls in love with on the trip, and they have this whirlwind romance and then he's wrongfully accused, and they have to work together to solve the murder—"

"—and confront the murderous sisters and then ride off into the sunset together," Becky says, nodding vigorously. "I love it so much."

"Yeah, it's a good story. I think I could write it well. Maybe…"

"But?" she prompts, and her voice softens. "Is it because you'd have to give the main character a happy ending with him?"

I sigh again. "That makes me sound terribly petty, doesn't it?"

"I'm not sure it does, since the woman you'd be denying happiness is, you know, *fictional*."

I chuckle. "Yeah, you're right."

She reaches for another pillow to prop up behind her back, grunting as she does so. "Can we go through what happened one more time?"

"Do we have to?"

She points at her belly. "I could pop any second, my feet hurt, and I'm swollen absolutely everywhere."

"Okay, all right," I say with a grin. "We can do whatever you want."

"That's right," she says. "So, the conversation you overheard. Are you sure you heard what you think you did?"

I brace my head in my hands. "Yes, of course, I am. He mentioned reading the contract during his trip. *She asked me to*, that's what he said. It was pretty clear who he was talking about."

It's easier to discuss now than it had been the first time, just a few days after I returned to Pinecrest and met a bubbly Becky who wanted to hear all about my holiday romance.

It's still painful, but back then, it hurt on a physical level. A blade slicing clean through the roots of a new hope that had just started to grow.

Becky groans. "I hate that you can't just call him and ask. What the heck were you thinking, either of you, not exchanging numbers?"

I sigh again. "I don't know. I thought it was kind of romantic, at the time. We'd just be a vacation fling and a beautiful memory. And I was going to give him my number when I doubled back from the airport—that's why I overheard his conversation in the first place!"

"Men," she says and shakes her head.

I pick at the blanket. "The worst part is, I am angry at him, and I know that's not fair because wasn't I using him as a rebound, too? Trying to get over Caleb, to be intimate with someone new, to pass the days?" My voice is rising, and I force myself to take a deep breath. "So why am I so *furious* that he wanted the exact same thing?"

Becky smiles. "Because somewhere between all the snorkeling and rum drinking and sex-having, you caught feelings."

"Ugh."

"It's true. We both know it."

"I know," I say and look down at my lap. My jeans are

frayed at the hem, and there's a speck of glitter there from my kindergarten class earlier today. "I didn't want to."

"I know, Eden."

"What really gets me is that now I know how good it *can* be," I say, pointing a finger at her like it's her fault. "I know how incredible the sex with a near-stranger can be, but the odds of that happening again are zero. Z. E. R.O."

She nods, frowning. "Yeah, unfortunately, that's not super common."

"So I'll have to start dating," I say and throw my hands up like I've been consigned to the worst fate imaginable. "And every date I'm going to compare to Phillip."

She taps her nails against the porcelain of her mug. "Have you googled him?"

"Googled?"

"Don't pretend you haven't."

"Okay, yeah, I have."

She shines up. "And?"

"I found his law firm. A picture of a much younger him from an article in his college's newspaper."

"Impressive."

"And that's pretty much it. He's not on social media."

"No contact info?"

I sigh. "No. And even if I found any, or tried to contact his law firm, what good would it do? You know what he said to his sister. He was relieved that our fling was over."

The hurt burns in my chest. Anger, too. Both at him… and at myself. For believing again. So stupid.

"You could just tell him off about that," Becky suggests. "Send a letter through his law firm and tell him off for being a pig."

I narrow my eyes at her. "You just want to watch the world burn."

She nods, not denying it. "Of course, I do. I'm in pain, and I want everyone else to be."

"I'm still waiting for his postcard to arrive."

Her eyebrows fly high. "Oh my God. I forgot to check in on the postcard watch today. So, it hasn't arrived."

"It has not," I say. Every day after work, I text Becky to let her know that the postcard hasn't arrived. When I forget, she texts to ask. "But at this point, I'm not holding my breath."

"You should. International mail can be super slow and weird."

"Yeah, but what would it even say? Hope you have a nice life?" I shake my head. "Look, I think I'm better off just consigning it to the past. I caught feelings. It happened, but I won't let it happen again. Not for a while. After… after Caleb and Cindy, and now after Phillip, it's enough."

She nods. "Sensible. So, the businessman character is definitely out?"

"Definitely," I say. "I think the main character might have a surfer love interest instead, or maybe the hotel owner, or the manager? That could be hot."

Becky makes a humming sound as she listens, but I know she's secretly rooting for the brooding businessman. She's made that clear before.

And so was I, once. But I can't anymore.

I reach for my own cup of tea. "Anyway," I say. "What day are you planning on finally having this baby?"

Becky leans her head back against a pillow and groans. "God, I wish I knew! I wake up hoping that it's today."

Seeing her experience up close has given me a whole new level of respect for mothers. Pregnancy is no walk in the park, from the early weeks of nausea to the current pain in her pelvis. "She's probably just so snug in there," I say. "Never wants to leave."

Becky looks down at her stomach and runs a hand over it. "Well, her landlord is getting ready to evict her," she says, but her voice is softer now. "I also can't wait to meet her. I want her out here with us."

My heart swells. "Me too."

Becky takes a deep breath. "This is going to be a wild year for us, you know."

"Me included?"

She nods, her face serene. "Yeah. Because you're on your own journey now. I can tell."

I tap my fingers along my knee. "With…?"

"Everything," she says and waves a hand in the air. "Finally getting this place decorated and all yours. Writing this book and self-publishing. Living your dream, *yours,* and not Caleb's. Going on that trip was the first step. That was your dream. I want you to do more of that."

I chuckle. "Yeah, I'm so glad I ended up going."

"Me, too," she says, smiling wide. "The girl Patrick and I drove to the airport isn't the same as the one who came home."

"Really? I was moping in both directions," I say.

She laughs. "Yeah, but one was sad, and the other was angry. You've gotten your fire back."

Maybe I have. Maybe my vacation self had found it, and brought it back to me.

I have a job I enjoy. A book I'm excited to write. A family I love, a goddaughter on the way, and a new house that's all mine.

So what if a teeny, tiny little postcard hadn't arrived?

I'll just have to live with the memories of him instead.

Chapter Twenty-seven

I'm driving home from work when I get the call.

It had been a good day. A great one, even. My kindergarteners are currently exploring the solar system, and we'd spent the better part of the day creating papier-mâché replicas of Saturn.

During my lunch break, I'd grabbed my prepackaged salad and ate it in my car. It wasn't sad at all—it was necessary, because it let me write on my laptop all through lunch. I'd never have gotten the peace and quiet in the break room.

The killer sisters are quickly becoming the most interesting part of the story for me. I'm focusing more on them and the mystery and less on the romance.

Maybe because I still haven't solved the other little puzzle at the heart of it all… who's going to be the main character's love interest.

I've tried to brainstorm other characters. I even got really far into writing a version where the hotel manager was the romantic interest, but it didn't feel right. Nothing did. Does.

Except…

The one version of the story I'm not supposed to write; that hurts to write. The one where Phillip is my inspiration. The worst part is that I know it would be easy, like falling into a memory and pulling emotions out of experience rather than thin air.

But I don't want to think about him, because every time I do, I get angry.

At myself. At the situation. And then at him and for what he said on the phone to his sister, and because I could hear the relief in his voice. He was genuine. He meant every one of those words.

I suppose I'd gotten in the way of a lot of work for him those two weeks. And maybe it had been fun, being with me. Diverting, even. I couldn't deny that he had been... well... he'd wanted to have sex. A lot. He was attracted to me.

That counted for something, and I couldn't pretend it didn't. I had my confidence back in that area, at least.

It was just the *more* he didn't want.

And that's totally fine, if I think about it logically. Convenient, even, seeing as we don't live in the same state and are both getting out of our respective relationships. But I'm still angry and hurt that he came to that conclusion when I was starting to feel the opposite.

But... Onwards and upwards.

So I'm still in a good mood when I'm driving back home from work. Saturn, book writing, and the warmth of May in the air.

The call is from Becky. I put her on speakerphone and keep driving.

"Hey?"

"It's Patrick." His voice is rushed. "It's happening."

"It's happening?"

"Yes. We're on our way to the hospital now."

"Okay. I'll go pick up Ziggy," I say. Their Jack Russell mix hates being left alone, and none of us know how long their stay at the hospital would be.

We'd worked out this game plan months ago. Becky goes into labor; I go get the dog.

"Thanks," he says. There's a low groan in the background and then I hear Becky's voice, frantic and angry.

"Tell her not to forget his treats!"

"Right. Treats, Eden, remember—"

"I'll get his treats," I say. "Don't worry about Ziggy. Good luck in there."

"Thank you," Patrick says on a long exhale, laden with emotion.

"Tell her I love her, and I'll be thinking of her, and all of you. She's strong."

"She is," he says. "She really, really is. Okay. Talk to you soon, Eden."

"Good luck guys."

He hangs up and I speed down the familiar streets, like I'm the one rushing to a hospital instead of picking up a smart, spoiled pup.

I have to stop at home to grab Becky's spare key from my hallway dresser. I'm in and out of my house in less than five minutes.

Only, as I unlock my car door, I realize that I've forgotten to check today.

I open my mailbox and pull out a wad of flyers from local supermarkets, fast-food places, and big-box stores. An envelope falls out, landing on the sidewalk.

It has my full name written on it in black ink.

And it's postmarked in Barbados.

I stare at it for a solid minute, as if I can't really believe it's there. I'm not sure I want to find out what's inside.

Ziggy. Right.

I grab the envelope and jump into my car. My heart is beating fast as I open it, accidentally tearing through the beautiful stamp. I pull out the postcard and several twenty-dollar bills come with it. One of the twenties is a bit crumpled in the corner.

What?

The postcard has a picture of a turtle on it. That makes me smile because, of course, he'd chosen that one. I flip it over.

Eden,

Please find the money you paid me back for our first dinner enclosed. You said you couldn't let me pay for it, because that would have made it a date. Well, this is me saying it was. Our first.

These weeks with you have been some of my happiest. I know you're still getting over an ex, and you just wanted a rebound, not to mention the long-distance thing. But all I know, standing here and writing a postcard because you had this wild idea (and I can't seem to say no to any of your wild ideas), is that I need to see you again.

My phone number is below. One text from you, and I can be on the next plane out to Washington.

Phillip.

I read through it one more time before I carefully place the postcard, envelope, and the bills that had once been mine on the passenger seat.

I drive to Becky's house in a haze. The route is familiar and, maybe that's a bad thing because it gives my brain space to turn over Phillip's words. They don't sound like they come from a man who was glad to say goodbye to me, who said it was a *relief*. They seem to say that he was interested in more.

Just like me.

He sent this five weeks ago. Maybe he's been walking

around thinking I received it after a week but hadn't called, and he's been wondering why.

How can I tell him that I eavesdropped on his conversation? Should I even do that?

Can I make that call?

Ziggy is a bouncing ball of energy when I enter Becky and Patrick's house. His paws rest on my shin and I scratch him behind the ears, his tail swishing fast.

"You're about to get another family member," I tell him. "I bet you're going to absolutely lose it when they bring her home."

He licks my hand.

I grab a set of his things. Leash, his favorite bowl, crate for the car, a bag of dog food, and his treats. I'm gathering it all up by the door when Ziggy comes zooming into the kitchen, tail wagging, holding old tennis ball in his mouth. He drops it between his paws and looks at me expectantly.

"We can't play fetch now," I say and reach for it. He darts away, tail wagging even faster. "I promise we'll play when we get to my house, okay?"

I drop his ball into my bag of stuff, and he cocks his head, looking at me with dismay. *You're supposed to* throw *it,* his gaze says.

We've just made it to my car when my phone rings again. I see Becky's number, and my heart goes haywire.

"Is everything all right?"

"We forgot my go-bag!" Becky yells. Her voice is strained, and I can hear the stress in it. "It has all my stuff in it. Could you—"

"Yes, I'll drive up to the hospital with it right away," I say. "Don't worry."

"Thank you," she says. "You're the best."

"No, in this situation, you are. How are you feeling?"

"Like I'm being split in half, and not in a nice way."

Beside her, I hear Patrick's amused snort.

I chuckle. "Sounds like you're keeping your spirits high."

"I gotta," she says. "It's the only thing I have left to work with."

We hang up, and I grab the bag from where it sits, packed and prepared, on the bench in their hallway. Patrick must have been going out of his mind to miss such a key detail.

Ziggy is quiet in the backseat during our drive to the hospital. Between all of us, he seems to be handling this situation the best.

My heart is pounding like I'm actually racing to the hospital with the pregnant Becky instead of her go-bag in the passenger seat.

Phillip reached out.

Becky is giving birth.

I should call him.

Please let everything go smoothly.

I make it to the hospital parking lot and give Ziggy a bowl of water and crack a window. He rests his head on his paws and gives a doggy sigh. *Okay, I'll wait here.*

I'm walking toward the entrance of the hospital when I see her. Standing outside, drinking a can of soda in the warm sunlight.

Of course this is happening. She's a nurse, and she works at this hospital. Nature's timing is impeccable. Cindy looks up. Our eyes meet, and her mouth opens in surprise.

I don't slow down, Becky's bag in my hand. There are many more important things going on right now than our non-friendship.

"Eden," she says.

"Hey, Cindy," I say with a nod.

We haven't spoken, not really, since everything exploded. Those days had been some of the ugliest in my life. Fighting, first with Caleb and then with Cindy. Having her sob in front of me like I was the one hurting her; when it was she who's been sleeping with my fiancé for months.

"How've you been?" she asks.

I slow down, glancing at the hospital door. "Good."

Maybe it's the adrenaline, or all the other things going on, but I don't feel nervous. "I'm writing again."

Her eyes widen. "Oh! That's really good to hear. I heard you're all moved in into your new place."

"I am, yes. It's great."

"I bet. You were always great at making a place a home." She gives me a smile. It's the kind that says *I know this won't fix anything, and you know it, too. But I still know you, and you still know me. Even after everything.*

And I can't argue with that.

"You doing okay?" I ask.

She shrugs. "Yeah. I got into the midwifery program, actually. I'm starting in the fall."

"Really? Congrats."

"Thanks," she says, her expression tightening. "I know it doesn't matter, but I really am sorry, Eden. What I did… there are no excuses."

"I know you are," I say. "It's just that…"

"I did it anyway," she says and takes a deep breath. "I know."

I take the chance to ask the question I've wanted answered since those first ugly weeks. "So, have you and Caleb been…?"

She shakes her head. "No, not at all."

"Right," I say. I don't know if I expected the answer to make things easier or harder, somehow. To hear that they tried to make a real go of it, or that they blew up my life just for some casual sex.

I find that it doesn't really matter, though. Actions speak loudest. Because intentions? They whisper.

I bet he tried with her. Just as he'd tried to get me back. Apologizing for his behavior and seeing who would be willing to take him back.

Cindy shrugs. "I know, it's such hypocrisy, but I didn't want to have a relationship with him. Not when I'd seen how he treated you. With my help."

"Yeah, you dodged one, I suppose."

"I'm in therapy," she says. "To try to understand why I… well. I'm sorry, that's all."

"Thanks," I say.

She nods again. "So, how's Becky?"

"She's giving birth," I say and hold up her bag. "Like, right now. I have to head inside."

"Shit, really?"

"Yep."

"Oh my God," Cindy says, and a real smile transforms her face. She looks like the friend I remember, the one who had cried beside me when Becky first told us she was pregnant. "That's incredible."

"Yeah. I have to go."

"Of course," she says. "I know she won't want to hear it, and you won't tell her, but I wish her all the best. Both of them."

I nod. "Yeah. I know."

"Bye, Eden."

"Bye."

I walk away from another facet of my past, and into the hospital. So much to process and absolutely no time, none at all.

At least there's no hurt. Resentment, perhaps. The weight of shared history and certainly distrust. But talking to Cindy hadn't brought up all those old feelings.

I make it through the sterile hospital hallways and finally arrive at Becky and Patrick's room, where she's munching on the ice chips.

Beside her, Patrick looks like he's been electrocuted.

He glances over at me. "Hi, Eden. Thank you."

"No problem! Ziggy's in the car. I'll take him for a nice long walk later."

"Thanks," Becky says with a wide smile. She looks perfectly serene, nodding her head along with the sound of music playing from her phone.

"You okay?" I ask her.

"She opted into trying laughing gas," Patrick says, "before the epidural kicks in."

"Yep. It's amazing," Becky says and holds up a breathing mask. "Hey, you look a bit peaky. Everything okay?"

"You're not allowed to care about anyone but you today," I say and pat her leg over the hospital blanket. "Yourself and the baby girl. And possibly Patrick."

She gives her husband an amused look. "Yeah, I think I might have to."

"Let me know if you need anything else. I'm on standby. And don't worry, I remembered Ziggy's treats."

Becky chuckles and puts a hand on her stomach. "Good. This might take a while. My contractions have slowed now."

I head toward the door. "You got this, though."

She nods like that's obvious. "Yeah. Hey!" she says and reaches for the laughing gas. "Postcard watch?"

I grimace. "It arrived today."

"No freaking way!"

"Yes, but we'll talk about it in a week or two. It's really not—"

"Give me the five-minute version," she says in a voice you don't argue with.

So I do.

Afterward, I drive home with a clear purpose. To call Phillip. Maybe it's just to ask about the phone call I heard. Maybe it's to ask about what he'd written on the postcard.

Maybe just to tell my side of the story.

I arrive home after dark and get Ziggy out. He dances around my legs and gets me tangled in his leash.

There's a car parked across from my house. It's not usually there, but I don't think much about it, digging through my purse for my house keys. I find Becky's instead and have to keep digging.

"Hey," a voice says.

Ziggy barks twice, standing by my feet.

I look up. On the sidewalk, in front of my house, is Phillip Meyer. He's got his hands in the pockets of a pair of dark jeans, and wearing a crisp, blue shirt with the sleeves rolled up.

"Sorry to show up unannounced," he says and smiles that crooked smile. "How have you been?"

Chapter Twenty-eight

"You're here," I say.

He nods. "Yeah."

"In my hometown. At my house."

"Yeah," he says again and frowns. The beard is gone, and his hair is shorter and neat around the edges. He looks achingly familiar and also like a handsome stranger. "I can come back another time. Or never, if you'd prefer."

"No, don't leave."

"Okay," he says and smiles again.

Ziggy pads toward this strange new man, outside of a house he's rarely at, and sniffs at Phillip's loafer-clad feet. Slowly, his tail starts to wag.

"You have a dog?" Phillip bends down to pet him, running a big hand down Ziggy's back.

"No," I say.

The world feels off-kilter. Like it has permanently shifted beneath my feet, and I can't find my footing.

I just stare at him.

Phillip chuckles. "Right. You stole this one, then?"

"No. It's my best friend."

"The dog?"

"No, sorry, I mean it's my best friend's dog. He's staying the night with me because my friend's in labor."

His eyebrows shoot up. "Damn."

"Yeah. It's a lot," I say. "And your card just arrived. Your postcard, I mean. Just today."

"Wow." He runs a hand over his jaw, contemplating that. There's something contained about him and cautious. It mirrors exactly what I feel.

"Did you get mine?" I ask. My mouth feels dry.

"Yeah, about three weeks ago."

"Oh."

"I liked it," he says. "You told me you'd be my guide in Pinecrest… if I ever needed one."

"Yeah. I did." Then I shake my head, feeling absurd. Ziggy is sniffing at my rose bushes, my best friend is in labor, and here's Phillip, standing right in front of me. "I'm confused."

"By what?"

"You," I say. "This. The postcard, you showing up here… all of it."

His smile disappears. "I see. If you want me to go, I will. It's no problem."

"No, stay. It's just, after we said goodbye in Barbados, I actually turned the cab around."

His eyes widen. "You did?"

"Yeah. I went to your bungalow, and I was going to give you my number and tell you that I wanted to keep in touch. Somehow. But you were on the phone."

His eyebrows have drawn together, and there's a little furrow right between them, like he's thinking back. "Yeah, that's right."

I take a deep breath. "Thing is, now I'm wondering if I was crazy. Because you're *here*. You're at my front door, and you wrote all that nice stuff in your card—"

"Oh," he says, his forehead smoothing out. "You heard me talking to my sister?"

"Yes. You were saying things, and at first, I thought it was about your ex, but then you mentioned a contract."

He blows out a sharp breath. "It *was* about my ex. My

sister had been at my apartment earlier that day, to make sure Lauren had taken all of her stuff, and got the keys back. After that, I texted Lauren and told her that she can't call me again, for any reason. I wanted a clean break."

"Really?"

"Yeah."

"But you mentioned something about being asked to read a contract, and that's what you did for me. I asked you to read mine!"

He chuckles. "Yes, because I *offered* to, Eden. I wanted to read yours. But she'd emailed me a contract for some minor endorsement deal she wanted me to look over. Apparently, she thought she could still get free legal advice from me. I said 'hell no' to that."

"Oh. In the same week?"

"Yeah. Recently, she's been trying to become a social media influencer and was always taking pictures of—God, Eden, the last thing I came here to talk to you about was my ex."

My breathing is becoming fast. "So, you really weren't talking about me?"

"No, I really, really wasn't," he says. "Saying goodbye to you was… well. I wish I'd been smoother."

"You were smooth. You looked unbothered."

"Well, I wasn't. I wanted to ask for your number. To see you again. But you told me you were only looking for a rebound, and you had a cute math teacher at work asking you out—"

"I never said he was cute!"

"That's what I heard, at any rate," Phillip says and takes a step closer. "The entire flight back home to Chicago, I hated myself for that. For not asking you."

"I hated you my entire flight home, too," I mutter.

He smiles. It's the crooked one. "I would have deserved it, too, if I'd really been speaking about you."

"How did you find me? How… how are you here?"

"I landed in Chicago, and nothing felt right. We'd had a two-week conversation, and I wasn't ready for it to end."

"Me, either," I whisper.

He reaches out and runs a strand of my hair between two of his fingers. His eyes soften. "You, with your wild ideas and talk of vacation selves, and forcing me out of my comfort zone at every single turn. Your beautiful brown hair, and your quick mouth, and these dark eyes. I could look at them forever."

I can't breathe.

"My law firm was hired by a company here in Washington. There's a tech merger going on, one of the biggest nationwide deals in months. An advisory position opened up."

"Here?" I ask.

He nods, and this time his words turn cautious. "I sent in my application nine days after I returned to Chicago. It went through just last week."

"So you… live here now?"

"I'm on a three-month extended stay in Seattle, yeah."

"Wow," I say. "Okay. Wow."

"A good wow? Or a horrified wow?"

"Good, I think. But how did you find me? And my house?"

At that, his expression turns chagrined. "Well, I might have done a bit of investigative work. I wasn't sure if my postcard would ever arrive, and I…" He breaks off and runs a hand through his hair. "I've been thinking about you nonstop since Barbados."

"Oh," I breathe.

"I had to know. I had to say the things I didn't when we were saying goodbye, even if you would want me to leave after. I memorized your address from the postcard, and… here I am."

I take a step closer. "I really can't believe you're here. For weeks, I've been thinking that you didn't care. That saying goodbye for you was easy."

"It wasn't," he says. "Not at the time, and definitely not in the days after. I knew I had to find you."

"You did."

"I did," he says and runs his fingers over my cheek. It's tentative, like he isn't sure he's quite allowed to touch me, yet. "There was only one thing that held me back."

I lean into the warmth of his hand. "There was?"

"You met my vacation self, as you liked to call it. I wasn't sure if you'd like my normal self, too."

"There's only one way to find out."

"I do work a lot, Eden. I love it."

"I know you do."

"I'm not sure if I've ever felt this way about anyone."

"Me neither," I whisper. "I haven't stopped thinking about you, too. Even when I hated you because I thought you'd said those things about me."

"I'm sorry I ever made you doubt," he murmurs. He tips my head back, and the intensity in his eyes takes my breath away. "You're the most wonderful thing I never saw coming. I need more of it in my life."

He reaches into the back pocket of his jeans and pulls out a thin, glossy guidebook. On it, the word Washington is in bold, black letters. "I need a guide, you see."

"Oh."

He smiles. "And this book is shamefully lacking in annotations."

"It doesn't even look bookmarked," I say.

"It's not. Not a single one."

"You poor thing," I whisper and rise up on my tiptoes.

He leans down an inch. "Does this mean you'll let me take you out?"

"Yes," I say, and he closes the distance between us.

Phillip kisses me softly, his lips familiar again in an instant. I knot my hands behind his neck and kiss him back. In my chest, my heart feels like it's pounding out of my ribcage. I've dreamed of being in his arms again. With my eyes closed, I can almost hear the ocean waves break against the shoreline, and the distant sound of cicadas.

It feels like coming home and going on vacation, the best of both worlds.

Excitement floods through me. I get to spend more time with him. After weeks of wondering, and worrying, there is a future to this. I'm not going to have to live on memories alone.

His kisses turn even softer and slower, like he's afraid I'll break or spook, like this is still too fragile to believe. I want to tell him it's not.

That I've never felt more alive.

But I think time will have to do that for us.

"Where are you staying?" I ask, threading my hands into his hair. God, he smells good.

His thumb brushes over my lower lip. "At a motel in Oakwood."

"That's over an hour away."

"Yeah. Halfway to Seattle."

I grab his hand and twine my fingers through his. "Come on, then. Let me show you my bungalow."

He smiles. It's brilliantly wide, promising many more to come, and his hand tightens around mine. "Lead the way."

Chapter Twenty-nine

Three Weeks Later

Phillip leans back on the couch with my laptop braced on his knees. He'd only bothered to put on his pants, and his bare chest is still in full, delicious view.

"This is good," he says.

I fold my legs up beneath me. "Honestly?"

"Honestly," he says. His face is set in the concentrated frown I've come to love.

He's reading the first ten chapters of my work-in-progress. Apart from Becky, I've never shown my writing to anyone since *One Fatal Step* came out and sold two hundred and seven copies. In total.

"I think it's better than *Fatal*," he says.

Oh, he's read that one, too. He'd bought it even when I told him I'd give him a copy for free. And when he returned the following weekend from Seattle, he'd already read it cover to cover.

"Okay, you're just saying that," I say.

"No, I mean it. It has a really strong start. And," he says, looking over at me, "I'm really liking this mysterious businessman."

I chuckle. "You are, are you?"

"Yeah."

"Well, he'll soon be suspected of the murder."

"Mmm. But our intrepid heroine—who is falling deeply in love with him, by the way—is going to save the day."

"She is. In about two hundred more pages." I fold up the long sleeves of my shirt. *His* shirt, really. It's the only thing I'm wearing.

It's Friday, and he arrived a few hours ago to spend the weekend here. With me. In my house. In Pinecrest. We had takeout, then we'd had sex on my couch, and now he's reading my manuscript.

I can't quite believe it. That I get to live this life, that he's here, and that happiness has taken up permanent residence in my chest.

He taps his fingers along the side of my laptop. "I might have some notes about the legal process, later. About the investigation, but also about what laws actually apply to a foreign national murdered abroad."

"Lay it all on me," I say. "You can be my law consultant on fictional criminal cases."

"Will I make it into the acknowledgments?"

"Maybe," I say.

He shakes his head. "Scratch that. I want into the dedication."

I laugh. "You're getting greedy."

"Yes," he says and puts the laptop down. He looks at me across the room with unbridled lust. "I thought that was obvious by now."

I chuckle, stretching my bare legs in front of me, and loving the way his eyes dip down. "Yeah, I've noticed."

"Then why are you over there?"

I get up off the armchair and walk around the coffee table, sinking onto the couch beside him. He lifts my legs and tucks them over his lap.

"Much better," he says. He's let his stubble grow out again. I love how it looks, rugged against his shirts and suits.

I prop myself up on a pillow. "I like it when you're here."

"I like it when I'm here, too," he says and puts a big hand on the outside of my thigh. His skin is warm on mine.

"Would you want to meet one of my friends on Sunday?"

"Yeah," he says. "Who?"

"Becky. She had her daughter the same day you showed up, remember?"

"I remember," he says. "Your goddaughter."

I nod. Little Riley is only three weeks and four days old, but she's already the cutest-looking baby. I haven't seen her or her mother much; only to return Ziggy and then to drop off a few meals and a big bag of groceries during their first week. Becky's the one who wants to meet up for a slow walk in the park this Sunday. *And by slow,* she'd written in her text, *I mean snail's pace.*

"Yeah. She'll come along," I say.

"Sure Becky won't mind me crashing?"

"I'm sure. She really wants to meet you."

"Ah," Phillip says. "The best friend test. Should I be scared?"

I grin at him. "Don't worry, you'll pass with flying colors."

His thumb starts to move in slow sweeps over my bare thigh. "You've told me how she encouraged you in Barbados, to go for it with me. I owe her a thank you."

"Mmm, probably," I say. His dark-brown hair is mussed from earlier, and his eyes dance with the same happiness I'm feeling.

I can't believe he's here… and that he's mine.

His eyes narrow. "You're looking at me like that again."

"Like what?" I ask, but I'm smiling, too.

His fingers dig softly into my flesh. "You know exactly like what… like you did earlier."

Yes. And we both know what had happened then, after eating takeout, right here on this very couch. "Whoops," I say.

He smooths his hand up my thigh and beneath my shirt,

his shirt, and over my bare hip. "You didn't put your panties back on."

I wriggle closer, but I keep my legs shut. His touch sends shivers up my body. "Nope," I say. "But I'm curious about something."

"Tell me," he says.

"What did your family say? About you taking this three-month position out here?"

His hand stills on my hipbone, the heel of his palm pushing down right at the top of my thigh. Just inches away. "Eden," he says.

I give him an innocent smile. "Come on, I'm really curious."

"They were surprised," he says and leans his head back against the couch. "But I think it made sense to them—after they thought about it—that I might want a change of scenery. You know, after everything."

"I get that," I say. "My parents were almost expecting me to move away after the whole debacle with Caleb and Cindy."

"I bet they're happy you didn't," he says, and I nod. My parents and I are close. They haven't met Phillip, yet, but they've definitely heard of him.

His fingers tap a slow rhythm on my hip. "Tess kept pushing me to tell her why I was moving."

"Did she?"

"Yeah. She's like a bloodhound when she can scent a secret."

I scoot closer to him, tilting my hips up. "And did you? Tell her?"

Phillip smirks. "Yeah. Eventually."

"Oh."

"She was surprised at first and then not surprised at all. 'When you least expect it,' she said, 'that's when you find it.'"

My breath catches. "Yeah. I have to say, I didn't expect to meet you on my honeymoon trip."

He chuckles. "Neither did I, baby."

"But I'm glad I did."

"Me, too," he says softly. His hand brushes over my stomach, but it doesn't move lower. I tilt my hips up again. "Touch me," I say.

He chuckles. "Bossy, aren't you?"

"I'm getting there," I say, and it's the truth. With Phillip, nothing is off-limits. No conversation topic, no joke, and nothing I might want to explore. He's there for all of it, giving just as well as me. It's the kind of freedom I've never experienced.

He inches up the button-down I'm wearing, exposing me fully. I watch him as he watches me. The air on my skin feels cool, but his gaze is hot.

Fridays are usually just like this. He gets into town after a week of work, and we celebrate the start of the weekend exactly like this. At home, indulging in one another.

Then, we spend our Saturdays and Sundays exploring the area, going grocery shopping, or watching movies.

After each weekend, I long even more for the next one. For him.

Phillip's fingers start to tease and stroke me, right where I need them, and my eyes drift half-shut. There's still residual pleasure in my body from earlier, I'm sensitive, and it doesn't take long for my breathing to speed up.

"You're so beautiful," he mutters. "It tugs my heart, all the damn time."

And I believe him.

Because I feel the same way about him. It doesn't matter if it's seeing him wake up in the morning or bantering during long car rides, or even when he's focused on work emails.

"That's it," he murmurs and slides a finger inside me. "God, you're pretty."

My back starts to arch. His fingers hasten, circling and stroking and pumping, and then he bends over and puts his tongue to my clit.

I come.

He strokes me through all of it.

I return slowly back to myself, my legs still splayed across his lap, and his shirt half-unbuttoned and bunched up around my chest.

His hands soothe my hips. "That's it."

"Wow," I whisper and look into his warm eyes. The dark-blue is liquid, and a soft smile lurks at the corner of his lips. "I love you."

His hands pause. My words hang in the air between us, a tangible, shimmering thing. One that can be accepted or rejected.

His mouth tightens. "You do?"

"Yes," I say. My hair must be a mess, and I'm half-naked, and I feel more like myself than I have in a long, long time. "It's okay if you're not there, yet, or if you don't want to say it. But I want you to know how I feel."

"Really?" he asks.

"Yes, so much, I don't know what to do with it all. It's taken me by surprise… but I love that, too."

He shifts us, moves so he's half resting on top of me. His face is close to mine, and his weight is delicious on top of me. "Eden," he murmurs and kisses me. "Eden, fuck."

"It's okay," I say. "It's fine. This doesn't change anything."

"It's not that." He rests his head against my neck. For a long time, he doesn't move, and I can feel the rapid beat of his heart against my breast.

Then he lifts his head, and his eyes are glazed. "I love you, too. I have for much longer than I realized. It crept up on me, slow at first, and then so fast that I was deep in it before I knew."

"You do?" I murmur.

He nods once, and his hand comes up to cup my face. "Yes. I don't think I've ever experienced this, or felt this much before."

"Not like this," I say.

"Not like this," he agrees. "I know how bad it can hurt when things fall apart. And now? Feeling like this? I don't think I could handle it, Eden. If I lost you."

I wrap my legs around his hips and rest my forehead against his. "You won't."

"No?"

"No," I murmur and dig my fingers into his hair. "Besides, this, with you and me? It's an adventure. We've been on those before."

"We have," he agrees, his lips brushing over mine. They're hot. "But that was hiking in a forest and watching sea turtles hatch."

"So maybe this is a bigger one," I say. "I know what it's like to be hurt, too."

"I know you do," he says, and there's anguish in his voice. He's told me several times that I have to point Caleb out if we see him around town. Not that I know what he'd do if I did. "Trust me, I won't ever put you through that. Never."

"That's right," I say and run my fingers through his hair. "I know you won't."

He kisses me again. It's filled with promises of the future, the excitement of the unknown, and all the words we've just spoken. I kiss him back. Because the adventure we're setting off on?

It might just be my favorite one, yet.

Epilogue

Three Years Later

I look at Phillip out of the corner of my eye. He's flipping through my notebook, filled with the scribbles I made during our plane ride. I'd even brought highlighters, and the notes for each chapter have their own colorful headings.

The taxi driver takes a corner fast, and I grab the headrest in front of me.

"Hold on!" the driver says with a chuckle. "More turns ahead." The car's engine protests as we head up the road. To our left is a barren hillside, and to our right, shrubbery. "Okay, now you have to look. When we come up here, on the right."

As he rounds the corner, the shrubbery gives way to a clear view of the glittering blue Aegean Sea. It stretches as far as the eye can see. And perched below us, on the cliffs, are white houses. Square like sugar cubes and built along the sunbaked slopes, cascading down to the azure waters.

"Oh my God," I whisper. We'd seen the blue ocean as we flew in, but this view is so much better.

"It's good," Phillip says. "I really like the premise, trapping them all together like that."

I tear my eyes away. "What?"

He holds up the notebook. "The plot? I like it. You have a great story idea here, with them all snowed in at a luxury ski resort."

"Really?" I say, grinning. "You think so?"

"Definitely. A worthy sequel to your last book."

"Thank you. I'm sorry I made you read it now, on this winding road."

He chuckles. "I offered."

"Are you seeing this? The view?"

"Yes." He reaches over and takes my hand. "It's stunning."

"I can't believe we're really here."

"I can," he says and smiles crookedly. "What I can't believe is that you've come up with an entire plot for your next book with all the craziness of the past few weeks."

I shrug. "Me either. Maybe that's why, though? My brain needed an escape from the party planning and seating arrangements?"

"And it went straight to a murder," he says, but there's only amusement in his voice. I've fully converted him into a true crime junkie. He was half of one already, as I'd once pointed out to him. Documentaries about real-life whodunnits and assassinations fall squarely into the same camp. In turn, he's opened my eyes to a whole new world of documentaries regarding historical crime—or even crazier, financial crime. It's just as interesting.

Now, he's officially the legal consultant on my stories. He made *The Sunshine Murder* leagues better than any of my previous books, just by letting me pick his brain.

Sure, sometimes the suggestions are unhelpful. *Why would his jaw be tensing so much when he looks at her?* he'd asked once, lowering my manuscript and frowning.

Because it shows he's secretly pining for her!

He hadn't bought it, but there are some things you just have to be a romance reader to appreciate.

The taxi driver pulls to a stop in front of the resort. It's a vision of white, lime-washed walls with hints of blue and terracotta. Two giant, knotted olive trees flank the wooden door that marks the entrance to the Winter Corporation's new five-star location on the Greek island.

"How does it look old," I say, "when it opened half a year ago?"

"Excellent architects," he responds.

Inside, the lobby has the kind of understated minimalism that signals true luxury. The air smells like lavender, and the front desk is made out of a single block of weathered wood. Under our feet, the marble is shining. I bet it was quarried locally.

An attendant arrives to take our bags, and I slip my arm through Phillip's. His linen shirt is soft beneath my fingers. "I can't believe this is real."

He presses a kiss to my temple. "Staying in a Winter Resort isn't a once-in-a-lifetime thing anymore," he says, and he sounds just the tiniest bit smug.

Our room needs another hour to be ready, the attendant explains with a wide, serviceable smile, but would we like to enjoy a late lunch on the terrace?

"Definitely," I say.

The receptionist steps around the beautiful counter to escort us there. "It's right this way, Mr. and Mrs. Meyer."

Phillip presses another kiss to my temple. "That's right," he murmurs. "You're all mine now."

My hand tightens around his arm. "And you're all mine."

The terrace overlooks the deep-blue Aegean Sea that stretches as far as the horizon. A few seagulls lazily glide overhead on currents of warm air. Next to the terrace is the hotel pool, surrounded by outdoor chaise lounges with shade umbrellas and tall olive trees in terracotta pots, providing much-needed relief from the scorching sun.

"Pinch me," I whisper. "Right now."

"Absolutely not," he says. "That would be very un-husbandly."

We are escorted to a table right at the edge of the terrace, overlooking the steep drop down to the adjacent white houses.

"After lunch, we'll be more than happy to show you to your suite," says our guide and gives us another beaming smile. "Nikos will be right out to take your order."

She leaves, and I set my bag on the chair. Then I wrap my arms around Phillip and press my lips to his.

He chuckles against me, but kisses me back. "Hello," he murmurs.

"Hi," I whisper back. It's been a very long twenty-four hours. An international flight, very little sleep, and a connection in Athens. But now we're here. Just the two of us in paradise, on another adventure. There's a guidebook in my bag. Less annotated than my last one, true. But the bookmarks in this one?

We put them there together.

"Happy?" he asks. His eyes are warm. They're the same color as the sea below. Dark-blue and sparkling.

"Yes," I say. "Stupidly happy."

He kisses me again, gently. "Good," he says. "That's my goal."

"Are you?"

He pulls out my chair and I take a seat, watching him. His face is relaxed. No frown between those brows. He's handsome, and he's mine now. Forever.

"Yes," he says and gives me a half smile as he sits down. "I'm not sure I can contain it all."

"Just enjoy it." I reach out a hand across the linen-clad table, and he takes it. His wedding ring is a thick, gold band on his left finger. It mirrors the thinner gold wedding ring and the diamond engagement ring on mine. "You know, this is technically our second honeymoon."

"It is," he says and squeezes my hand. "And it'll be our best one yet."

ACKNOWLEDGMENTS

Every book takes a village, but this one took an entire island.

Firstly, there would be no book without L. Thank you for getting the job in Barbados, for taking it, and for letting me stay at yours for two months. The monkeys walking along the balcony railing were great companions while I explored Eden and Phillip's story.

The island itself and the amazingly generous people I met there were invaluable. Thank you for the experiences and for sharing the natural beauty of the island, for rum tastings, beaches, scuba diving, shipwrecks, sea turtles, and the most delicious grilled fish I've ever had.

Not to be forgotten (trust me, I tried) is the wild rooster who very conscientiously woke me up at dawn every morning. You helped me seize the days, and I've never had a better (or louder) alarm cock.

And of course, any mistakes in the depiction of Barbados in this book are entirely of my own making, and no one else's.

Thank you, Andie, for the brilliant feedback and editing. You made this book so much better. Thanks to Leni Kauffman for designing the amazing cover, and bringing Eden and Phillip to life. I absolutely love how they look!

And to the readers who pick up my books… I can't thank you enough. You're the reason I have a career and the courage to write this book, my first ever romantic comedy. Without you all, this book would be nothing more than an empty page longing to be filled.

Thank you!

OTHER BOOKS BY OLIVIA

LISTED IN READING ORDER

The New York Billionaire Series

Think Outside the Boss
Tristan and Freddie

Saved by the Boss
Anthony and Summer

Say Yes to the Boss
Victor and Cecilia

A Ticking Time Boss
Carter and Audrey

Suite on the Boss
Isaac and Sophia

12 Days of Bossmas
Christmas anthology

The Seattle Billionaire Series

Billion Dollar Enemy
Cole and Skye

Billion Dollar Beast
Nick and Blair

Billion Dollar Catch
Ethan and Bella

Billion Dollar Fiancé
Liam and Maddie

Brothers of Paradise Series

Dark Eyed Devil
Lily and Hayden

Ice Cold Boss
Faye and Henry

Red Hot Rebel
Ivy and Rhys

Small Town Hero
Jamie and Parker

Standalones

How to Honeymoon Alone
Phillip and Eden

Arrogant Boss
Julian and Emily

Look But Don't Touch
Grant and Ada

The Billionaire Scrooge Next Door
Adam and Holly

ABOUT OLIVIA

Olivia picked up the pen in 2019, and she hasn't put it down since! With over a million books sold, Olivia writes fast-paced, swoon-worthy stories filled with banter and spice. Join the heroes as they meet, clash with, or stumble into the ambitious heroines that make them fall, and fall hard.

Join her newsletter for updates and bonus content.
www.oliviahayle.com.
Connect with Olivia

facebook.com/authoroliviahayle
instagram.com/oliviahayle
goodreads.com/oliviahayle
amazon.com/author/oliviahayle
bookbub.com/profile/olivia-hayle

Printed in the USA
CPSIA information can be obtained
at www.ICGtesting.com
LVHW092300010324
773315LV00005B/867